THE WEST LONDON MURDERS

An absolutely gripping crime mystery with a massive twist

BIBA PEARCE

Detective Rob Miller Mystery Book 2

Originally published as
The Revenge Killer

Revised edition 2021
Joffe Books, London
www.joffebooks.com

First published in Great Britain in 2020
as *The Revenge Killer*

This paperback edition was first published
in Great Britain in 2022

Cover art by Nebojša Zorić

ISBN: 978-1-78931-833-3

CHAPTER 1

Aadam Yousef was in a good mood. After months of hard work, everything had fallen into place. His business was thriving, he'd finally found someone to marry his fat, socially awkward daughter and take her off his hands, and he'd just bought a banging new BMW. To top it all, he'd had a great afternoon and was feeling totally relaxed.

The doorbell rang. Aadam smiled to himself and stood up. Time to get to work. He checked his reflection in the living-room mirror and was pleased with what he saw. He still had all his hair, his teeth were straight and white, and he had a strong aquiline nose that spoke of good breeding, even though nothing could be further from the truth. He'd grown up in a dingy two-bedroom flat with threadbare carpets and not enough heating in winter. His father was a cleric, his mother — well, she was nothing. She couldn't even cook that well. Maybe that's why his father had been so rough with her. She drifted in and out of the shadows of his memory, a fragile figure in a dark headscarf, eyes downcast, too timid to utter a word. It was his grandmother, his father's mother, who'd had the biggest input into his upbringing. He had spent many happy weekends at their double-storey house in Finsbury Park with his cousins, eating as much as they could and riding their bicycles up and down the street. It was Teeta who had decided which school he'd go to and what subjects he'd study. She'd always treated him with respect, even more so than his father, who — she never missed an opportunity to point out — had made such an unfortunate marriage.

The doorbell chimed again.

"Coming," he yelled and walked down the passage to open it.

"Hello." His smiling guest's breath turned to steam in the cold afternoon air. Aadam was looking forward to spring. He had a big back garden, perfect for barbecues.

He shook their hand. "Hello, good to meet you. Please, come in."

He stood back to let his guest into the house. His cleaner, a sexy Polish bitch, had been that morning so it looked better than it did most days. Having grown up with his mother picking up after him, Aadam hadn't learned the value of cleaning up after himself. He didn't see the point. Wasn't that what wives were for? And if you were blessedly single, like he was, then you hired a cleaner to do it for you.

He led his guest into the lounge, a spacious room with a leather lounge suite, a glass coffee table and an enormous flat-screen TV suspended on the wall. The television was also new and, after the Beemer, his second favourite possession. He'd bought it with last month's windfall. He knew the boss had said not to splurge on boys' toys, it would draw too much attention, but he didn't think a little reward here and there would do much harm. It wasn't like he was on anyone's radar. Hounslow was full of middle-class Muslims like him.

"Would you like a drink before we get down to business?" It was gone four o'clock, an acceptable time for a drink. He may have grown up in a strict Muslim household, but he wasn't a believer. The only thing he believed in was money, and lots of it, so that he could enjoy himself. Wasn't that what life was all about? Hence his choice of occupation. But for his friends and family who had no idea what he did for a living — they thought he worked for a property

2

development company — he played the part of the devout Muslim. He even went to Friday prayers. He had to be seen to be doing the right thing. He was an upstanding member of the community, after all.

He chuckled to himself. He'd always enjoyed subterfuge. Most people were idiots — they believed what they saw, what they wanted to believe. What had religion ever done for his father? He was a hard-working cleric who'd spent his life serving Allah, and for what? A squalid council flat in North West London. No thanks. This was England, after all. Capitalism thrived here. For a man who knew what he wanted, it was easy to make money, and the police were either too soft or too stupid to figure it out.

"I'll have a Scotch," said his guest.

He poured them each two fingers and sat down on the couch.

His guest downed it in one go and that's when he noticed the gloves and that he hadn't offered to take their coat. How remiss of him. He offered now, but his guest refused, instead rising and handing him the empty glass. "I think it's time we got down to business. I don't have all day."

"Of course. I'm interested to hear your proposal."

He was about to get to his feet when he felt a hand on his shoulder followed by a sharp pain in his chest. He staggered back on to the couch, confused. That had never happened before. Was he having a heart attack?

He looked up. His guest was holding a knife.

"What the . . . ?" He glanced down and saw a red stain appear in the centre of his £450 Giorgio Armani shirt. It was mesmerizing, the blood dark red against the pale-blue material, growing bigger as he watched.

Another thrust and the blade pierced his chest, where he imagined his heart might be. He howled in agony but then felt a snap inside him. It was hard to breathe.

He clutched his chest and stared up at his guest. "Why are you doing this?" he tried to ask, but it came out as a frothy gargle.

Panic set in. He was a big guy — maybe he could overpower his attacker. He tried to stand but his knees buckled and he collapsed. He'd lost control over his body. The whisky glass fell to the floor, the amber liquid staining his cream carpet. He was annoyed about that, he'd just had the place recarpeted.

His guest straddled him and lifted the knife again. The frenzied expression sent a fresh surge of adrenalin through Aadam's body. "No!" He held up his hands up in an attempt to protect himself.

It was too late. His guest plunged the knife into his abdomen, pulled it out and thrust it into his chest again. He gasped as the strike took his breath away.

Stop, he wanted to say, to plead, but his attacker was beyond reason, caught up in their mad bloodlust. As Aadam's vision began to close in, the blows kept coming, each more frenzied than the last, until the pain finally faded away and he lapsed into blissful oblivion.

CHAPTER 2

DI Rob Miller was sitting down to breakfast when his mobile phone rang. He glanced at his perfectly cooked poached egg, crispy bacon and toast, then at his phone.

"Leave it." Yvette perched prettily opposite him, her satin nightgown falling off one shoulder, her hair over the other, a cigarette between her fingers.

"You know I can't." He reached for the phone. "DI Miller."

Yvette blew a pillar of smoke into the air and leaned back, watching him with a deceptively calm gaze. He knew that look. Beneath the serene exterior, she was simmering with annoyance.

"I've got a case for you, Rob. It's a homicide in Hounslow. Uniform are already there, but it's yours if you want it." It was his boss and head of the Putney Major Investigation Team, Detective Superintendent Lawrence.

Hounslow, in West London, fell under their remit and even though Rob's team weren't officially "on call" that week, they were picking up the overflow.

"Sure, I'm in." Rob didn't need to think about it.

"Great, how soon can you get there?"

It was rush hour on a Tuesday morning. He glanced at the clock on the kitchen wall. "Thirty minutes." If he gunned it.

"I'll text you the address."

Yvette stubbed out her cigarette in the heavy glass ashtray and stood up. "I take it you'll be gone for the rest of the day?"

"Yeah, probably." He stuffed the egg and bacon between two slices of toast. Breakfast to go.

His wife of seven months pursed her lips in a perfect pout. "Of course."

Rob put his makeshift sandwich down. "Yvette, we talked about this. I have to go back to work. They won't give me any more time off." He'd been half-arsing it for months now because Yvette didn't like being left alone for too long. Despite the extenuating circumstances of his situation, they'd been more than lenient. "It's time."

She lit another cigarette from a box on the countertop. He noticed that her hand was shaking. "I know, but I don't have to like it."

Rob squeezed her shoulders. "Relax. You're safe here and you've got Trigger for company." The golden Labrador at her feet thumped his tail in agreement.

She nodded bravely and his heart went out to her. He knew she was still terrified of being by herself. Ever since she'd been abducted last year, she'd transformed from haughty and confident to clingy and insecure. Ironically, the experience had brought them closer together. She relied on him more than ever now, but while he enjoyed the attention — it made up for all the cold silences of the past — it also put more pressure on him.

"I'll call later and check on you."

She inhaled slow and deep until the smoke filled her lungs, then tilted her head back and blew it up towards the ceiling. It seemed to fortify her. "Okay, you'd better get going then."

She was trying. He kissed her on the cheek, pulled on his jacket, picked up his sandwich and left the house.

* * *

"It's a messy one," DS Mallory warned as Rob got out of the car. He'd parked halfway down the street behind the crowd of ambulances, police vehicles and forensic vans. The street had been cordoned off with police tape and, despite the cold, several bystanders were hovering beyond the line, craning their necks to see what was going on. Uniformed officers were keeping them back.

"Go back indoors, please," Rob told a nosy neighbour who was loitering on his doorstep. "We'll be around in due course to take your statement." The grey-haired old man shuffled back inside and closed his door.

"SOCO are processing the scene now." Mallory handed Rob a disposable forensic suit in a plastic bag identical to the one he was wearing.

Rob removed his jacket, tore open the packaging and pulled it over his clothes. "Who's the victim?"

"A forty-year-old Asian man called Aadam Yousef. The house is registered in his name, as is the fancy BMW in the drive." Rob took in the sturdy double-storey property with its sloping driveway housing what looked like an 8 Series Coupé in metallic blue. He wondered what Mr Yousef did for a living.

"Was there any ID on the body?"

"His wallet was in his back pocket, yeah."

Rob nodded. He zipped the suit up, then pulled on the shoe protectors. He grabbed a pair of latex gloves out of a box on the back seat of his car. "Right, let's go."

They gave their names to the uniformed officer at the entrance and proceeded into the living room. The curtains were open, yet the room felt dark and oppressive. There wasn't much natural light — the heavy cloud cover didn't help — and the furniture was mostly black. Rob surveyed the leather sofa and matching armchair, chrome-rimmed glass coffee table and the enormous flat-screen television that covered half of the far wall.

"Is Yousef married?"

Mallory shook his head. "He doesn't appear to be."

It figured. The décor was masculine and functional. He thought of Yvette's chic Parisian style, full of pastels and soft edges, and how guests always commented on what a fabulous job she'd done. This place hadn't seen a woman's touch in a long time.

Mallory nodded to a dark shape on the floor. "His body's over there." A crime scene photographer was taking pictures, his camera flashing every few seconds, creating a strobe effect.

Rob crouched down to inspect the victim. He was a big guy, over six foot, and lay in a pool of his own blood. His face was contorted in pain, but his eyes were empty. Multiple stab wounds punctuated his torso. "Can we get some extra light in here?"

A forensic technician set up a portable spotlight and switched it on. Immediately, a bright puddle swamped the dead man.

"Good morning, detectives."

Both Rob and Mallory glanced up. A middle-aged woman with a clipped voice and intelligent eyes stood there holding a silver case. "Do you mind if I get to work?"

"Hi, Liz." Rob straightened up to give her room, but he didn't move away from the body. He'd worked with Liz Kramer before. She was terse but efficient and didn't suffer fools gladly. Any stupid questions and she'd shut you down. He'd learned that the hard way.

She set her forensic case on the carpet and got to her knees with a little grunt. "I haven't seen anything this bad in a while." She inspected the puncture wounds that covered his torso.

"There's a lot of blood," Rob agreed. A faint metallic smell permeated the air around the body.

"The victim has been stabbed multiple times," said Liz. "I'd say the fatal one was probably this one, over the heart. It looks like it severed the aorta, hence the rapid blood loss."

Mallory scrunched up his nose. "Why didn't the killer stop there? Why stab him so many times when one would do?"

Liz smiled grimly but didn't look up. "That's your job, gentlemen, the mental state of the killer is not my remit. But I'd say there are seven, maybe eight puncture wounds covering his chest and stomach. Some bled more than others."

"Do we know when he died?" asked Rob.

"Probably sometime yesterday afternoon or early evening, judging by the viscosity of the blood and the state of the body, but I'll know more after the post-mortem."

A yellow sign with a number three on it stood on the coffee table beside a plastic evidence bag.

"What's this?" Rob asked one of the scene-of-crime officers. They always reminded him of worker bees in their white suits, buzzing around collecting evidence and marking out the crime scene. Right now, he was one of them.

"It's an empty glass, sir," the young man said. "I'm no expert, but it smelled like it contained whisky."

Rob scanned the room and walked over to an elaborate serving trolley that doubled as a liquor cabinet. It was covered with assorted bottles of spirits — white rum, tequila, vodka, whisky and gin, as well as a cream liqueur and two bottles of Bordeaux. On the shelf below were a range of glasses. He picked up a bottle of Scotch and sniffed it. He tried the top. It was loose. "Could have been this," he said to the technician. "Let's bag it, just in case."

Another marker lay on the floor beside the victim's body. The carpet was lightly stained, but it was hardly noticeable next to the puddle of blood. "Another glass?"

The technician nodded. "Yep, also empty. Most of it spilled on the carpet."

Rob looked at Mallory. "Our victim had a guest?"

His DS nodded. "It looks that way. There are no obvious marks on the glass, no lipstick, nothing to indicate who the guest was."

"Maybe we'll be able to grab some prints or DNA off it." Rob sounded more positive than he felt. The guest's glass was on the table in front of the leather armchair. "Have we processed this chair for DNA?"

The technician nodded. "Yes, sir. We didn't find much. It's fairly new — you can still smell the leather — but we took samples anyway."

"Good." If the killer had sat there before they'd launched their brutal attack on the unsuspecting victim, there might be a hair or skin sample left behind.

There was a shout from the kitchen.

They filed in. A crime scene officer was bending over the sink. "There's blood in here. Lots of it. Looks like the killer used it to wash the blood off his hands or clean the murder weapon."

A thought hit Rob. "Could it be the killer's blood?"

"Not sure. I'll take samples." The forensic officer bent down to fetch the appropriate equipment from his kit bag. "We'll get them analyzed for you."

"Thanks." Rob glanced at Mallory. "It would be very convenient if the killer cut himself in the process and left us some DNA in the sink."

"Too convenient," Mallory muttered. "He probably just cleaned the blood off himself before he left the house." He twisted his head to nod back towards the living room. "*That* would have made quite a mess."

"We can hope." Rob cast his eyes around the kitchen. "Check this out." He pointed to a block of wood that had six different knives sticking out of it. "None missing." He opened the drawers but didn't find any more sharp knives, only your usual run-of-the-mill cutlery. "Have you been upstairs?" Rob asked.

"No, not yet. I didn't get here much before you."

They climbed up the narrow staircase and paused on a wide landing. Above them, subdued winter light streamed in from a rectangular skylight. Rob squinted up at it. The loft had been removed to create extra-high ceilings, which made the top floor appear more spacious. That would have been an expensive job.

"This must be the main bedroom." Rob indicated an open door on the right, through which a wooden king-sized bed was visible. They entered the room. The bed had pride of place in the centre, flanked by two bedside tables, both in the same dark mahogany as the bed frame. The duvet cover was a steely grey, a shade lighter than the pillows, and it was perfectly made. There was not a single crease in the smooth material.

"Does he have a cleaner?" Rob enquired, walking around the room.

"I'll find out," said Mallory.

The carpet was clean with faint striations in it that told Rob it had recently been vacuumed. The heavy curtains were open, tied back with tasselled cords. Not his taste, but it did the job.

"The bathroom's through here." Mallory was holding open a slatted door that had been made to look like it was part of the built-in cupboards. He switched on the light and the extractor fan immediately whirred to life.

"Really?" Rob walked through the narrow entrance into a tiled bathroom complete with walk-in shower, basin and toilet. It was much larger than he had expected, then he realized it must have been a smaller bedroom next door that had been converted. No bath, he noted. The bathroom was sparklingly clean, and the mirrors were clear and unsmudged. He doubted Aadam Yousef was the type of man to get his Marigolds on and whip out the Windolene. No, this had been professionally cleaned, and not too long ago. He'd guess as recently as yesterday morning. Yousef hadn't had time to mess it up.

The bathroom cabinet contained men's toiletries, paracetamol, ibuprofen tablets and an electric toothbrush. Nothing remotely feminine.

"I think it's safe to say he lived alone," Rob muttered, closing the cabinet. Mallory switched the light off and the fan lapsed into blissful silence.

The guest bedroom didn't look lived-in. There was a double bed but the mattress was bare. The only items in the built-in cupboard were some winter coats pushed to one side. There were no personal items on the dresser beneath the window, nothing to indicate the room was in use.

"What's in those?" Rob nodded towards two cardboard boxes piled on top of each other in the corner.

"Extra bedding," Mallory replied with a shrug. "Nothing of interest."

Rob frowned. "When did Yousef move into this house?"

"The title deed said two years ago. He obviously didn't use this room."

Rob opened the top of the box and peered in. "Pink," he said. "It's a woman's bedding. Find out if he used to be married or had a daughter or sister living with him prior to moving in here."

"I'll get right on it," Mallory said with a curt nod. One of the things Rob liked about working with Mallory is that he never took notes, but still seemed to remember everything he'd been instructed to follow up on. He'd once told Rob he had an eidetic memory — Rob wasn't entirely sure what that meant — but it had come in handy at school and the police academy. He could recite even the most obscure laws, rules and regulations that most officers forgot the second they left college.

They moved into the study.

"Bloody hell," muttered Rob. Unlike the bedrooms, it was a mess. The desk was cluttered with papers, a laptop lay open to one side and there were two used coffee cups making rings in the wood. It was a nice desk, too. Yvette would go ballistic if he did that. He resisted the urge to move them. "I'm guessing the cleaner wasn't allowed in here."

"That's for sure." Mallory ran a latex finger along the windowsill and held it up. "Look at this." It was covered in dust.

"Let's get SOCO in here. It might give us an indication of what line of business he was in."

Mallory flicked through the papers on his desk. "These are all household bills. I can't see anything pertaining to a business."

"Invoices?" asked Rob.

Mallory nodded. "Yeah, electricity, council tax, car insurance . . ." He put them back down. "Everything's in Yousef's name and there's nothing addressed to a limited company or business of any sort."

Rob scratched his head. "We need to find out what Yousef did for a living. This house and that car didn't pay for itself."

"Nothing in his wallet indicated he was employed. No key cards or name badge, no company business card. Only a debit card and a driver's licence, both in his name."

"Okay, let's run him through the database when we get back to the station and see what pops up."

Rob opened a desk drawer and let out a low, slow whistle. Mallory peered over his shoulder. "Burner phones?"

"Yeah, and a stack of them at that." He rifled through the pile of devices, all different sizes and makes. "I count nine."

He opened the other drawers. "There's more. What the hell was this guy up to with so many prepaid phones?"

"It can't be good," muttered Mallory.

Was this what had got him killed? Something he was into? An illegal scheme or business deal?

Not finding much else, they went downstairs just in time to see the ambulance service wheeling out the black body bag.

"When's the post-mortem?" Rob asked Liz, who was still on her knees packing up her kit.

She rubbed her forehead. "I can't do it before three o'clock tomorrow. I've got a queue running. It was a busy weekend."

Rob nodded. He would have liked it done sooner, but it couldn't be helped. She had her hands full. He'd heard about the multi-vehicle pile-up on the M3 near Thorpe Park that had resulted in several fatalities. The motorway had only just reopened.

"Thanks, Liz." He turned to Mallory, who was talking to a member of the SOCO team about bagging everything in the upstairs study. "Let's head back to the station. There's nothing more we can do here."

CHAPTER 3

The Putney major crime team was housed in an uninspiring grey four-storey building at the bottom of Putney Bridge Road. Despite its unflattering exterior, it had recently undergone an extensive refurbishment and now boasted a shiny reception area, a decent cafeteria and three floors of open-plan office space including stylish, glass-walled incident rooms that made briefings feel more like business meetings.

Rob stood at the head of the twelve-seater table in Incident Room One waiting for his team to filter in. Mallory, his right-hand man was pinning photographs of their victim on to the whiteboard behind him.

"Come on, we haven't got all day." He kept his voice light but he was impatient to get started.

DS Jenny Bird and DS Will Freemont, two experienced sergeants, sat on either side of him, followed by DC Celeste Parker, all of whom had worked on the Surrey Stalker case with him last year. New to the department were DC Mike Manner, a tall black man with a distinctive London accent, and DC Jeff Clarke, a young northerner who'd transferred down south to be closer to his wife's ageing parents. Rob didn't know either of them very well.

Since the new incident rooms had been installed, Rob couldn't decide whether to sit at the head of the table or stand like he used to when addressing his team. He figured since he'd be pointing to the whiteboard most of the time, he'd be better off standing. Mallory finished attaching the photographs and walked around to sit at the foot of the table.

"Thanks, Mallory," he said. "Right, let's get started. The victim is forty-year-old Aadam Yousef from Hounslow. He was found by his neighbour, a Mrs Banerjee, who looked through the window, spotted him lying on the floor and called the police. He was stabbed several times and the knife wounds were extensive. I'm not sure exactly how many there were — the post-mortem will confirm — but at first glance, at least seven or eight."

There was a gentle murmur around the table.

"This is what we know so far." He turned to the whiteboard. "Yousef lived alone and, as far as we can tell, was unmarried. There was a box of pink bedding in the spare room, so he may have had a guest or a family member stay there at some point. Jenny and Will, can you get hold of his phone records, social media accounts, emails and so on? We need to identify his next of kin and if he was seeing anyone, or if he had any children from a previous relationship. Anyone who can give us a better idea of who this guy was."

The two sergeants nodded and made notes on their handheld devices. It seemed notepads were a thing of the past. It felt right, in keeping with their high-tech new image. In fact, he was the only one with a paper and pencil in front of him on the table. Mallory didn't use anything.

"We need to find out what this guy did for a living. We found a stash of burner phones in his study. Judging by his new house and fancy BMW, he had recently come into some money. I want to know the source of that income."

Mallory sat up straight. "I'll get on to SOCO and see if we can get access to his laptop and the phone records."

"Celeste, will you coordinate a door-to-door with Hounslow Police? Maybe the neighbours or someone in the local community can shed some light on Yousef's business dealings. Oh, and find out who his cleaner was. We urgently need to talk to them. They would have been there the day of the murder, I'm sure of it. The place was spotless."

"I asked the neighbour, she didn't know," cut in Mallory.

Rob pursed his lips. "Okay, there might be something in his paperwork or telephone records. Everyone keep an eye out for contact information for a cleaner."

Nods all round.

"What about CCTV?" asked Celeste.

"Yeah, I'm getting to that. The house is off the A4 on the way to Heathrow, so there's bound to be some coverage. That's a major thoroughfare. Mike, can you and Jeff look into that?"

Celeste grinned. Rob always gave the CCTV to the rookies, and last year it had been her. Trawling through hours of footage was dog work, but it got results. Often it was the CCTV footage that led to a successful prosecution. He said as much now, and the two young men nodded, although Jeff looked disappointed. He probably wanted to get stuck in to the real police work, but this was important, and everyone had to earn their stripes.

"Yes, guv," they said in unison.

He noticed Mike had a jagged scar on his jawline. It wasn't noticeable unless he tilted his head backwards and the light caught it. Rob made a mental note to chat with both the new guys when he had time. He liked to get to know his team, and he knew nothing about these two. Mike had appeared a couple of weeks ago, having transferred from Southwark Police, where he'd been a uniformed officer. He looked like he could handle himself, with a broad chest and shoulders that had been honed in the gym. It would be interesting to find out why he'd made the switch to the major crime team.

Jeff was easier to read. Young, eager and motivated, he wanted to work his way up the ranks as quickly as possible.

16

Ambition wasn't a bad thing, but Rob wanted to make sure he covered all the basics on his way up the ladder.

"Now, I want to take a moment to talk about the nature of the crime. We're still waiting on forensics, but by all accounts, this was a vicious, personal attack."

Mike leaned forward in his seat. "So, Yousef knew his attacker?"

"Yep, no doubt about it," said Rob. "There was no forced entry. The victim let his attacker in, even offered him a drink. There were two whisky glasses found at the scene." He pointed to the evidence pictures on the board behind him. "One was on the table, empty, and the other on the floor where the victim dropped it when he was attacked."

"That doesn't mean he knew his killer." Jeff spoke out. "That could have been their first meeting."

"True." That was quite astute. The number-one rule in policing was assume nothing. "But he was expecting him. The house was freshy cleaned, the living room was spotless and they were enjoying a fairly expensive single malt. You don't give that to just anybody."

Jeff nodded slowly. "Maybe his phone records will show us who came round."

"Maybe." Rob sent a pointed look in Jenny's direction. She nodded. "Stabbing someone over and over again takes real anger," he continued. "This was not a cold, calculated attack. That's not to say it wasn't pre-planned, but the attacker wanted that man dead, and he wanted it done in the most violent way possible."

"Are we assuming it's a he?" asked Jenny.

Another good question. "No, we can't assume anything yet. Forensics might help with that, however. Yousef was a big man, so unless he was taken by surprise, I can't see a woman getting the upper hand over him. Also, there was no lipstick on the empty glass, and no evidence of sexual activity on the body."

"And women don't usually drink whisky," said Mike. At Jenny's raised eyebrow, he added, "Do they?"

Celeste crinkled her nose. "No."

"Maybe he was drugged?" This from Will.

"It's a possibility. Again, we'll have to wait for the toxicology report for that."

"It was definitely pre-planned," said Mallory from the foot of the table.

All eyes turned to him. Rob motioned for him to go ahead. He liked to give Mallory free rein. He was a good detective and showed a lot of initiative. Rob had been encouraging him to apply for a promotion to Detective Inspector, but Mallory seemed reluctant to push himself forward.

His sergeant got to his feet. "The murder weapon, for one thing. The killer brought it with him. That takes a certain level of premeditation. Then, there's the blood found in the kitchen sink. It looks like the killer cleaned the blood off the knife before leaving the house, but we'll know this for sure once we get the blood results back. And he made an appointment with Yousef. As DI Miller pointed out, they knew or knew of each other."

"He washed off the knife?" repeated Mike.

"Yeah, committing a crime like that would have been pretty messy," said Rob bluntly. "He couldn't go out with a bloody knife."

"What about his clothing?" asked Jenny.

"There would definitely have been blood spatter," said Rob. "Let's see if CCTV picks up anything. I've got the Hounslow Uniform division searching all the bins and skips in the area looking for the murder weapon or any items of clothing with blood on them."

Mike and Jeff both nodded. The importance of the CCTV footage was becoming more evident.

Rob wrapped up the meeting soon after that. There wasn't much more they could discuss until they got the results back from the lab and the post-mortem had been performed.

* * *

18

"Rob, a word," came Detective Superintendent Lawrence's rumbling voice from the other end of the squad room. He wasn't yelling, but his natural volume was so loud it rose above everyone else's.

Rob made his way to his boss's office. It was also made of glass and resembled a square bubble in the corner, affording no privacy whatsoever. Lawrence liked it that way. He'd once told Rob that it made him feel more connected to the action. He was a very hands-on boss, often following up on leads when they were short-staffed. Secretly, Rob thought Lawrence would be happier in the thick of things than driving a desk.

"Close the door."

Rob did as he was told. The office may have been completely see-through, but it was soundproof, so even if Lawrence was yelling down the telephone — a common occurrence — they couldn't hear anything from outside the room if the door was shut. The only indication of the shouting was the Superintendent's mottled expression and the veins standing out in his thick neck.

"How is Yvette?" He leaned back in his executive swivel chair and surveyed his senior investigating officer.

"She's improving, sir," said Rob. He knew where this was going. Lawrence was worried about his ability to commit to the investigation.

"I'm glad to hear it. She took a bad knock last year."

You could say that again. After spending a week in hospital, she'd proceeded to have a full-blown nervous breakdown, and had had to go home to France for a month. He'd taken some time off and visited her at her parents' farm on the outskirts of Lyon, and they'd gone for long walks, talked a lot about the important things in life, and eventually got married in a tiny church in Saint-Étienne. It was a small wedding with only her parents and sister and brother-in-law attending. They'd agreed that they'd have a bigger ceremony in London when she was feeling stronger.

"I think she's on the mend now."

Lawrence sighed. "Listen, Rob. You know I'm not one to beat around the bush. Are you able to commit a hundred per cent to this case? Because if you can't, if you need more time, I can assign—"

"I'm fine." Rob cut him off. "Yvette understands I have to work. I can't put my career on hold for ever. We've talked about it. She's okay with it."

Lawrence exhaled and Rob realized how relieved he was. "I'm glad to hear it. It's good to have you back in the game."

Even though he'd been at work these last few months, he'd been on light duties, which had been frustrating from a professional point of view. He'd had to take a back seat while his team dealt with homicides and other serious crimes.

After the much-publicized apprehending of the Surrey Stalker, Rob had given several interviews to the press and become something of a media star, albeit temporarily. That was another reason he'd escaped to France. The constant swarm of photographers and journalists outside his house had been doing his head in. Now he was back, he wanted to get stuck in again. He couldn't let the rest of the team continue to carry him.

"When's the PM?" asked his boss.

"Three o'clock tomorrow." Rob wondered how SOCO were getting on with the lab results.

Lawrence read his mind. "Any DNA from the scene yet?"

"Not yet." Rob shook his head.

"Chase them up. Tell them it's a priority. I've managed to keep this under wraps for now, but it won't be long before the press get wind of it."

"Great." Rob was well aware that once the media realized who was in charge of the case, the old news articles would resurface again.

"I'll get you to give a statement, once we know more," Lawrence said with a wry grin. "At least the public will be pleased to hear you're in charge."

Rob grimaced. Nothing like raising expectations.

Lawrence chuckled. "It's about time the public had a little faith in the police department."

"I hope they won't be disappointed."

"Let the evidence show you the way, and trust your gut, Rob. It's stood you in good stead before."

It wasn't often that his boss offered such nuggets of wisdom. "Will do." He stood up. "Thanks, boss."

Lawrence grunted. "Keep me posted."

CHAPTER 4

Liz Kramer rang and said she could squeeze in Yousef's post-mortem later that day, after all. The coroner had postponed the inquest into the motorway collision, which meant there was a rare gap in her schedule.

Rob observed from the viewing gallery as Liz began, inspecting the body from all angles. Lying naked on the metal table, Aadam Yousef appeared smaller and more vulnerable than he had lying fully clothed on his living-room floor.

Liz clicked on the recorder and began to speak. "The victim is a well-nourished forty-year-old male previously identified as Aadam Yousef. He is of Arabic descent. Initial observations show . . . nine stab wounds to the chest and abdomen."

Nine. Christ.

Her assistant, a fresh-faced young woman in a lab coat, handed her a ruler. Liz laid it across the chest. "The entry wounds are three centimetres across and smooth, which means the knife was non-serrated."

"All made by the same knife?" he asked, pushing the button that allowed him to communicate with the room below.

Liz glanced up and nodded. "Some haven't gone in as far as others, but they were all made by the same knife."

"Like a kitchen knife?" Rob asked.

"Yes."

That didn't help much. Everyone had access to a kitchen knife. He wondered how the officers he'd dispatched to search the bins were getting on. It would really help if they could find the murder weapon. However, he didn't think it was going to be that easy.

The rest of the examination was unenlightening. Liz took samples from beneath Yousef's fingernails but, although they were dirty, it didn't look like there were any skin samples there. No defensive wounds either, so Yousef hadn't put up a fight, a fact Rob found very interesting, given the size of him.

"Is it possible he was drugged?" he asked the pathologist.

"I've taken samples for Toxicology, but we won't know until the results come back."

"When will that be?" There was no harm in applying a bit of gentle pressure.

She arched an eyebrow. "Probably tomorrow now, unless the lab decides to rush it through."

Rob grimaced. "That would be great. I'm under pressure on this one."

"Aren't we all," was her response.

* * *

True to her word, though, the toxicology results landed on his desk at seven o'clock, as he was about to head home. He'd already rung Yvette and told her he was on his way. The rest of the team, other than Mallory and Mike, had left for the day.

He sat down again and looked them over. They were pretty straightforward. No evidence of sedatives or anything else in the man's bloodstream. He had not been drugged. Rob raised his eyebrows. That meant the attacker had relied on the element of surprise to down his victim. The first thrust must have debilitated Yousef to such an extent that he'd been unable to fight back. He pictured the scenario in his head

— the initial stab taking him by surprise, Yousef falling to the floor clutching his chest, dropping his whisky glass in the process. A second blow, even more debilitating than the first. Yousef rolling in agony, gazing up at his attacker with wild eyes. The attacker standing over him, repeatedly stabbing in a frenzy of rage until Yousef was dead, perhaps even continuing after the life had drained out of him.

He exhaled slowly, then went to discuss it with Mallory.

* * *

Yvette was sitting on the couch, her legs folded beneath her, watching an episode of *The Durrells* when he got home. She didn't get up. Trigger, on the other hand, met him at the door, tail wagging. *At least someone's pleased to see me*, he thought.

"How was your day?" He went into the lounge and sat beside her. The air was thick with smoke.

She shrugged. "Boring. How was yours?"

"Why don't you go out? See your friends?" She hadn't gone back to work since the attack, even though eight months had passed.

"You know I don't like to leave the house." He knew she was suffering from agoraphobia but had refused to speak to anyone about it. Personally, he didn't like shrinks, but in this case, he felt it was warranted. She'd been through a particularly traumatic experience and didn't seem able to pull herself out of it.

He sighed. "Darling, it's not good for you to be stuck inside all day."

"I have Trigger." Her eyes were still glued to the television, although she had turned down the volume.

"That's not the same as human interaction." He paused. This was always a sensitive subject but she was getting worse and he had to act now before it was too late. "Listen, there's a woman at work, her name's Becca and she trained as a trauma counsellor before she became a police officer. She worked with me last year on the Stalker case."

He saw Yvette go rigid at the mention of the Stalker.

"I think you should talk to her."

"I don't want to speak to anybody," she said sulkily, her lower lip protruding in a pout. She still looked sexy despite not having brushed her hair or applied any make-up. That, in itself, was a sure sign she wasn't in her right frame of mind. Yvette usually took so much care with her appearance.

"I really think you should. Let me set up an appointment for you," he pressed. "She can come here so you don't have to go anywhere." His voice was firm, but kind. He didn't want her to turn into a hermit — it wasn't healthy. A wave of guilt passed over him. It was his fault she'd been abducted, his case that had overflowed into his personal life, and she'd been the one who had suffered.

Yvette reached for her cigarettes. The ashtray on the coffee table was overflowing with butts. She didn't reply, which he took to be a good sign.

"I'm going to have a shower and then I'll make supper. Have you eaten anything?"

She shook her head. Her shoulders had become more pronounced of late and her hips stuck out above the tracksuit pants that she wore. She'd replaced food with cigarettes and was losing weight. Her beautiful, magazine-worthy body was becoming angular and thin.

He felt an upwelling of emotion and leaned over and kissed her on the cheek. "I love you. We'll get through this. I promise."

She turned to face him, her slanting eyes haunted. "Will we?"

He took her into his arms and mumbled into her hair. "Of course we will."

* * *

After supper, he took the case file and a beer, and sat in his favourite armchair to read. Trigger followed him in and lay down on his foot. He fondled the dog's ears. When Yvette's sister, Naomi, had first suggested they get a dog, he hadn't been sure. He'd never had a pet before — his mother had been allergic to animal fur — but Trigger had grown on him and he'd got used to the Labrador's silent, loyal companionship, and it was great protection for Yvette. While he was at work, Trigger stuck to Yvette like glue, but as soon as he got home, the dog switched loyalties and followed him around everywhere, even into the bathroom. It was like having a four-legged shadow.

Mallory had typed everything up and added it to the system, but Rob preferred a hard copy. He liked to spread out the pages and look at the full picture like pieces of a puzzle, move them around and consider them from all angles. All the notes had been printed out and added to the file, along with the preliminary forensic and toxicology reports.

Yvette had gone to bed, or rather, she'd gone upstairs to watch TV. They had a flat-screen mounted on the bedroom wall, which was a new thing. He had objected at first, but he had to admit, it made life easier. At least he had somewhere to work in peace, and Yvette could still watch her soaps and romcoms without him rolling his eyes and making inane comments.

He opened the manila folder and withdrew the SOCO report from the crime scene. It wasn't complete — they were still waiting on some lab results — but it had come in late and he hadn't had a chance to read it yet.

Two sets of prints were found at the crime scene, those of Yousef and an unknown person who wasn't on the database. It could be the killer, but the same prints had been found in the kitchen and upstairs bedroom, so Rob was banking on the cleaner. They needed to find them.

The guest's whisky glass had been clean, not even Yousef's prints were on it. Now that was odd. Yousef would have poured the drinks and his fingerprints were all over his own glass. Had the guest been wearing gloves? It was possible, given that it was a cold January. Except the glass had been empty with no saliva or lip marks on the outside and no whisky residue inside, which begged the question: did the killer wash the glass in the kitchen sink along with the murder weapon?

The armchair had been swabbed for hair and fibres but had turned up nothing of interest. It was surprisingly clean for an armchair, but as the forensic technician had pointed out, it was fairly new.

He read through Yousef's personal bank statement found in the study. His account had a few thousand pounds in it, nothing remarkable. Rob gnawed on his lower lip. Where had the money for the house and car come from? Had he paid in cash? There had to be another, secret account or a business account that they didn't know about. Even the shirt Yousef had been wearing when he died cost more than Rob's weekly budget. He made a note to get Mallory to look into that in more detail. It would mean getting a warrant, which might pose a problem since Yousef was the victim, not the perpetrator, but then he'd had several pre-paid phones stashed in his drawer — that ought to count for something. Hopefully, it would shed some light on why he'd been murdered.

A few of the transactions caught his eye. Every week Yousef paid 200 quid to a 'T Barszcz'. He read the name out loud and made a hash of it. How did you pronounce that, anyway? Were they the cleaner? He took out his phone and googled the surname. It was Polish.

Next, he read the preliminary lab report. It turned out the blood in the kitchen sink belonged solely to Yousef. Rob leaned back in his chair and took a swig of beer. So, the killer left Yousef lying on the lounge floor, went into the kitchen and washed the blood off the knife and possibly cleaned the whisky glass before putting it back on the table and leaving the premises undetected. Those were both bizarrely calm gestures in light of what had happened, and in complete contrast to the frenzied nature of the attack.

Rob wondered what his old friend Tony would make of it. Tony Sanderson was a criminal profiler of some repute and had worked for most of Britain's law enforcement agencies at some stage over the last few years. He made a note to meet Tony for a drink. They were due for a catch-up anyway, and it would be useful to run this past him, unofficially, of course. The budget wouldn't stretch to hiring a professional criminologist, and certainly not one of Tony's stature.

Upstairs, the television fell silent. Yvette was going to sleep. She didn't come down to say goodnight and he didn't go up. Instead, he took out the crime scene photographs and spread them over the coffee table. He studied the image of Yousef lying on the plush carpet, his blood pooling beneath him, the spilled glass only inches from his outstretched hand. He'd been smartly dressed in navy jeans and, according to the forensic report, a Giorgio Armani shirt. He'd also been wearing cologne — Rob had smelled it when he'd inspected the body. The gold TAG Heuer watch on his wrist was visible, and apparently, he'd had a wallet in his back pocket containing £300.

The house contained several other expensive items, namely the enormous cinema-style TV screen, the laptop in the study and an assortment of watches the scene-of-crime officers had found in a drawer in Yousef's bedroom. Their victim liked the good things in life.

Rob yawned loudly, and Trigger, who was sleeping at his feet, glanced up in surprise. They could rule out burglary. This was a personal, premeditated attack. Someone had had it in for Yousef. Now he just had to find out why, and hopefully that would lead him to who.

CHAPTER 5

Rob was at the station early the next morning. He'd left Yvette to sleep, and after feeding Trigger had driven the four miles to the major crimes office in Putney. It was a crisp, blue-skied winter's day and before he went inside, he turned his face towards the sun, enjoying the warmth. A smattering of frost covered the ground in shaded areas and in the background, someone was scraping ice off their windscreen. He preferred it like this — cold and sunny — to the dreary rain-drenched few months they'd had. Christmas had seen one of the worst rainfalls on record, which hadn't brought much in the way of joy and glad tidings.

Superintendent Lawrence was already in his office. Rob grinned. No matter how early he got in, the DSI was already there. Rob put the bulky file on his desk, took off his jacket and slung it over the back of his chair.

First things first. Coffee.

He made his way to the fancy new coffee machine that had been installed in the small waiting area, raising his hand in greeting at his boss as he passed. Lawrence was on the phone and didn't respond, although his eyes followed Rob as he walked across the office. The squad room was unnervingly

29

quiet without the whirring of the printers and the collective hum of the computers and office chatter.

The coffee machine sputtered quietly as it poured him a semi-decent cappuccino. The smell reminded him of the inside of one of the cafés he and Yvette frequented in Lyon, and he inhaled before taking his first sip.

"Rob, you'd better get in here."

Lawrence's voice startled him. He hadn't heard him open the glass doors to the waiting room. He followed his boss into his bubble office. By the look on his face, this wasn't good news.

"What's up?"

The Superintendent's office was fitted with the same standard-issue desk and computer as the rest of the squad room. He hadn't wanted any special treatment. Rob respected him for that. Apart from the desk and executive chair, there were two small armchairs huddled around a coffee table for more intimate discussions. Rob had only seen him use them when the Deputy Commissioner came for a visit. The only window in the room looked out on to the high street, and on the other exterior wall hung several framed certificates and a photograph of a group of men in maroon berets. The Parachute Regiment. Apparently, Lawrence had enlisted straight out of school and had survived three tours in the Middle East before a leg injury saw him medically discharged. And that information had come from the Deputy Commissioner, with whom Rob had had informal drinks after they'd caught the Surrey Stalker. He'd never once heard his boss mention it. The picture on the wall was the only clue he'd served at all.

Lawrence studied him. "You're not going to like it, Rob."

A bad feeling gathered in the pit of Rob's stomach. He sat down, put his coffee on the desk and waited for his boss to explain.

"I've just been on the phone to the National Crime Agency. They have a particular interest in your victim, Aadam Yousef."

"Yousef? How come?"

"It turns out he was on their watch list. They've been keeping tabs on him for several months in connection with a county lines drug network."

Rob stared at him. "You're serious? Organized crime?"

"It looks like it. Your vic may have been pretty high up in the criminal hierarchy."

"How high up?" asked Rob, his gaze locked on his boss's face.

"They think he's part of an illegal supply chain selling thousands of pounds' worth of drugs to small-time dealers and county lines networks across West London."

"Christ. So Yousef is a drug kingpin." It was starting to make sense. The new house. The BMW. The cinema-like TV and the new furniture. This guy was raking it in.

"So it would seem. Oh, and they're sending a representative to work with you on the case."

He liked the way the boss had thrown that in there, almost as an aside. "A representative? Who?"

Lawrence's face broke into a smile. "Someone we know, actually. She's gone up in the world since the Stalker case last year."

Rob felt his stomach lurch.

"Jo Maguire," said the Superintendent with a flourish. "At least it's not a stranger," he added. "You guys worked well together, if memory serves. Things could be a lot worse."

They had worked too well together, that was the problem.

Rob forced a smile, but it turned into a grimace. "When's she arriving?"

"This afternoon. They're not wasting any time on this one. These county lines gangs have been getting a lot of bad press, especially because they target youngsters and vulnerable adults. There's even talk about charging them under human trafficking legislation in addition to drug dealing, because it offers a longer prison sentence."

Rob had read about that. The theory was if they lumped the drug gangs with child abusers and human traffickers, the lowest of the low, they'd lose some of their sheen, particularly on the inside.

"Okay," he said. "But this is still our case, right? We're not handing it over to the NCA?"

Lawrence didn't meet his eye. "For now. If this murder is related to their wider operation, then we may not have a choice. Apparently, they've had several players under surveillance for months in preparation for a massive country-wide crackdown."

"Of course it's connected." Rob's coffee suddenly tasted sour. "The guy's a drug dealer. Someone obviously wanted him dead."

"I'm sorry, Rob, but it is what it is. We have to play ball."

Rob sighed. That much was true, but he didn't have to like it.

* * *

As soon as he left Lawrence's office, he went outside for a cigarette. So what if it was only eight thirty in the morning? He lit up and drew the smoke deep into his lungs.

Jo Maguire.

Fuck.

He didn't think he'd ever see her again. She was head of the Lewisham Major Investigation Team, or she had been when they'd worked together on the Stalker case. Now, apparently, she'd moved to the National Crime Agency. He wondered what had brought on that move, then decided it was none of his business. She'd always been ambitious. Besides, she was a good detective — she deserved it.

He exhaled, watching the smoke mingle with the cold morning air. His affair with Jo seemed like ages ago, even though it was only last spring. Yvette had moved out, told him it was over. He'd been confused, and if he was honest, bitter that his fiancée hadn't understood the demands his work placed on him. He took another drag. Not much had changed in that regard. Then there was Jo, a five-foot-ten blonde bombshell with an easy, down-to-earth manner and cute dimples to go with it. Within hours, she'd had the whole department, himself included, eating out of her hand. And now she was back.

And now, he was married.

He shook his head and studied the glowing butt of his cigarette. Yvette had never needed him more. The guilt washed over him again, as it always did when he thought about what had happened. It was thanks to him she was stuck inside suffering from panic attacks, unable to leave the house.

"Is it that bad?" quipped DS Luke Anstead, a colleague Rob had worked with before but was now assigned to a different team. They'd given up smoking together last year as a New Year's resolution and had lasted four months before, under mutual agreement, they'd given up giving up.

Rob flicked his butt into the gutter and fell into step beside him. "You're in early today." They entered the thick glass doors of the MIT building, both nodding towards the duty sergeant.

"Yeah, Amy has taken the kids to her parents' in Essex, so I've got the house to myself. For once I didn't have to wait in line for the bathroom this morning."

Rob chuckled. He couldn't imagine a house full of kids. Yvette had made it quite clear when they were dating that she didn't want children. As an ex-lingerie model, he could understand why. She'd made her money off her figure. Given his job and the long hours he worked, he'd agreed, but every now and then he thought it might be nice to have a son to take to the Arsenal game or a daughter to . . . what? He didn't even know what girls did. Ballet?

Now they had Trigger, they were getting quite domesticated, but Yvette was in no state to have children, even if she wanted to. With that in mind, he said goodbye to Luke and made his way to the second floor, where the Family Liaison Team was based. He spotted Becca Townsend immediately. She was laughing with another female officer, a cup in her hand. For someone who dealt with grief all the time, she was a remarkably upbeat woman. He supposed you had to be, or it would drag you down.

"Hi, Becca," he said.

She gave him a wave. "It's nice to see you, Rob. How have you been?"

Becca had worked with the relatives of the victims on some of his past cases, and he'd gotten to know her fairly well. A soft-spoken, matronly woman with sympathetic eyes and a warm smile, she was just the type of person Yvette would listen to. He hoped.

"Do you have a minute?"

She nodded. "Come on, let's go in here." He followed her to a small incident room with a four-seater table surrounded by soundproof glass.

"Now, what's bothering you?" She gave him an encouraging smile.

He took a deep breath. "It's Yvette."

She nodded knowingly. "Is she still having trouble?" Becca knew what had happened — it wasn't a secret.

"Yeah, I think she's getting worse. She won't leave the house, she's not eating, she's smoking way too much. It's been eight months now, shouldn't she be getting over it?"

He was the type of person that took the bull by the horns. If he was afraid of it, he'd confront it, but then his job was to run head first into danger while everyone else was running the other way. Perhaps he was used to it, but watching Yvette's decline, he'd never felt so helpless.

"Is she having panic attacks? Flashbacks?"

He ran a hand through his hair. "I'm not sure about flashbacks, but she's definitely having panic attacks."

"It sounds like she might have a touch of PTSD," Becca said. "She needs help. Closeting herself away and refusing to face the world will only make things worse."

"Will you talk to her?"

Becca raised her eyebrows in surprise. "I'm sure the department would pay for a therapist."

"She won't see a therapist. She's met you, and I think she'll talk to you. You're a trained trauma counsellor. Please Becca. I don't know what else to do."

Becca nodded slowly. "Okay, I'll have to clear it with my boss, but if he says yes, I'll go to see her tomorrow afternoon. I have some free time then."

He took her hand. "Thank you, you're a star."

She grinned. "Anything for you, Rob."

Rob went back upstairs feeling like a weight had been lifted from his shoulders. If anyone could get through to Yvette, it was Becca. He knew it wouldn't be a quick fix, but he was looking forward to having his wife back.

* * *

The cleaner's name was Tatiana Barszcz and she was from Warsaw. She'd been in the UK for seven years and worked as an independent cleaning contractor. She lived in Hounslow, close to the airport, and a squad car was bringing her in for questioning right now.

There were several CCTV cameras in the streets around Yousef's house but annoyingly none that picked up his end of the road, his driveway or the front entrance. The pathologist had put the time of death between four and eight o'clock on Monday evening and so the CCTV team, aka Mike and Jeff, were scrolling through footage of the surrounding area looking for anything suspicious during that time frame. So far, they'd come up with absolutely zilch.

"The killer must have arrived by car," Rob told Mike and Jeff, both of whom were looking bleary-eyed and dishevelled after too many hours glued to screens in the warren, which was what they called the CCTV room. "And he must have come off the A4, so start there and work your way towards the house." The A4 happened to be one of the busiest roads in West London and the continuous flow of traffic on a Monday evening didn't make the task any easier. Still, one of those vehicles must belong to their killer.

"He might have come by train or bus." Jeff rubbed his eyes.

"It's possible, but unlikely." Rob had thought about that. "Carrying a knife on public transport would be risky, particularly with the current stop-and-search law in place, and having blood spatter on his clothing would have raised the alarm. I think, for now, let's assume he came by car, but obviously if you see anyone on foot who looks suspicious, let me know. We can't rule anything out."

"The cleaner's here," Mallory told him, once he'd grabbed his fifth cup of coffee of the day. This one had two sachets of sugar in it in lieu of lunch. "I've asked them to put her in Interview Room Two."

"Right, thanks. Let's head down there now."

"Mind if I come?" said a clear feminine voice behind them.

CHAPTER 6

Rob swung around.

"Hi, Jo," he said casually, as if he were greeting a colleague he hadn't seen for a while, not a woman he'd slept with, bonded with and, if he were brutally honest, fallen a little bit in love with. She still looked great — just as he remembered, except her hair was a bit shorter and swung around her shoulders, rather than up in a ponytail like she used to wear it for work. Her clear skin was almost devoid of make-up, save for a light swipe of lip gloss, and she wore an efficient black trouser suit with a soft cream blouse underneath. With a start, he realized he was staring.

He cleared his throat. "Sure, why don't you come downstairs with us now? You can watch from the viewing gallery."

She hesitated, and he knew she was dying to sit in on the interview, but having just arrived, she didn't want to muscle her way in. That wasn't her style. No, she charmed her way in, and he had no doubt that before long, the rest of his team would be bending over backwards to do her bidding. He'd seen her at work before.

"Okay, fine." Her cobalt-blue eyes lacked the sparkle he remembered. Instead, they were rather frosty as they glared at him.

He smiled. He knew it was petty, but he refused to give in so soon. This was his case. If the NCA wanted to take it over, he'd have no choice but to let them, but for now, he was the one in charge. "Good. Let's go then."

He led the way down the stairs to the ground floor, conscious of Jo's heels clicking on the concrete behind him. Mallory said nothing. As they walked past the viewing room, Mallory pointed it out to Jo, who, without glancing at either of them, pushed open the door and disappeared inside.

"Hello. I'm Detective Inspector Miller and this is Detective Sergeant Mallory. We're going to ask you some questions about your employer, Aadam Yousef."

The cleaner's eyes widened. Obviously, the police officers who'd picked her up hadn't told her what it was in connection with. "I'm not in trouble?"

"Have you done something wrong?" Rob asked her.

She shook her head. "No, sir."

"Then you aren't in any trouble." He smiled, and her lips turned up ever so slightly at the corners. He saw her shoulders drop as she relaxed. She was young, probably in her early twenties and would have been pretty if it wasn't for her pasty complexion and the dark shadows beneath her eyes. Maybe she worked too hard. Being a cleaner didn't pay much, barely minimum wage, and the work was physical and demanding. She probably didn't get outside much either, not that any of them did, to be fair. Anyway, her lifestyle was not his concern. "How long have you been working for Aadam Yousef?" he asked.

She thought for a moment. "Maybe six months."

"And how did you come to work there?"

"I used to work for another lady in that street, Mrs Abrahams. She runs a hostel. I believe she told him about me."

Rob glanced at Mallory, who nodded. He was storing away all the details in his hard drive of a memory.

"What's he like to work for? Is he a nice man?"

Tatiana hesitated, but only for a split second. "He's okay. Most of the time he lets me get on with it."

"Most of the time?"

She shifted in her seat. "Sometimes he watches me work. I don't like it, but he says he wants to talk. It gets lonely working from home."

Rob exhaled. "Do you know what he does for a living?"

She shook her head. "I don't know. I hear him on the phone a lot." She made a texting motion. "He is always taking calls, but I don't know what they are saying. He doesn't talk in front of me. Always outside or in his office."

Rob nodded. It fit with what Lawrence had told him about Yousef and the county lines gang. The calls could be to and from his network of drug dealers.

"Did you work on Monday?" Rob shifted the discussion to the day of the murder.

"Yes. I work every Monday and Friday for Mr Yousef."

"Was he his normal self that day?"

She frowned, confused. He rephrased. "Was he acting strangely at all?"

"No." She shook her head. "He was the same."

"You didn't notice him arguing with anyone, maybe on the phone?"

"No." She folded her hands in her lap. "Has something happened to Mr Yousef?"

A brief pause. "I'm sorry to tell you that he was found dead in his house on Tuesday morning."

Her hand flew to her mouth and she whispered something in Polish. Her hand was shaking.

"Are you okay?" he asked her. "Do you want some water?"

She shook her head. "I'm okay. I'm shocked, that's all." She fought to regain her composure, but he could see the questions were flying through her head.

"He was stabbed," he told her, watching her face carefully for clues. She was, after all, the last person to have seen him alive.

She paled. "By who?"

"That is what we're trying to find out," said Rob. "Anything you can tell us would be helpful."

"I—I don't know anything," she cried. "I did my shift and left at midday, like I always do. Mr Yousef transfers money to my account, but he also pays for an Uber when I leave. He was good like that." Her hand fluttered across her face. "I can't believe he is dead."

"Where did you go after you left Yousef's house?" Mallory spoke for the first time.

She glanced away from Rob. "I had another client in Whitton, so the Uber driver took me there."

"Could we have the name of your next client?" Mallory asked.

She nodded and fished in her jacket pocket for her phone. After a few moments, she slid the phone over the metal table. Mallory took the number down then pushed the phone back to her. Even though he'd memorized it, the written notes were a reminder to enter the number into the system once the interview was over. They'd be checking up on her alibi, but Rob was fairly confident she wasn't the murderer. To start with, she was small-boned and slender. It looked like a stiff wind might blow her down. He couldn't imagine her attacking a man of Yousef's size. Secondly, she had no motive. Killing Yousef made no sense. It would just leave her without a job, and from the sounds of things, he was a good employer.

A thought struck him. "You mentioned Yousef used to like to watch you work. Did he ever . . . ?" He petered off, unsure how to phrase it. "Did he ever make advances towards you?"

"What?" She didn't understand.

"Did he ever come on to you, try to touch you, anything like that?"

The violent head-shaking was back. "No! I'm not like that. I do honest work. I have a son."

"A son?" She didn't look old enough to have a kid. "Who looks after him while you work?"

"My mother." She was sulking now. He'd offended her.

"Where's the boy's father?"

40

She shrugged and made a face like she'd smelled something unpleasant. "He lives in Poland." Obviously, there was no love lost there.

"Okay." He raised a hand. "That's fine. I believe you."

She stared at her hands. "Can I go now?"

"One more thing." She glanced up almost fearfully. "Did Yousef say anything about expecting a guest on Monday night?"

"A guest?" She thought for a moment, her teeth biting down on her lower lip. "No, but he did ask me to clean the glasses on the drinks trolley. They get dusty sometimes, so maybe . . ." Her voice faded away. Rob knew she was trying.

He smiled. "That's great. Thank you, Tatiana. You've been very helpful."

"I can go now?" She glanced from him to Mallory and back again.

"Yes, you can go now. The lady at the front desk will sign you out."

She nodded and stood up. Rob held the door for her while Mallory showed her to the front desk.

Jo came out of the viewing room. "I don't think she had anything to do with it, do you?"

It was just like Jo to cut straight to the chase. "Nope, but we'll check with her second client just to be sure."

She nodded, her eyes scanning his face. "It's good to see you again, Rob."

He hesitated. "Good to see you too."

She gave a wry smile. "I heard you got married."

From who? he wondered. "Yes." He fingered his silver wedding band. Why did he feel like he ought to explain about Yvette's breakdown, the time they'd spent together in France, the impromptu wedding, the guilt? He didn't elaborate.

"Congratulations." He was surprised by the sincerity in her voice. He remembered how easy she was to talk to. There had never been any awkwardness between them, even after they'd slept together. She'd been as content as he was to leave things as they were.

"Thank you," he said, relaxing a little. They headed towards the front desk. Mallory had already gone up to the squad room, presumably to follow up on Tatiana's alibi and write up the statement. "We've even got a dog."

She laughed. He'd forgotten how nice that sounded. "What's next? Kids?"

His smile faded. "No, I don't think we'll ever go that far."

She changed the subject. "Tell me about Yousef."

"Haven't you read the files?"

"Yes, but I want to hear it from you."

He gave her a hard look. "Isn't it you who should be telling us about Yousef? Apparently, you know a lot more about him than we do. That's why you're here, after all."

Her face remained neutral. "Fair enough. Okay, let's have a pow-wow in one of your fancy incident rooms." He didn't miss the sarcasm in her voice. She'd wanted to sit down and discuss the case with him, but he'd removed that possibility. It was best to keep things official, get everyone on board. It saved repetition. It saved a lot of things.

Rob called his team together and they all filed into the incident room. Jenny and Will greeted Jo like an old friend, while the new additions to the team eyed her with a mixture of awe and curiosity. It wasn't every day they got a visit from the National Crime Agency. Even the Superintendent squeezed in at the back.

"This is sensitive information," Jo began, standing as he had done at the head of the table. "The National Crime Agency has launched a full-scale investigation into the county lines network, and we've been monitoring several individuals for some time now. Aadam Yousef was one of those individuals. We believe he's one of the gang's core suppliers, trafficking heroin and cocaine with a street value of roughly one million pounds into the rural towns of Surrey, Hampshire and Berkshire, maybe even as far as Wiltshire and Somerset. He recruited small-time local drug dealers to act as couriers. We've had access to one of his pay-as-you-go phones, and he's been receiving between 250 and 300 messages a day from drug users, which shows the scale of their supply and the harm they are causing."

She paused to let this sink in. His team were silent, all eyes on Jo. "His untimely demise," she added, "has resulted in a major setback to our operation. We were hoping he would lead us to his main supplier, the top dog in the organization, the one who's bringing in the drugs."

"Do you have any idea who that is?" boomed Lawrence from the doorway. The detectives in front of him jumped.

"No, not as yet. We have several people under surveillance but we've yet to identify anyone who could be the kingpin."

"What about the phones we found?" Rob asked. "Will they help?"

The smile lit up her face. "Yes, that was a great coup. We're already analysing the data and consolidating it with what we know. It will potentially give us access to Yousef's runners and mules across the country. When we do, we'll organize a massive crackdown."

There were nods of approval around the table. Jo held up her hand. "It goes without saying that this is highly confidential, and the news of Yousef's death must be kept under wraps for now. If his organization knew he was out of commission, it would jeopardize our operation."

"You'd better get a move on, then," drawled Rob.

Jo shot him an irritated look. "It won't be long now. We can't keep his death quiet for much longer. Customers will realize their supply chain has dried up and questions will be asked."

"What about the media?" asked Mallory.

"We've issued a gag order until after the bust," she said. Rob loved the way the NCA could pull those kind of strings.

"How can we assist?" Lawrence asked from the back.

Jo's gaze landed on Rob. "Well, for now we'll treat this as a standard homicide enquiry on the off-chance that it's not related to the county lines operation."

There was a soft murmur. It was business as usual, for now.

She smiled. "It's most likely someone within the network took him out — maybe a competitor — but we like to keep an open mind."

"Maybe it was the top dog who killed him," said Mallory. "Perhaps he didn't like the way he was running things."

"It's a possibility." Jo wiped a strand of blonde hair off her face. "We're hoping any leads you dig up might point us in the right direction."

"Well, we'll do everything in our power to assist," cut in Lawrence from the back.

Jo beamed at him. "Thank you, sir. Your cooperation is much appreciated."

Rob had to give it to her, she certainly knew how to get people on her side. The meeting broke up after that, and they all went back to their desks. Lab reports were still coming in on evidence found at the crime scene, but with no new leads. The search of the rubbish bins hadn't turned up any knives or bloodied clothing, and nothing of interest had been seen on the CCTV footage. Even the cleaner, Tatiana's alibi, checked out. She was at a job in Whitton all afternoon, like she'd said.

"The problem is, we don't know who we're looking for," Rob said when Jo asked again for an update. She perched on the corner of his desk, completely at ease with him, while he was conscious of her every movement. "It could be anybody. Man, woman, black, white, Asian. We have no idea. There's not a strand of DNA evidence at the crime scene and we've picked up nothing untoward on the CCTV cameras." He ran a hand through his hair. God, he'd kill for a cigarette. Maybe after this he could slip downstairs for a quick one.

"Have you spoken to Yousef's family?" she asked.

"No, not yet. I was going to do that this afternoon." He glanced at the time on his computer. 3.30 p.m. The afternoon was already halfway through.

"Can I come?" She flashed him a dimpled smile.

Play nice, the Superintendent had said. He couldn't very well refuse.

"Sure." He kept his tone light. "Let me grab a sandwich from the canteen and we can head out."

"Okay, I'll meet you in the car park in ten minutes."

His phone rang. He glanced down. It was Yvette.

"Make that fifteen," he said.

CHAPTER 7

Mohammed Yousef lived in a two-bedroom council flat in a depressing high-rise in Wembley, North West London. His block was one of four that blighted the urban skyline. On the way there, Jo told Rob that this was where a young Aadam had grown up, along with his mother, Soraya, who had since passed away.

"How do you know this?" Rob asked.

"His father, Mohammed, is a cleric and an active member of the local Muslim community. He teaches at an Islamic boys' school connected to the mosque."

"And?" prompted Rob. He could hear by her voice there was more.

"He's been cautioned for preaching borderline extremist views," she said. "A parent at the school brought his behaviour to our attention. Consequently, Counter Terrorism's been watching him for a while now, but he seems to have been behaving himself."

"Strange that his son could be so different," mused Rob. He parked the car. The grey concrete building towered above them, blocking out the sun. "Drugs, human trafficking, abuse . . . Doesn't that go against the principles of Islam?"

"Yousef puts on a good show." Jo climbed out of the car and glanced around her. A pair of shabbily dressed youths were kicking a football around, while a group of black teens eyeballed them warily. "He goes to the mosque every Friday and donates to the local Islamic charity."

Rob made sure he locked it — twice — so that everyone heard the beeps. "Come on, let's get inside."

Mohammed Yousef's flat was on the fourth floor on the side of the block that didn't get any direct sunlight. They felt the cold as soon as he opened the door.

"Good afternoon, Mr Yousef. I'm DI Miller and this is DCI Maguire from the Putney Major Investigation Team. Can we have a word?"

"What's this about?" The cleric was an elderly man, outwardly quite frail but with sharp, penetrating black eyes. Tufts of white hair poked out from beneath his headscarf and he was dressed in a white shalwar kameez.

"It's about your son, Aadam. Can we come in?" Jo's voice was softer, more empathetic.

He didn't look at her, but he opened the door and stood back. Jo met Rob's gaze as they filed into the dark interior. The message was clear. *You do the talking.* Mr Yousef didn't seem all that fond of women.

They sat in a dimly lit lounge on a worn sofa. Jo shivered and Rob wondered how the old guy hadn't frozen to death already. "Is your heating broken?" Rob asked.

"I don't keep it on during the day," he said.

Was money pretty tight? As a cleric, Rob would have expected him to live more comfortably than this.

There was no television, only a radio playing Middle Eastern music coming from somewhere else in the apartment. Beneath the window was a well-worn prayer rug. The window itself was grimy and looked as if it hadn't been cleaned in months. What a way to live. Rob felt sorry for the old man.

"What did you want to talk to me about?" The cleric peered at Rob through the dimness. "Has Aadam done something wrong?"

"What makes you say that?"

The old man stroked his beard and Rob thought he wasn't going to reply, but then he spoke. "Aadam was always getting into trouble as a child. He had a strong, independent streak. My wife and I couldn't control him."

Rob could believe it. "No, we're here to give you some bad news."

The old man watched him with beady eyes.

Rob cleared his throat. He hated this part. "Aadam was found dead at his house yesterday morning. We think he died sometime on Monday night."

There was a long silence. The tinkling rhythm of the unfamiliar music rose and fell in the background. Mohammed blinked several times in rapid succession, but his eyes remained dry, then he whispered something beneath his breath in Arabic. Eventually, the man asked, "How did he die?"

"He was stabbed."

Rob watched the expression on Mohammed's face. A flicker of pain, maybe? No, it was more like sadness or regret, but then it was gone, replaced by the calm, almost zen-like veneer he'd had when they arrived.

"I'm sorry for your loss," Rob said.

Yousef nodded. "Thank you. Is that all you wanted to tell me?"

"Actually, because of the nature of his death, we wondered if we might ask you a few questions. Would that be okay?"

Rob glanced at Jo, who gave a little shrug. He didn't know how to handle this man who seemed to have no reaction at all over the news of his only son's death.

A hint of annoyance in the tight lips, but he nodded.

"Thank you." Rob composed his thoughts. "When last did you see your son?"

Another pause. "About three years ago. He didn't visit often."

"I'm sorry to hear that. Weren't you close?"

The beady eyes regarded him disdainfully. "No."

"Was that when your wife died?" cut in Jo.

Mohammed glanced towards the window, his voice tight. "Yes, Aadam came to the funeral."

"Did you talk?" asked Rob.

"Not really. Like I said, we didn't get on."

"Why was that?" Rob wanted to know.

The old man glanced at him and for the first time, Rob saw a hint of emotion, a flash of anger in the dark gaze. "Aadam wasn't a true believer. He pretended to be, but I could see right through him."

Rob could see how that might be a problem in a devout Muslim household. "Were you aware of your son's involvement in anything illegal?"

The beady eyes widened. "Illegal? No. Aadam may have turned his back on Islam, but he wasn't a criminal."

That's what he thought. Rob met Jo's gaze and she gave a little shake of her head. Leave the father in peace. He doesn't need to know. His son was already lost to him.

"Do you know if Aadam had a wife or a partner?" he asked.

The old man shook his head. "Not that I know of, but like I said, I haven't seen him for a long time."

Rob nodded. "As Aadam's only living relative, you will inherit his estate."

"His estate?"

"Yes, he was quite a wealthy man when he died." Most of the money was ill-gotten gains from drug deals and would be confiscated, but there was still his house in Hounslow and its contents. The BMW.

"What about his daughter?" Mohammed said, looking uninterested at the prospect of being wealthy. "Won't she inherit?"

Rob caught eyes with Jo. "He has a daughter?"

"Yes, her name is Aisha. I've never met her but Aadam told his mother about her when she was born, and she told me. The girl must be about eighteen now."

Wow. The family had been estranged for a long time.

"Do you know how we can contact her?"

The old man sighed, then stood up. "I think I have her details here somewhere." He disappeared into the bedroom and they could hear him rummaging around. After about ten minutes, he came back holding a photograph of a chubby teenager with long dark hair and a shy smile. He handed it to Rob. "On the back."

Rob flipped it over. On the back was sprawled *Aisha* and, beneath the name, a telephone number.

"Do you think Aisha knows her father is dead?" asked Jo once they'd got back into the car. Rob was surprised to find the tyres hadn't been slashed or a brick hadn't been thrown through the windscreen. There was no sign of the youths that had been watching them when they arrived.

"Probably not," he said. "Do you want to call her and see if she's available to meet now?" Then he glanced at the dashboard and realized it was almost five o'clock. Yvette would be getting antsy.

"Don't you have to get home?" Jo asked, reading his mind. The drive back from North London would take over an hour in rush hour traffic.

Rob hesitated. He was torn. He didn't want to leave Yvette alone, but now they knew there was a daughter, they couldn't wait until tomorrow to tell her that her father was dead.

I need to know you can commit a hundred per cent. Lawrence's words echoed in his mind.

"I can handle the daughter," Jo said. "I'll take Mallory with me."

Reluctantly, Rob nodded. Mallory would be up for it. He was always able to work late. Did Mallory have a girl-friend? Rob realized he'd never asked, but then he never talked about Yvette either. He'd have to rectify that as soon as possible and take Mallory out for a decent drink.

"Okay, but keep me posted," he said.

Rob drove them back to the station. The traffic was dire, and as predicted, it took them a little over an hour. On the way, when he wasn't swearing at the traffic lights or fellow motorists, he asked Jo how she'd ended up at the National Crime Agency.

"Well, after the Stalker case, I was up for promotion, but my boss felt it was too soon. He said I needed more experience."

"And you didn't like that?"

"It wasn't that. In fact, he may have been right about the experience. It was more his attitude. He'd worked his way up the hard way and I was fast-tracked out of uni, so he didn't take too kindly to me getting promoted to the same rank as him. It meant one of us would be transferred out of the department, and the way things were going, it was probably going to be him."

Rob kept his eyes on the road.

"So, I put feelers out and when Neil Pearson at the NCA offered me a position, I jumped at the chance."

"Organized crime?"

"Why not? It's interesting work and we actually have a chance at catching the bastards. The ops are long and involved, we track these guys for months, so by the time the crackdown comes we have more than enough evidence to prosecute."

She had a point. He remembered a case that had been thrown out of court just last month because an inexperienced constable hadn't followed the correct procedure when documenting evidence. A silly mistake and a murderous thug had walked free.

Yvette had rung twice by the time they got back to the station. He texted her saying he was on his way, and left Jo and Mallory to go and see the daughter. Two next-of-kin visits in one night was a lot to ask of anyone, and he didn't envy Jo her task, although he did want to know what Aisha had to say about her father. Were they close? Did she know about his drug trafficking? Did she have any idea who could have visited him on Monday afternoon? Dammit, he should be there!

"I'll fill you in later," Jo promised. "Go home to your wife."

Yes, Yvette needed him. He'd promised her they'd get through this together, and they would. He owed her that much. So why did he feel so torn?

* * *

Yvette, accompanied by a frantically barking Trigger, threw herself into his arms the moment he walked through the door. "Oh, thank God you're back. I heard a noise in the garden and Trigger wouldn't stop barking. I think someone's out there."

He held her for a moment, then gently disentangled himself. "Trigger, hush. What noise?"

Trigger calmed down but continued to run in circles around him.

"A thumping, creaking sound like someone was climbing over the fence. I nearly called the police."

Rob walked through the kitchen to the sliding doors that led out to the small back garden. "I'll check it out." He unlocked the doors and slid them open.

Yvette wrapped her cardigan around her slim frame and took a few nervous steps backwards. Rob, followed by an overexcited Trigger, inspected the perimeter. He'd have to take the dog for a walk later to get rid of some of this excess energy.

"The fence is loose over here." He pulled one of the wooden slats towards him to demonstrate. "I'll fix it at the weekend. You probably heard it banging in the wind. It was a bit gusty today."

Yvette didn't look convinced. He sighed. "Darling, no one is going to break in. You're perfectly safe here. We're surrounded on all sides by the neighbours and all the doors have secure locks on them."

She fell into his arms. "I was so scared."

He kissed her trembling lips and she wrapped her arms around his neck. "Take me upstairs," she whispered.

Making love to Yvette was a bit like charging naked through a hurricane. He always felt windswept and a little off-kilter afterwards. He left her to sleep and went downstairs to make a sandwich. He was ravenous after having barely eaten the whole day. It seemed Trigger was too, even though his bowl had the remnants of supper in it, so they shared a ham-and-cheese toastie and then he took the golden Lab for a walk, just to the end of the street and back. He'd take him for a proper run in the park this weekend. It wasn't good for the dog to be stuck indoors all day either, even though Yvette let him out into the garden.

His wife was still in bed when he got back, so he sat in the lounge and watched the tail end of some true-life crime drama on television. He was just dozing off himself when his phone buzzed.

"Hi, it's Jo. I hope I'm not calling too late."

"No, not at all." He pressed the mute button on the remote. "What happened with the daughter?"

"Well, she was a lot more upset than Yousef's father was. She cried constantly from the minute we told her. It was almost impossible to get anything out of her."

"That doesn't sound good." He was glad he hadn't gone now.

"I said almost."

Rob waited, knowing she'd continue.

"It seems she had an inkling of her father's illegal activities. She'd been staying with him up until November last year while her mother was away. Her mother, Isabella, has gone back to Ukraine to look after *her* mother, who's got cancer. It's a bit complicated. Anyway, Aisha moved in with her dad."

"Hence the box of pink bedding in the spare room."

"Yes, but while she was there, she realized her father didn't work in property anymore. When she asked him about his new job, he said he'd moved into development and was working as a middleman selling new builds to prospective buyers."

"But she didn't believe him?"

"She said it was odd how many text messages he got every day. He was constantly on his phone."

"That ties in with the drug trafficking theory."

"She knew better than to ask too many questions, so when her boyfriend proposed, she moved out. They live in Twickenham now."

"Any leads on who visited Yousef on Monday afternoon?"

"Well, that's the interesting thing. Aisha didn't know any of his business associates, but she said he did have a man over a few times, went by the name of Mr Fox."

"Mr Fox? That's an alias, surely?"

"Probably, but we'll check it out. She said he was a well dressed guy, similar age to Yousef, so early to mid-forties, and he drove a black Porsche SUV. She remembered the car."

"Sounds promising. He could be our mystery guest."

"Yes, it's possible." There was a small pause. "Oh, I've managed to get a warrant for Yousef's bank records, both personal and business. He has several limited companies."

"That's great." He'd known there would be others. She obviously had more sway than him. "Hopefully they'll tell us something. Any news on the prepaid phones?"

"My team are still going through the messages. There are thousands of them. Most will link back to small-time dealers. They're mapping the lines to give us an indication of the extent of the operation."

"I'm only interested in calls made in the days leading up to Yousef's death. Anything that could shed some light on who he was entertaining that night." His focus was on finding the killer.

"We'll have those for you tomorrow. You can go through them yourself. Anyway, I'll let you go now. Just thought I'd update you."

"Thanks, Jo, appreciate the call."

She hung up, and he spent a long time sitting in his chair, staring at the silent TV.

CHAPTER 8

All the messages that Yousef had received on his various burner phones in the days leading up to his death were from buyers placing orders. Location-wise, they'd come in from all over the south-east of England. It was mind-boggling how far the tentacles of the network reached. All the outgoing texts were to dealers or couriers with coded instructions on how to fulfil the orders. Each line had an area-specific code name. None of the numbers were registered to a 'Mr Fox', or anyone else for that matter. They were all pay-as-you-go SIM cards and therefore untraceable.

"It would help if people had to show ID when purchasing a pay-as-you-go SIM," Mallory complained, staring at a computer graphic of a central hub with ten lines spreading outwards, and then hundreds outward from them. "At least then we could link the numbers with the names."

"Except the real criminals would probably use fake IDs and the only names we'd get would be of innocent people who we shouldn't be spying on anyway," said Jo, with a sigh. "On the bright side, we're making progress. There is a whole team of analysts at the NCA who are tracing these numbers. We have some of them under surveillance already, but what we really need is the kingpin, the guy who's bringing in the drugs and supplying them to Yousef and others like him to distribute to the smaller towns and rural areas."

"Mr Fox," said Rob.

She shrugged. "Maybe. We don't know if he's the guy. And even if he is, we don't know *who* he is."

"Where are we on those bank statements?" asked Rob. They were standing around Jo's desk, having an impromptu meeting. It had gone 9 a.m. and everybody was in, except for Superintendent Lawrence, who'd gone to a meeting in the city.

She was wearing a skirt suit today, which showed off her lovely shapely legs.

"I've had a quick look."

"And?" What wasn't she saying?

"And there are some leads that warrant following up. Want to grab a coffee and I'll fill you in?"

Mallory glanced between the two of them and stood up. "I've got to get on. You can fill me in later."

There was a split-second hesitation. "Sure. Downstairs?"

She smiled. "Why not? It's drinkable."

The canteen didn't do a bad Americano. It wasn't as good as the fancy new machine in the waiting area on the third floor, but it did the trick. Rob, who hadn't had breakfast, grabbed a blueberry muffin. They chose a table in the corner, away from everyone else.

Jo handed him a wad of papers. "These are from one of his company accounts."

Rob glanced down at the bank statement for Ferdon Ltd.

"It's a standard off-the-shelf corporation."

He nodded and let his eyes roam down the list of transactions. "Woah," he exclaimed, as the totals grew. There weren't any big deposits, but there were a lot of small ones. £200, then £500, then £300, and several of these in one day. All cash deposits. By the end of the month of December, Yousef had in excess of £500,000 in his company account.

He looked up.

"Keep going," she said.

He read on. On 1 January, Yousef had made a large outgoing payment of almost £375,000. He poked the outgoing account name — also a limited company by the looks of things — Apex Holdings. "That's your guy."

Jo was grinning. "Yep, although at this stage it's just a corporation name. We're getting a warrant to access the details. The Commissioner is prepared to do whatever it takes to take down this network."

"That's great, but is the owner of Apex Holdings the person who murdered Yousef?" He studied Jo over his coffee. "Why take out your main distributor? Yousef is making this guy a lot of money."

"Maybe they fell out," Jo suggested. She wrapped her hands around the paper cup. "Or maybe Yousef was skimming off the top."

Rob scratched his chin. "It's possible," he acknowledged, but something didn't feel right. From the bank statements it didn't appear Yousef was holding back. £375,000 was roughly seventy-five per cent of his year's earnings. It sounded like a fair deal, especially considering Yousef was doing all the grunt work.

"We're building a strong picture of the various county lines, each with their own distributor at the top. Before this breaks, we're going to conduct a massive raid, along with the local police in the affected areas." Her voice quivered with excitement. "We can bring the whole network down, Rob."

"That's great," he said, but he couldn't share her enthusiasm. Bringing down a complex drug smuggling network was fantastic, but would it solve his murder? Would the person who stabbed Aadam Yousef be brought to justice? He had the awful feeling this case was slipping away from him.

* * *

"I don't want to lose sight of our objective, which is to see the killer of Aadam Yousef prosecuted," Rob told the DSI later that day in his bubble. "While I understand the county lines drug bust is important, it's not my remit. We still don't have any proof that the two are linked."

"You think Yousef's death was unrelated?" Lawrence asked incredulously.

"No, that's not what I'm saying," Rob hastened to explain. "I'm worried if the NCA crack down on this county lines gang, we may lose the opportunity to convict Yousef's killer. He may well be charged with drug dealing offences, but not murder. He'll get five to ten years, if that."

Lawrence was silent for a moment. "So, what do you suggest, Rob? I can't tell the NCA to hold off until you have the proof you need. This is a nationwide operation. It will happen when it happens, and we have no say over that."

Rob felt in his pocket for his box of ciggies. He needed more time. "I have to find out who the main supplier is and whether he was the man Yousef met the afternoon he died."

Lawrence regarded him seriously. "Well, I suggest you do it fast, because once this crackdown happens, he'll either be in custody or in the wind. Either way, we will have lost him."

"Do we know when it's happening?" Rob asked.

Lawrence grimaced. "It's need-to-know, for obvious reasons, but if I were to hazard a guess, I'd say before the end of the week. We can't keep a lid on Yousef's murder for much longer."

He left the office and spotted Jo heading out, phone glued to her ear. Things were clearly heating up because she'd been on her mobile most of the afternoon. He followed her. Reception in the elevator was dodgy at best, so she took the stairs. Lucky for him. He slunk after her, hoping to overhear what she was saying.

She didn't go far. Instead of going outside, she hovered in the stairwell one flight down. Her voice resonated clearly in the confined space. It was hardly private, but then she thought she was alone.

"Great. Do we have a name?"

A pause as she listened to the caller.

"Is he our man?"

He knew she meant the head of the supply chain. The man who was receiving the shipments of heroin and cocaine that had been smuggled into the country.

"Okay, keep me posted. He may be a person of interest in a homicide."

The person on the other end spoke for a long time. Eventually, Jo said, "The Putney Major Crime Team. The senior investigating officer is DI Miller."

Another pause. "I understand the raid is our priority. Yes, sir. Thank you, sir." She hung up.

Rob, who'd been hanging over the banister at the top of the stairs, straightened up. He didn't bother to go back into the squad room. Jo's heels got louder as she climbed the stairs. She stopped short when she saw him standing there, waiting for her.

"When were you going to tell me?" he asked.

"You've resorted to eavesdropping now, have you?" She raised an eyebrow.

"I thought we were a team? I let you in on this investigation, shared our information with you, but you don't see fit to do the same."

She sighed. "It's complicated, Rob."

He didn't move. She couldn't get up the stairs without brushing past him. It was an intimidating stance, and he knew it. "What happened to inter-agency cooperation?"

"For Christ's sake, it's the NCA. You know how they operate. Everything is kept under wraps until we have enough evidence to act."

"And do you have it? Enough evidence?"

She didn't meet his gaze. "So it seems. They're still digging into our mystery man, but it looks like he might be the head of the organization."

"What's his name?"

She hesitated. "I can't tell you that."

"Why not?"

"You know why not."

He glared at her. "When is the raid?"

She sighed. "I can't tell you that, either."

Rob put his hand on the banister and looked down at her. "You can't, or you won't?"

"I can't jeopardize the operation, you know that. This department isn't involved in the crackdown, so therefore I can't tell you when it is. Not even Lawrence knows."

Rob's heart sank. "How long have I got, Jo?"

"You can't go near him, Rob. Not now."

"He's a suspect in a homicide investigation, he could even be our killer. Doesn't that mean anything to you?"

"Of course it does." Her cheeks flushed a bright pink, and he should have known better than to question her integrity. Her single-minded pursuit for the truth matched his, which was one of the things he loved about her. "But this is a major operation. You could risk months of hard work if you question this guy now. He'll know we're on to him. He'll shut down the network and all his distributors and couriers will scarper. It will all have been for nothing."

Rob was silent. He knew that — he was just being difficult. This guy was their main murder suspect and they had to leave him alone. Hands off.

He exhaled noisily. "So, Yousef's murderer gets done on drug charges and he's out in a couple of years. Is that how this is going to go down?"

"You can question him once we bring him in."

"By then he would have lawyered up and any evidence we may have found at his house will have been compromised by the raid, if he hasn't got rid of it by then."

Jo walked up to the top step. Her face was inches away from his. "I'm sorry, Rob. There's nothing I can do. This is the way it has to be."

He could feel the warmth from her body, the faint vanilla smell that he'd forgotten but now came flooding back. Suddenly, he was hit with an overpowering urge to kiss her. His eyes dropped to her lips as his pulse quickened. It was always like this with her. He remembered when they'd first met, the urge to touch her had been so strong, he'd been unable to resist.

"Please, let me pass." She put a hand on his chest. Without meaning to, he reached up and covered it with his own.

"I wish it didn't have to be this way," he murmured.

Her gaze softened, but she removed her hand. "Me too." She walked back into the squad room.

* * *

"Guv, come and look at this," said Mallory.

"What's up?"

"Mike and Jeff have made some headway with the ANPR cameras on the A4." Rob followed him into the warren, where the two constables were huddled over a spreadsheet.

Mike straightened his back. "We've narrowed down the cars that could have gone to Yousef's house on Monday afternoon."

Rob perked up. This was good news. "Really? How many?"

"Fifty-three." Jeff grinned.

"Fifty-three? What, all between 4 and 8 p.m.?" That was the window of the time of death.

Jeff's face fell and Rob felt bad for raining on his parade. It was good detective work. "Yeah, we added an extra hour to account for the killer getting to the house, so from 3 p.m. onwards."

"Smart thinking." He forced a smile.

"Camera W4652 covers the section of the A4 before Haslemere Avenue and camera W5934 covers the section immediately afterwards," Mike explained. "So we looked for vehicles that appeared on the first camera but not the second. That's how we figured out which turned off."

"Yousef's road is part of a one-way system," Jeff explained. "Which means there isn't another way in other than via this route. They would have had to have turned in there."

Rob clapped him on the back. "Great work, guys. I presume you're looking up the vehicle owners on the DVLA database?"

They nodded.

"Ask for a valid reason why they were in the area," said Mallory. "We'll need to check their alibis."

Rob nodded. "Yep, one of those vehicles must belong to our killer."

He wished he had a name that they could cross-reference. It would either help eliminate the drug kingpin from their enquiries and get the NCA off their backs, or it would confirm that he was their killer. Either way, it would beat not knowing.

"Keep it up, lads. We're getting there," he said. But with Jo keeping secrets, he wasn't sure they would get there fast enough to make a difference.

CHAPTER 9

Dennis Patterson was looking forward to this afternoon. He hadn't had a day off in months. His weekends were taken up with trips to the park, ballet lessons, ice skating and countless kids' parties and playdates.

His wife never seemed to tire of being around their two young daughters — she was amazing like that — but he felt frazzled and worn out. It was almost a relief to go back to work on a Monday, particularly when he was going out of town on a sales trip.

"Where are you off to?" Michelle had asked.

"West London," he'd told her. "There's a private clinic that's interested in a Legacy 5 Swivel Turbine handset." But she'd already zoned out. He was away one week out of every month, had been for years, so she was used to it. Her mother came over and helped out with the kids.

Dennis loved the feel of his Toyota RAV4 on the open road, country music playing on the car radio instead of the soundtrack to the latest Disney movie. He could eat what he liked when he liked and didn't have to chop carrots and cucumber into a hundred tiny pieces.

This afternoon, he thought, *I'm going to kick back and watch the football with a six-pack of cold ones, and no one is going to tell me to bathe the kids, make supper or not to drink too much.* Another bonus of these week-long sales trips was that he got to sleep through the night. No bad dreams of dragons or monsters to wake him up. No "Daddy, I need a wee," or "Can you read me a story?" It was bliss.

But first, his morning appointment. It was an impromptu visit by an old colleague who'd started his own dental supply company, mostly online sales from what he could gather, but that's the way things were going these days. He'd said on the phone that he was looking for a competent sales director with excellent product knowledge to join the business. While Dennis wasn't particularly interested in leaving his current job — he loved the freedom it gave him — he was curious about the proposal. It wasn't every day a man got headhunted. And who knew? If the money was good, he might just be tempted.

He showered and shaved, then, humming a Garth Brooks tune, put on his work suit and a freshly ironed shirt. He liked to make a good impression. When he was ready, he made the bed and straightened up the room. Again, first impressions were everything. He couldn't do business in a messy hotel suite.

When the knock on the door came, Dennis was prepared. He'd revised his CV, just in case, and had practised the answer to the inevitable "Tell me about yourself" question that was a staple, if predictable, part of all interviews. Confidence, that's what he was going for — the key component in any winning sales pitch.

"Hello," he said, opening the door. The smile faded on his lips and he frowned. "Where's Kevin?"

Kevin Mundy was his colleague and the man who was to be interviewing him this morning, although he'd called it an "informal discussion" on the phone.

"Who the fuck's Kevin?" said the stranger at the door.

"He's . . . Never mind. Who are you?"

"I'm an avenging angel," came the reply, followed by a penetrating punch to the stomach.

Dennis doubled over, gasping. "Hey!" He glanced down and his eyes widened with disbelief. A knife was sticking out of his abdomen. "What?"

Confusion descended, then a slow, burning heat, then — *Oh, God!* — the pain. Gulping, he clutched his stomach to pull out the knife, but it was already gone. The next jab was to the chest, close to his heart. It felt like he'd been hit by a sledgehammer, and suddenly it was hard to breathe.

"No," he panted, gazing at his attacker with wild, terrified eyes. "What are you doing?"

He fell to his knees and tried to stop the bleeding, but it was too late. The knife fell again, this time slicing through his torso, just below the shoulder blade. Tears sprung to his eyes as blood gushed from his wounds, but he couldn't staunch the flow. He collapsed forward on to his stomach and fought to keep from blacking out. His breath was coming in loud rasps, and it felt like he was drooling, but he suspected it was blood. He coughed, spurting frothy red foam on to the carpet.

Excruciating pain burst between his shoulder blades as the attacker, who wasn't done yet, stabbed him in the back. He cried out, but it was only a gurgle. The knife fell again and again until Dennis couldn't hold on anymore. It hurt too much and he wasn't getting enough air. The world was blurring at the edges now. It wouldn't be long before it faded completely.

Why are you doing this to me? he wanted to ask, but he couldn't speak. Strangely enough, his last thoughts weren't about his wife or his kids, but the football match he'd been looking forward to watching this afternoon. Now he'd never know whether Sheffield United, a team he'd supported since boyhood, would make it through to the next round of the FA Cup.

It was dark all around him, like the lights had gone out. He couldn't make out a thing, couldn't see through the pain. Yet there was no respite. The blows kept on coming.

CHAPTER 10

It was around noon the following day when they got the call. Mallory, who'd been on the first floor with the uniformed police, rushed into the squad room panting. "Guv, you're going to want to hear this."

Rob swivelled around in his desk chair. "What?"

"Dispatch just called it in. A body's been found at a hotel in Hammersmith with multiple stab wounds."

Rob stared at him for a moment. "Like our victim?"

"Same. The first responder counted at least six puncture wounds, maybe more. The guy didn't stand a chance. He said it's a bloodbath."

Rob leaped up. "We'd better get down there."

"I'm coming too," cut in Jo, who'd emerged from the Superintendent's office and overheard the tail end of the conversation.

Rob frowned. "We don't know if this is drug-related. It might have nothing to do with the NCA's operation."

She fixed her blue eyes on him. "It's the same MO, isn't it?"

Rob relented. He didn't have time to argue, and she was right, there was a chance it was related to the county lines gang. This guy could be a link in the supply chain, another distributor or a courier of some sort. If he were her, he'd want to check it out too. "Okay, fine, but we're leaving now."

"I'm ready." She grabbed her bag and jacket and followed them out of the room. That was one of the things he liked about Jo. She didn't fuss. Yvette always took at least an hour to get ready before she left the house, back in the days when she went out. Jo, on the other hand, could get up and go at a moment's notice and look fantastic doing it.

"Where was the body found?" she enquired as they marched downstairs and out into the car park.

"Hammersmith," Mallory told her. "At the Pear Tree Hotel, but we don't know much more than that."

"Pear Tree Hotel?" She wrinkled her forehead. "Never heard of it."

"Me neither."

Traffic was scarce and the drive took them less than twenty minutes via Hammersmith Bridge. As they parked, Jo glanced up at the four-storey Victorian terrace. "It's more of an exclusive bed and breakfast than a hotel."

Yet the metallic plaque on the wall beside the door read *Pear Tree Hotel*, and beneath it was a silhouette of a tree.

"I see SOCO is already here." Rob nodded to the forensic van parked outside the building. The entrance had been taped off and a police officer armed with a clipboard was stationed outside.

"Names, please."

They showed him their warrant cards and he wrote down their details. "He's on the third floor. Make sure you kit up, it's messy."

They went into the foyer and were immediately handed a set of protective coveralls. They pulled them on before proceeding up the stairs.

The hotel was quite nice inside. The carpeting was new and clean, the walls freshly painted — the acrid tang was still evident in the air — and the inset lighting created a stylish, sophisticated effect.

"I don't think this is the type of establishment that rents rooms by the hour," Rob said to Mallory.

They reached the third floor. Another police officer directed them to room eleven. He looked pale and his mouth was set in a grim line.

There was a crooked *Do Not Disturb* sign hanging on the door, despite it being ajar. Heart pounding, Rob entered the room, followed by Mallory and Jo. He mentally prepared for the worst. Even though he'd seen his fair share of dead bodies, the initial shock never lessened. There was something about the loss of a life that was so profound that he couldn't get used to it.

The victim lay just inside the doorway. A crime scene photographer circled him, bending forward as he honed in for close-ups, then backward to get a wider-angle shot.

"Could you give us a minute?" Rob asked. The space between the bed and the door was too small for all of them at the same time. The photographer straightened up and took a step back.

They crowded around the body, careful not to disturb anything. The officer downstairs was right — it was a mess. The victim's shirt was drenched with blood and, as with Yousef, it had pooled beneath his body in a sticky puddle. He lay on his stomach — that was different — with multiple stab wounds visible on his back. The puncture wounds looked to be the same size as those inflicted on Yousef. Could it be the same weapon?

Jo looked from the body to Rob. "Is it like the last one?" she whispered.

"Similar," he replied. "Yousef was found on his back, and was stabbed in his chest and abdomen. This guy has been stabbed several times in the back, as you can see."

"So not the same, then?"

Was that a twinge of disappointment in her voice? Jo must have been hoping for a connection, for more clues as to who was involved in the county lines drug network.

Mallory bent down. "It looks like he's bleeding from the front, too. It could just be the way he fell that made the attacker continue stabbing him in the back."

"Can we get a pathologist in here?" called Rob.

At that moment, Liz Kramer marched into the room carrying her metal case. "Hello, Rob. We have to stop meeting like this."

"Liz." He gave her a small smile.

She bent down beside the body. "Have we finished taking the photos in situ?" she asked. The photographer shook his head.

"I told him to wait," said Rob.

Liz gave him a sideways glance. "Okay, proceed please, Michael."

The photographer got back to work. He seemed to be taking an awful lot of photos.

"Liz, we need to know if he was stabbed in the stomach or chest as well as the back." Rob crouched down beside her. Mallory and Jo backed out of the room to give them more space.

"Give me a chance," she said without looking up. "I've just got here."

Rob sighed. Patience wasn't one of his virtues. He stood up and surveyed the hotel room, walking slowly around it. It was clean, the bed was made and there were no clothes sprawled on the floor. A purple suitcase stood on the far side of the bed. He lifted it up. It was empty.

Rob inspected the items on the dresser. Standard-issue notepad and pen alongside the hotel telephone. No personal items. "There's no sign of a scuffle," he said. Just like with Yousef, it looked like this guy had been surprised by his attacker.

"Do we know who he is?" Mallory asked from the doorway.

"There's nothing on the body," said Liz.

"Not even a phone?" asked Rob.

Liz shook her head.

Rob opened the closet opposite the bed and peered inside. Two suits hung on hotel hangers, along with two pressed shirts, and at the bottom, a pair of trainers. This guy was a damn sight neater than Yousef, that was for sure. He felt around in the suit pockets and pulled out a leather wallet. "Ah, we have an ID."

Both Mallory and Jo turned to him expectantly.

He opened it and studied the driver's licence. "Allow me to introduce Dennis Patterson from Harrogate."

"Harrogate?" said Mallory. "He's a bit far from home, isn't he?"

Rob pulled another card from the wallet and showed them it.

Dennis Patterson. Sales Representative. Avar Dental Technologies.

"He's a sales rep," said Jo. "Must be down here on business."

"And he's got a family." Rob held up a worn photograph of a smiling brunette holding by the hands two identical little girls with pigtails. Twins. He didn't want to think what effect this would have on them. It was just as well the family were far away so they wouldn't see him like this.

Rob slipped the photo back into the wallet and handed it to a forensic officer, who put it in an evidence bag and sealed it up.

"Any sign of a laptop?" asked Mallory, who was still standing outside the door.

Rob poked his head right into the closet and felt around. Nothing at the bottom. Then he reached up and felt on the top shelf above his head. His fingers closed around a flat, rectangular device.

"Bingo." He lifted it down. The cord, weighted by the plug on the end, snaked off the shelf after the laptop and nearly hit him on the head, but he managed to dodge it in time.

"I'll take that," said the scene-of-crime officer, and promptly bagged it too. Every item had to be logged and recorded before being taken into evidence. There, they would be inspected and photographed, and a detailed report sent to the senior investigating officer. Failure to follow protocol could result in a mistrial, especially if that piece of evidence was something the prosecution relied on in court.

"Definitely no mobile phone," said Rob.

"Who doesn't carry a phone with them?" asked Mallory.

Rob tensed his jaw. "The killer must have taken it. Dennis Patterson would have had one to call his family."

"It was the same scenario with Yousef," said Jo. "You found several burner phones at the scene, but not a personal device. None of the phones we analysed had his daughter's or father's numbers on them."

Rob pursed his lips. "Maybe the killer's number is on the phone, that's why he takes them. To slow us down."

"He must know we'd access the records eventually," said Jo.

"Yes, but not if it's a burner. We'd have no way of knowing what the number was." He thought about what Jo had said about Yousef. "And let's face it, no self-respecting drug dealer is going to have a mobile phone registered in his name, not even for personal use."

Mallory leaned against the door frame. "So, the killer contacts the victim by phone, or vice versa, presuming it's the same person. They come over and attack their target, unleashing all this pent-up rage, before calmly washing the murder weapon in the sink and taking off."

"Was there blood in the sink?" Rob asked a forensic guy.

"A small amount," he confirmed. "I had to use the UV light to find it, but we took samples and photographed it. You'll get the report in due course."

Rob felt his pulse rate accelerate. "It's definitely the same person." He went into the small bathroom to see for himself, but like the crime scene officer had said, the blood wasn't visible to the naked eye. The killer must have rinsed the sink afterwards.

"What about sexual activity?" asked Jo.

The forensic guy shook his head. "The bed doesn't look slept in, but we'll check all the same."

Rob nodded. They couldn't leave anything to chance. They watched as two forensic officers pulled back the sheets and shone the UV light on the bed.

"Can we turn the lights off for a moment?"

Jo flicked the switch and the hotel room was bathed in darkness.

"Don't mind me," called Liz from the floor.

All eyes were on the bed. It was illuminated under an eerie purple glow. Since all bodily fluids are fluorescent, they can be picked up much easier using an ultraviolet light source.

"Nothing," the technician said. "The sheets are clean." The lights went back on.

"Right, do you want to help me roll him over?" Liz glanced up at Rob.

Rob crouched down and they gently rolled the victim on to his back.

Liz leaned forward and inspected his torso. "Yes, there are also puncture wounds on the chest and abdomen. They appear to be the same size and shape as your last victim. Also non-serrated, about three centimetres in diameter. Is that what you wanted to know?"

Rob nodded gravely. "So, it's the same killer?"

Liz nodded. "I'd say so. I'll have specifics for you after the post-mortem."

Jo and Mallory stared at Rob. Now they had confirmation, they weren't quite sure what to make of it.

"Do you know how long he's been dead?" asked Rob.

Liz hesitated. "Well, the body's at room temperature, hypostasis is developed and rigor mortis is fully completed, so I'd say roughly twenty-four hours ago, give or take."

Rob glanced at his watch. "That makes the time he was killed yesterday, around midday." Jo took out her phone to check the time. "Where is the receptionist?" Rob asked no one in particular. "I didn't see anyone downstairs when we came in."

Jo swivelled on her heel. "Let's go find out."

"Can we bag the 'Do Not Disturb' sign and check it for prints?" Rob asked.

The scene-of-crime officer nodded. "I was getting there."

With the crime scene under control, Jo led the way back down to a small lounge opposite the check-in desk. It was empty. The guests had been told to leave for the day and no was allowed back in until the police were finished processing the scene. Mallory found the receptionist in the back office, crying. She'd also discovered the body. In her mid-thirties with shoulder-length brown hair and red-rimmed eyes, she spoke with a soft Eastern European accent.

"He was supposed to check out at ten o'clock" she told them, her voice quivering. "When he didn't come down, I went up to see if he was okay. Sometimes our customers sleep late and forget they have to check out."

This was obviously a common occurrence.

"I called to him but there was no answer. I was worried he might have left without settling his bill, so I opened the door with my key card and—" She gave a little gasp — "That's when I found him lying on the floor." She shook her head, her eyes filling with tears again. "There was so much blood."

Jo leaned forward and squeezed her arm. "It's okay. What did you do then? Did you touch the body at all?"

"Oh, no. I ran out of the room and called the police."

"Good. You did the right thing."

"Had he stayed in the hotel before?" Rob asked.

She shook her head. "I didn't recognize him."

"How long have you worked here?"

"Five years." She sniffed and rubbed her nose on her sleeve. "I never thought anything like this would happen."

"Were you on duty yesterday?" asked Rob.

"Yes, I work five days a week. There is another girl that comes in on the weekends, and we also have a night manager."

Rob leaned forward in his chair and gazed directly at her. "Did you notice anyone come into the hotel yesterday morning?"

"You mean a guest?"

"Anyone. A guest or a visitor of a guest, maybe even a stranger."

She thought for a moment, gnawing at the edge of her lip. "Most of our guests go out after breakfast. I don't remember anyone coming in."

"Were you at your post all morning?"

She nodded, but didn't quite meet his eye.

Rob thought about pushing her, but then decided against it. She'd been through enough and she'd just deny leaving the front desk. Her job depended on it.

"Okay, Miss . . . ?"

"Kurylenko, but you can call me Daria."

"Okay, Daria. You've been great." He saw Jo glance at him in surprise. "Just one more thing, did you take a copy of Mr Patterson's ID documents when he checked in?"

She straightened her back. "Of course. And his credit card details."

"Okay, we'll need a copy of those," said Rob. Even though they had the contents of his wallet, which would give them much the same information, it didn't hurt to be thorough. "Also, do you know if he made any calls from his hotel room?"

"I don't think so, but I can check for you."

"Please."

She got up and walked across the lobby to the front desk, then disappeared into the office again. After five minutes, she was back. "This is a copy of what I have." It was a printout of the guest register complete with Patterson's driver's licence and credit card details. "He didn't make any phone calls from his room."

"Perfect." Rob nodded at the others to leave. "Thanks again."

CHAPTER 11

They waited to cross the busy street outside the hotel.

"Why didn't you ask her why she left her post?" asked Jo.

"I knew she'd deny it," he said. "And I didn't want to push her. It could mean her job."

Jo studied him for a moment. "You know she was lying."

"Yes, but she had a cigarette box in her back pocket, so she probably went out for a smoke."

"Or a toilet break," added Mallory. "She was the only one on duty."

True. The killer could have waited for her to leave the front desk and then slipped in unannounced. There was no automatic locking system on the front door. The Pear Tree Hotel, for all its chic interiors, wasn't that modern. The front door was left unlocked during the day, with all visitors asked to report to reception, and locked at night when the night manager was on duty.

"Mallory, contact the owners and ask if there's a camera on the premises," said Rob. "I didn't see one as we went in."

"Neither did I," echoed Jo.

"And let's get on to the council. There's bound to be CCTV coverage in the street. Hammersmith is riddled with them."

"Let's grab a coffee." Jo pointed to a Starbucks across the road. It was situated on the corner of a busy junction and the smell of exhaust fumes was heavy in the air, replaced by the comforting aroma of roasted coffee beans once inside. They ordered and took a table by the window.

The warm, cosy shop was a welcome change after the gruesome scene in the hotel room. Mallory cradled his English breakfast tea. "Are we assuming that the person who killed Yousef also killed Dennis Patterson?"

There was a pause.

"Yes, we are," said Jo. "The similarities can't be ignored."

"But Yousef was a drug dealer and Patterson was a travelling salesman. Yousef lived in West London and Patterson was from up north." Mallory sighed. "I don't see the connection."

"I have to admit, neither do I." Rob took the lid off his Americano to help it cool down.

"Maybe Patterson was a courier," suggested Jo. "He did travel around the country selling dental products. It would be the perfect cover for a drug dealer."

"Did you see how neat and tidy that guy was? Everything was unpacked and put away, even though he was only staying a few days. Besides, he's got a decent job. I can't picture him as a drug mule."

Jo sipped her cappuccino. "It takes all types," she muttered.

She was right. Drug gangs used everyone from kids to vulnerable adults to distribute their merchandise. Just because Patterson was a neat freak and a family man, didn't mean he wasn't working for them.

"He could have been blackmailed." This from Mallory.

Jo perked up. "Good point. That's a possibility. We'll have to speak to his wife."

"She's in Harrogate," said Rob. "We'll get one of the detectives up there to talk to her and we can tune in via video link."

"Okay." She drummed her forefinger on the edge of her cup. "There must be a connection somewhere — why else was he murdered?"

Rob fell silent for a moment. "There is a possibility that this has nothing to do with the county lines gang."

Both Jo and Mallory stared at him.

"What if we're looking at this the wrong way? Maybe we should be trying to figure out what Yousef had in common with Patterson, not vice versa."

"Patterson was a married white dental salesman who, from what we can see, didn't do drugs. Yousef was an unmarried drug dealer of Arabic descent." Mallory spread his hands. "They didn't have anything in common."

Jo studied Rob intently. "Do you really think Yousef's death was non-drug-related?"

"I'm saying it's a possibility."

She sighed.

"We have to keep an open mind," Rob continued.

Silence again as they thought about this. Eventually, Rob said, "Let's see what Forensics comes up with. They might pick up something when they dust for prints or maybe the killer was careless and left a sample of his DNA on the body."

"Hotel rooms are a disaster, forensically speaking," Jo pointed out. "So many people go in and out of them and you'd be surprised at how badly they're cleaned."

"Ugh." Mallory shuddered.

"But we can hope." She tilted her head and smiled at Rob.

"Well, someone was in that room other than the victim," he said.

"I'll get Patterson's phone records," Mallory suggested. "He looks like the type of guy to have a contract."

"Agreed," said Jo.

Rob chugged down his Americano. "Maybe that will tell us who his mystery guest was."

"We don't know whether he was expecting a visitor," Jo said. "The killer could have surprised him."

"Except he was wearing a business suit and the room was immaculate. The cleaners hadn't been in yet, so he must have tidied it himself. I think it's safe to assume he was expecting someone."

"But who?" murmured Mallory.

"The same person Yousef was expecting," finished Rob.

"If it wasn't drug-related, who could it be?" Jo wrapped her hands around the cardboard cup like she was trying to draw warmth from it.

"What sort of person does home appointments?" asked Rob.

"Accountant. Business consultant. Tax advisor," suggested Mallory.

"Loan shark. Prostitute. Masseuse," said Jo, her thoughts darker than Mallory's.

"There's no indication that these were sexually motivated attacks," said Rob. "And I'm still not convinced a woman would be able to overpower a man like Yousef. Patterson is smaller, but he's still got some bulk on him."

"And he was married," interjected Mallory. "Would he be fooling around with prostitutes?"

Jo raised an eyebrow. "Who knows? He might."

"I can't see it." Rob agreed. "Your loan shark theory sounds more plausible. Patterson could have got himself into debt and needed a way out. When he couldn't pay back the money, they came after him."

"But Yousef didn't need money. He was minted." Mallory said.

Rob sighed. "We're chasing our tails here. Let's wait until we get the victim's bank statements and speak to his wife. She might be able to shed some light."

* * *

"I'm going to call Tony Sanderson to take a look at the two murders," Rob informed them on the way back to the station.

Mallory was driving, with Rob sitting beside him and Jo in the back. She leaned forward between the seats. "Is he your profiling friend, the one who wrote that book?"

"*Mind Games*, yes. I thought he might offer some useful insights. Maybe even help us link the two murders." Granted, it was a long shot, but he was desperate. Their two victims couldn't be more different and if there was a connection between them, Rob couldn't see it.

"Hmm . . ." Jo didn't sound convinced.

"I thought you'd be all for it," said Rob. "You didn't waste any time bringing one in on the Stalker case."

"That was a serial killer, but these are drug-related murders. I'm not sure your profiler is going to be of much use. Especially since . . ." She paused.

"Especially since your raid will bring in our chief suspect, anyway." She still hadn't told them who it was, although he knew they had a name, thanks to the information provided by Companies House.

She nodded. It was clear Jo thought this man was responsible for both murders.

Mallory pulled into the police car park. As they climbed out of the vehicle, Jo's phone rang. She glanced at the screen, then excused herself to answer.

"Bloody raid is going ahead," Rob muttered under his breath. He'd been watching Jo's face and he could tell by her flushed expression and barely concealed excitement that he was right. Mallory raised his eyebrows. Rob kept his gaze trained on Jo. "Tonight, by the looks of things."

"At least we'll be able to question him once he's in custody," Mallory pointed out reasonably.

Rob sighed. "Yeah, after everyone else has had a crack at him."

CHAPTER 12

"So this is where it all happens, eh?"

Rob grinned at his old friend. "Hey, Tony. Good to see you, mate. Thanks for coming in so early on Monday morning."

"No problem. I have some time before my first lecture."

Rob got to his feet and they hugged, much to the astonishment of the rest of the team. Rob wasn't known for overt displays of affection, but then he and Tony went way back. They had first met at the police academy in Hendon. Tony had been studying criminology at the time and had come to see what a day at the police academy was like. Rob had been asked to babysit him and they'd been firm friends ever since.

Tony scanned the open-plan squad room with its rows of neat white desks, flat-screen computers and spot lighting and nodded approvingly. "Very impressive. I feel like I ought to whisper like in a library."

Rob laughed. "No, it's not like that. Come on, let's talk in the incident room. It's more private." He led his friend across the room to where a glass office stood empty. The walls were soundproof, and although you could see inside, it felt totally separate from the rest of the floor.

"So, I hear congratulations are in order."

It took Rob a moment to realize he was talking about Yvette. "Thanks, yes. We got married in France. It was a very quiet affair."

Tony grinned. "I heard. Well done on catching that bastard last year. I did try to call a couple of times, but your mobile was off."

"Sorry, we needed some downtime."

"I understand. It must have been tough. You guys did well to see it through."

Had they? Maybe that's all they'd done — seen it through. And now, where were they? Still picking up the pieces?

He didn't say any of that. "How're Kim and the kids?" Tony had a boy and a girl, two years apart.

"Kim's working flat out at the hospital and the kids are growing up fast," he said with a smile. "They're nearly in their teens now. I believe that's when the fun really begins."

Rob laughed. It was good to see Tony again. It had been a frustrating weekend. The raid had gone ahead like he'd predicted in the early hours of Saturday morning and continued throughout the weekend. Jo had left to go back to the NCA headquarters shortly after they'd got back from Hammersmith as she wanted to be where the action was. She'd called briefly on Sunday morning to say they'd arrested over fifty people in a county-wide crackdown, including alleged county lines drug boss, Asir Ahmed, who would be charged with conspiring to supply class A drugs.

So, they'd got 'Mr Fox', Yousef's boss and possible killer.

While Rob was pleased the organized crime group had been brought down, he still wanted to question Asir Ahmed in connection with Aadam Yousef's and Dennis Patterson's murders. He'd asked when he'd get the chance, but Jo had been vague and non-committal. It wasn't her call. He'd have to go through the official channels, she'd told him, which could take days, if not weeks.

Feeling depressed, he'd taken Trigger for a long walk in Richmond Park and then fixed the loose board in the back fence. Yvette actually ventured out into the back garden and sat gingerly at the table, wrapped in a blanket and watched as he'd hammered the board back into place. Her session with Becca must have helped. It was a start.

"Is this your new case then?" Tony nodded towards the whiteboard upon which photos of the two crime scenes were pinned.

"'Fraid so."

Tony stood in front of the board and studied the gruesome images. "Multiple stabbings?"

"Yeah, both victims. Same MO."

"Looks vicious."

"There was a lot of blood. Both victims were stabbed at least six or seven times."

Tony nodded slowly. He was one of England's foremost criminal profilers and had worked with most of the law enforcement agencies in the country. The UK wasn't as advanced in the behavioural sciences department as the United States, but they were getting there. Profilers with Tony's experience were rare and therefore in great demand. It was a good position to be in. In addition to consulting, Tony was a lecturer at the University of Surrey, where he taught their master's programme in criminology.

"The killer continued to stab them after they fell?"

"Yes, according to the pathologist over half the stab wounds were inflicted post-mortem." They could tell by the way some had bled more than others.

"You can be certain of one thing — this was a frenzied attack committed by someone fuelled by rage."

No offence to Tony, but it didn't take a genius to figure that much out.

"There must have been a lot of blood spatter," Tony said. "Hard to get away without being seen when you're covered in blood."

"That's the thing." Rob sat down. "We think the killer cleaned the murder weapon and possibly himself before leaving the crime scene."

Tony's eyebrows shot up. "Okay, tell me more."

Rob explained about the blood in the sink at both scenes. "At Yousef's house it was obvious, as if the killer had rinsed himself off. Unfortunately, we didn't find any DNA. At the hotel where Patterson was murdered there were minute traces, but it was still there. Again, no DNA."

"So, your killer is forensically aware. They're cleaning the blood off the weapon, their hands, maybe even their clothes before leaving the scene."

Rob nodded. "It seems that way."

"Any CCTV?"

"No, nothing we could find. The killer made sure of that. Yousef lived in Hounslow while Patterson was in a hotel in Hammersmith. As far as locations go, there is no link."

"Do you think the killer had a vehicle?"

"I'd say so, wouldn't you?" Rob asked.

Tony nodded. "Again, with the blood spatter it would make sense."

"We're working on narrowing down the vehicles outside Yousef's house, but we still have a way to go. Hammersmith is pointless since the hotel was on a major road. The volume of traffic is too large to sift through. We might be able to cross-reference if we get a lead."

Tony read through the forensic report. "Your killer is a careful, meticulous individual, a planner. These murders were set up perfectly. The victims granted the killer access, even dressed up for them, so I'd say you're looking for someone articulate and well dressed, someone who can pull off a professional image."

"If only we had some DNA, but there was nothing left at either crime scene. Either the killer was meticulously clean, or they wore gloves and a hazmat suit."

"Or they were a woman."

"What?" Rob stared at him for a long moment. He'd dismissed the killer as female due to the aggressive nature of the attacks and the strength required to overpower the victims. He said as much now.

Tony drummed his middle finger on the table. "The attacks are well planned, the appointments set up in advance. The murderer times it so the victims are alone and there's nobody else around. Any evidence of the meeting is removed, for example their mobile phones are missing, the whisky glass rinsed out, removing all traces of DNA, and in the second murder, the traces of blood in the sink were negligible."

Rob was still unconvinced. "Could a woman inflict this level of carnage?"

"Of course. Don't underestimate the fairer sex. I agree, it's unusual for a woman to go for such a violent method of murder, but it's not unheard of. And while this is messy—" Tony gestured to the whiteboard — "it's not showy. There are no blood-written signatures on the walls, no jibes aimed at the police, no dismemberment or shocking effects, which tells me there was no ego involved."

Rob frowned. "Okay . . ." It was hardly conclusive.

"Then there's the level of control. The killer has a deep-seated rage against the victims, but she's cool-headed enough to get access to them before she lets loose with the knife. After that, she's back in control again. Boom."

Rob rubbed his forehead.

"So much so that she even remembers to clean off the knife and possibly herself before leaving the scene of the crime. She probably wore some sort of protective clothing, a trench coat or jacket, nothing obvious, and removed it before she left so as not to attract undue attention." He gave Rob a wry glance, "Women are far better at that level of control than men, but obviously I'm generalizing."

Okay, what Tony was saying did make sense, but it was still just a theory. "Would a woman be strong enough to attack a man of Yousef's size? The guy was nearly six foot three."

Tony pursed his lips. "Yes, if the element of surprise was on her side. Your victims never saw this coming. They trusted her and gave her access to their house and their hotel room." He gestured to the board.

Rob shook his head, struggling to get to grips with this new angle.

Tony gave him a moment to let it sink in. "It's hard to picture a woman as a violent killer because they're viewed as nurturers and homemakers," he said softly, "but women can be as violent as men. They're known as the 'quiet killers' for just that reason, because they often slip under the radar."

"Quiet killers?" There wasn't anything quiet about these murders.

"They often target family, children in their care or people with whom they already have a relationship," he said. "And like I mentioned before, their methods are less showy — for example, they don't mutilate their victims' bodies and there isn't normally any sign of sexual abuse."

"Our victims weren't family members or people in their care," Rob said.

"But you can bet they had an existing relationship with the murderer."

Did they? Rob wasn't sure. "We know the victims let the killer in, but we're not sure whether they knew him — or her — personally."

"It might be who they represent that your killer is familiar with." Tony's gaze dropped to the case notes.

"You mean like a drug dealer?"

Tony nodded. "Yes, or someone who is abusive towards women, or who neglects their wife or partner — a cheating husband, for example."

Rob exhaled slowly. "Are—are you saying that the murderer is going after a type? That we could have a serial killer on our hands?" Oh boy, the Superintendent was going to love this.

Tony flipped over the page. "It's too soon to say. You've had two very similar murders, but technically a serial killer is only termed as such after three or more victims are found with the same signature or MO."

A cold feeling dropped down the centre of Rob's body, like he'd swallowed a stone. "In that case, we have to wait until he — sorry, *she* — kills again."

Tony met his gaze. "I'm afraid so."

* * *

"If it happens again, at least we'll know it can't be Asir Ahmed," said Rob optimistically. He was sitting in Lawrence's office across the desk from his stony-faced boss.

"Is Tony absolutely sure about this?" Lawrence growled.

Rob shrugged. Criminal profiling was to him a mixture of common sense and calculated guesses, but he couldn't be too critical — he'd seen Tony in action. "He's about as sure as he can be at this stage. Obviously, it's not an exact science."

Lawrence sighed. "So, we're looking for a female knife-wielding serial killer."

"Yes, someone who's hell-bent on revenge."

The Superintendent leaned forward across his desk. "Revenge?"

Rob had talked to Tony for most of the morning, ana-lysing every aspect of the case. By the end of their discussion, he, too, was convinced they were looking for a woman. The ease at which she'd gained her victims' trust and been able to take them by surprise, the meticulous manner in which she'd planned the attacks, the way in which she'd cleaned the mur-der weapon and removed blood-spattered clothing, all spoke of a cunning female mind. The only thing uncontrolled was the murderous act itself. Stabbing was violent and messy, and the killer must have had a strong motive for causing that much pain, for succumbing to that level of anger.

"Yes, because the attacks are so violent. Tony feels it's the only thing that can generate that level of rage."

"Do we have any idea who this person is? If it's not Asir Ahmed, that is."

"I'll question Asir as soon as I'm allowed to." Rob gave his boss a pointed look. "But until then, I think we should continue with this line of enquiry."

"Any leads?"

Rob hesitated. "Not as such. We're looking at vehicles that turned into Yousef's road the afternoon of his death and we're narrowing it down slowly, but it's going to take time. We're also waiting on lab results from the second crime scene and the post-mortem is due to take place this afternoon."

"Keep me posted."

Rob returned to his desk. Jo hadn't made an appearance today, but that was to be expected. After the NCA's big bust over the weekend, she would have had her hands full questioning suspects and following up evidence. He felt a little sad that he wouldn't be seeing her around anymore and realized it was because he missed her. Shaking the feeling off, he went outside to call Yvette.

CHAPTER 13

Dennis's wife, Michelle, was in her mid-thirties with a pale, dazed expression that told Rob she was still in shock. Over the weekend she'd been informed that her husband had been killed in a London hotel room while on a sales trip. According to the family liaison officer that Rob had spoken to, she'd taken it very badly. It was only today that she'd felt up to answering some questions.

Rob and Mallory sat in front of Rob's computer while they tuned in to the interview via a video link. Mrs Patterson had agreed to come to the Harrogate Police Department accompanied by an FLO, to be questioned by a local detective.

She gave her name for the recording and for those watching. She'd been told that a live link was being sent to the detectives investigating her husband's murder in London.

"Michelle Patterson," she said. Her voice was steady but so soft they had to strain to hear what was being said. Rob pressed the volume key and turned it up as far as it would go. The local DI had been briefed on the investigation and knew what to ask. Rob had spent twenty minutes on the phone with him prior to this interview.

"What was your husband doing in London?" the DI asked.

"He was on a sales trip for his company, Avar. He sold dental equipment."

"Was he happy in his job?"

"Yes, I think so. He never complained about it. I—I got the impression that he quite enjoyed going away. It gave him a break from the kids." She stifled a sob.

The interviewer gave her a moment. "Did he go away a lot?"

She nodded. "He was away for one week of every month. It was part of his contract."

"Did he always go to London?"

"Oh no, they sent him all over. Sometimes it was Sheffield or Manchester, but this time it was London."

"Did he tell you where he was staying?"

"You mean which hotel?"

The DI nodded.

"No." She shook her head. "I don't think so. I didn't pay much attention to his travel plans, but then he went away so often and with the twins . . ." Her eyes filled with tears. She was probably wishing she had paid more attention now. The FLO patted her hand.

"Are you okay, Michelle? Can I get you anything?"

Michelle shook her head. "I'm okay. I just—I just can't believe he's gone."

The FLO nodded sympathetically.

The DI continued with his line of questioning. "Did you speak to your husband while he was away?"

"Yes, of course. He rang every evening to see how the twins were."

"Did you speak to him on Wednesday evening?"

She thought back. "Yes, I did. He rang around eight, after I'd put the girls down. We talked for a few minutes, that's all." She sniffed again. Rob felt terrible for her. Now she'd have to bring up the twins by herself. A single mum.

"And, how was he?"

"What do you mean?"

"Did he appear normal? Was he agitated or upset at all?"

"No, nothing like that. He was plain old Dennis." She seemed bewildered. "Why are you asking me that?"

"It's for the purposes of the investigation," the FLO said lightly, patting her hand. "You're doing great."

"Mrs Patterson, did your husband mention meeting anyone else in London, other than for work? A business associate or friend who he might not have seen in a while?"

She bit her lip, the tears in her eyes threatening to overflow at any minute. "No, he didn't. He asked after the girls — they're at nursery school now — and we talked about that and how my day was." She swallowed. "I didn't ask him about his day or how things were going in London. I never do." Now the tears rolled down her cheeks. "I'm a terrible wife."

"No, you're not." The FLO cast a glance at the DI. "You couldn't have known what would happen. You're just a busy mum with two toddlers. None of this is your fault."

She nodded, but the silent tears kept falling.

"Would you like to take a break?" the DI asked.

Michelle sniffed. "No, let's carry on. I want to get this over with."

He nodded. "Thank you. I know this is difficult. So was Wednesday night the last time you spoke to your husband?"

"Yes."

"He didn't text you or try to contact you on Thursday morning?"

"No."

She rubbed her eyes. "Was that when . . . ? Was that when he died?"

People had trouble with the D-word, Rob observed. It was almost as if once they said it, it suddenly became real and they had to deal with the fact that their loved one was never coming home.

"We don't know the exact time of death," the DI said tactfully, which was true. He hadn't been privy to that information. "But it was sometime on Thursday, yes."

A pause as Michelle absorbed this information.

"Mrs Patterson, I apologize if this question offends you, but were you and your husband happy together?"

Her eyes widened. The DI clarified. "Did you have a good relationship?"

"Yes! I mean the twins were hard work, but we were a team. He was a very hands-on dad."

"What about your relationship? Were things okay between you?"

"Yes, why wouldn't they be?" She was worried now, her forehead wrinkled with lines.

"No reason. We just have to ask."

Rob had specifically asked to find out if they were having marital problems because, as Jo said, prostitutes, escorts and masseuses all made home visits — something they had to look into now that they were searching for a woman. In this respect, however, it seemed Dennis Patterson was a loyal family man. Rob didn't think he would have been the type to mess around with prostitutes and the like, but then you never could tell. It wouldn't be the first time he'd been surprised.

"What about your finances? Were they secure?"

Michelle spluttered. "Yes, why do you ask? What's going on, detective? Is there something you're not telling me?"

"She knows her husband was murdered, doesn't she?" Mallory glanced from the screen to Rob.

"I assumed so, but maybe not."

The DI hesitated and looked at the FLO, who nodded. He cleared his throat. "I'm sorry to have to tell you this, Mrs Patterson, but your husband was murdered."

"Murdered?" She blinked several times as if she didn't understand the word. Then her hand flew to her mouth and she stifled a gasp. "You mean someone killed him?"

"Yes, that's correct. We're trying to establish who might have had a motive to do that."

She looked like she was hyperventilating. The FLO put an arm around her shoulders and told her it was going to be all right, that the police were going to do everything in their power to find out who did this.

"Who would want to murder Dennis?" she breathed, her eyes even more glazed than before. Rob could sense her bewilderment from 200 miles away. It was a good question. Dennis Patterson was an unassuming, middle-aged sales rep. He wasn't particularly good-looking, he didn't have a high-flying job, and he didn't gamble, according to his bank statements. In fact, he seemed a pretty average guy. So why had he been targeted by a female serial killer, if that was who they were dealing with? It still sounded slightly surreal, and not for the first time Rob questioned whether Tony knew what he was talking about. Maybe he'd jumped to that conclusion because it was his job. Maybe he'd worked with serial offenders for so long, he saw them everywhere. He sighed and leaned back in his chair.

"She ought to have been told beforehand," muttered Mallory. He looked away from the screen and took a sip of his now-cold coffee, pulled a face and put it down again.

"They probably didn't want to upset her any more than was necessary," said Rob. "The FLO said she was pretty cut up."

Once she'd got herself under control, the Harrogate DI continued.

"So you don't owe any money or have any big expenses to pay off?"

She shook her head. "No, not that I know of. We have a mortgage, of course, but Dennis took care of that." She lowered her face into her hands. "I have no idea what I'm going to do now."

Rob's heart went out to the poor woman. On top of her grief she had to deal with their finances and loss of income. Life really did suck sometimes.

"You can't think of anyone who would have a reason to harm your husband?"

She lifted her tear-streaked face. "No. He was a decent man and a good husband. I can't imagine anyone wanting to hurt him."

"Okay, well I think that's everything for now," the detective said. "Thank you for coming in, Mrs Patterson. We appreciate that this is a very difficult time for you."

She gave a small nod and glanced up at the camera in the corner of the room. It was the first time she'd looked directly at it, but Rob didn't miss the pleading expression in her eyes. It was as if she was begging him to get to the bottom of this, to find out who had killed her husband and ruined her life. He gave a little nod and promised himself that he would. Whatever it took.

* * *

"Yes!" Rob pumped the air. "It's about time we had some good news."

DS Jenny Bird, who had just arrived back after attending Dennis Patterson's post-mortem, smiled.

"Have we got a lead?" asked Will, who'd been ploughing through Patterson's work emails, none of which were very exciting. "I need a break. Dental equipment is quite possibly the most boring topic on the planet."

"The pathologist found a skin scraping under one of Patterson's fingernails that doesn't belong to him. It could be our killer!"

"Excellent." Will high-fived Jenny.

Everybody was pleased. They needed a break in the case. Ever since the press had been informed of the hotel stabbing, Rob had been shielding calls from investigative reporters sniffing around to find out if there was anything more to the story than the watered-down statement issued by the police department.

Dennis Patterson had appeared on the second page of London's dailies in a short article stating that the North Yorkshireman had been found stabbed to death in a boutique hotel in Hammersmith. DI Rob Miller had been named as Senior Investigating Officer and anyone with any information asked to contact the Putney Major Investigation Team. Rob knew Vicky Bainbridge, the Homicide and Serious Crime Command's press liaison officer, had quietly released the statement the night before. At least nobody had linked it to Yousef's death, which, miraculously, had been kept under wraps — thanks to the NCA's gag order.

"Let me know when that sample comes back," Rob told Jenny. "Before we run it through the database, I want to know whether it belongs to a male or a female."

It would help if they could prove whether Tony's theory was right and they were, at least, on the correct track. It would make Rob feel a little less like he was shooting into the dark. At the moment everything they had was hearsay. They needed something concrete, something that would stand up in court.

CHAPTER 14

Rob stood outside the National Crime Agency HQ in Lambeth finishing his cigarette. He'd rushed through here first thing this morning only to have had a very unsatisfying interview with Asir Ahmed, the drug kingpin arrested in connection with supplying class A drugs to the county lines network. Ahmed, who'd had his lawyer present, admitted to knowing Aadam Yousef, but said he hadn't gone near his house on Monday 27 January. He'd been at home working and his wife could back him up. When Rob had asked him about Friday, the day Dennis Patterson was killed, he'd claimed he was at Friday prayers and about fifty other men could vouch for him.

"How did it go?" Jo came down the steps to join him. Her cheeks were flushed and she appeared a little out of breath. "I heard you were here, so I ran down to catch you before you left."

He smiled, pleased she'd taken the trouble. "It went okay. He's not a very nice bloke, is he?"

She laughed. "No, he's not."

Ahmed was a medium-sized Asian man with greasy hair plastered against his scalp and strange, bulging eyes that were never still, even when he was looking straight at you. They shifted constantly like a goldfish swimming around a bowl looking for a way out.

"He's got alibis for both murders."

"Can you check them out?" Jo asked.

"I will, but I'm pretty sure his wife will vouch for him no matter what and anyone I talk to at the mosque will corroborate his story for Friday. At his one, they tend to close ranks against outsiders, particularly the police. I've had dealings with that mosque before."

Jo nodded. "You still don't know whether he was responsible?"

"No, but I don't trust him. I know that much." He felt his stomach rumble. "Do you want to grab something to eat? I'm starving and will probably have to work late tonight."

She glanced at her phone. "Sure, I can spare half an hour."

They went to a small deli-style bistro down the road from the NCA building. It wasn't a great area, but the bistro seemed okay and sold a variety of sandwiches and salads. They took a seat in the back. There were a few other customers reading the newspaper and drinking coffee, but it wasn't busy.

"The coffee's pretty good," Jo said. "Another hour and there'll be a queue out the door. It's the only decent place to eat around here."

They went up to the counter and ordered. Rob had a chicken mayo baguette while Jo had a toasted cheese-and-ham panini. Armed with their coffees, they returned to the table.

"It's strange not seeing you around the squad room," Rob said.

She smiled but didn't meet his gaze. "I know. I wanted to say goodbye, but things kicked off so fast on Friday afternoon that I didn't get a chance. That's why I wanted to catch you now."

"How did the dawn raid go?"

"Well, out of the fifty or so people we arrested, some were distributors and others small-time dealers, but I think we managed to smash at least ten of the county lines that Yousef and Ahmed were running."

"Congratulations. That's a career bust."

She grinned. "Well, I can't take all the credit. We've had teams working on it for months."

"Still, it'll look good on your CV."

She nodded. There was a brief pause. "It was good working with you again, Rob. Even temporarily."

"It was." He hesitated, searching for the right words. "Listen, I wanted to explain about Yvette."

"You don't owe me an explanation," she said quickly. "It's none of my business."

"I feel like I do," he said. "I wanted to explain why I married her so quickly after you and I . . ."

"Rob, honestly, it's okay. I'm fine with it."

He could see she was uncomfortable, but he pushed on. "Still, it would make me feel better to get this off my chest."

She sighed. "Okay, if you must, but it's really not necessary."

It was to him. "Things between me and Yvette hadn't been great, as you know, but I felt responsible for her attack."

"It wasn't your fault," Jo insisted.

If only he could believe that. "If it wasn't for me, it would never have happened."

Not even Jo could argue with that one. She watched him closely, her eyes filled with compassion. "You can't blame yourself, Rob."

He sighed. "Anyway, she took it badly. The trauma was too much for her. She had to go to her parents' house in France to recover. She still won't go out."

"I'm sorry to hear that. I didn't know," said Jo.

"I took some time off to be with her," Rob continued. "We got married while we were in France. She needed me and it seemed like the right thing to do under the circumstances." He hesitated. "Had she not fallen apart like that, I don't think we would have rushed into it the way we did."

Jo was silent for a moment. The waiter brought them their sandwiches, but Rob didn't feel hungry anymore.

"Do you love her?" Jo asked softly, once the waiter had gone.

Rob hesitated. He'd asked himself the same question many times during the course of their often-turbulent relationship. "Yes," he said quietly. "Yes, I think I do."

"Well, that's okay then."

He looked up in surprise.

"For a moment there, I thought you were going to say you married her because you felt guilty about what happened, and that's no reason to get married." She bit into her sandwich and chewed vigorously.

Rob shook his head. Jo never ceased to amaze him. "I didn't take you for a romantic."

She grinned, "Well, maybe you don't know me as well as you think you do."

"Hmm . . ." He bit into his baguette. It was good, and suddenly his appetite returned. As always, Jo made everything okay.

"Now, have you got any other leads in Dennis Patterson's murder yet?"

Rob told her about the DNA they'd discovered underneath his fingernail. Her eyes widened. "Wow, that's a big breakthrough. Have you run it yet?"

He shook his head. "The results will be sent through this afternoon. Hopefully our perp has some priors and we can wind this up relatively quickly, although I have to admit, it's unlikely she's in the database." Like anything was that simple.

"She?" Jo mumbled, her mouth full.

He realized she hadn't been there when Tony had dropped his bombshell. "Yeah, Tony Sanderson profiled our murderer and told us we could be looking at a female killer." He left out the word "serial" for now. *A serial killer is only termed as such after three or more victims are found with the same MO.* Tony's words rang in his ears.

It wasn't often Jo was at a loss for words. "I didn't see that one coming," she admitted, putting down her panini.

"I know. Neither did I, but it makes sense if you think about it. The meticulous planning, the ease at which she gains entry, the cleaning up before she leaves . . ." He shrugged. "I can see where he's coming from."

"But it's just a theory at this point." Jo's expression was doubtful. "You don't have any actual proof."

"Even if the fingernail DNA isn't on the database, it should be able to tell us whether the killer's a man or a woman," Rob said.

Jo nodded slowly. "If it's a woman, you can rule out Asir Ahmed."

He smirked. "Yep, which means you'll finally be shot of me."

She smiled at him over her cappuccino. "That's a shame. I was beginning to enjoy having you around."

He raised his eyebrow.

"As a friend," she added hastily.

He grinned back. "Friends, I can do."

* * *

Unfortunately, but not surprisingly, the DNA found under Patterson's fingernail wasn't in the database. Rob wasn't deterred, however, because it meant if they ever did bring a suspect in for questioning, they could match them to the sample. The good news, though, was that it was very definitely female.

"He was right!" Rob poked his nose into the Superintendent's office. "Tony was bloody right. I swear, I don't know how he does it."

Lawrence stopped what he was doing and leaned back in his chair. He didn't have to ask Rob what he was talking about. "Well, I'll be . . . I never did put much stake in that profiling business, but Tony's fast becoming the exception."

"That's why he's so expensive," Rob reminded him with a grin. "Anyway, I just thought I'd let you know. Now we can forget about Ahmed and focus our search on a female killer."

"Let's keep this close to our chest for now," ordered Lawrence. "We don't want the media to find out about it."

"Agreed."

"What are the next steps?"

Rob came into his office and stood against the glass wall. "We'll keep digging through both Yousef's and Patterson's lives until we find a connection. There must be something linking them to this mystery woman."

"Well, let me know if I can help."

Rob nodded. His boss liked to get his hands dirty every now and then. For a moment he wondered how he would fare in Lawrence's position. In charge of the department, forced to answer to the powers that be, having to put his trust in his team and not being able to do any of the grunt work himself. He shook off a shiver. No, that would never be him. Besides, he was hopeless at schmoozing. He didn't have the charm or the patience for it. DI was probably as high up the food chain as he was going to get — and he was okay with that.

"Will do."

* * *

Rob had just returned to his desk when his phone buzzed. He glanced down. Yvette. He thought about sending it to voicemail, but then changed his mind. "Hey, babe, you okay?"

She was sobbing softly. "Rob, can you come home?"

His heart leaped into his throat. "What's happened? Are you okay?"

She was breathing heavily and he recognized the signs of a panic attack.

"Yvette, calm down and talk to me. What happened?"

"Bec—Becca came over and we had a session, but it brought it all back. I can't stop shaking and I feel like I'm about to pass out."

Rob glanced at the time on his phone. It had just gone four o'clock. "It's a bit early for me to knock off," he said. He was going through Patterson's phone records, looking for anyone he may have arranged a meeting with on the day he died.

"Please, I need you."

He heard a low whine in the background and knew Trigger was worried about his mistress too.

He sighed and glanced up as a shadow passed over his desk. Mallory was standing in front of his computer. "I can hold the fort here, guv, if you've got to go."

Torn between wanting to stay and having to get home to his wife, he nodded. "Okay. I'm leaving now. I'll be home in ten minutes."

"Thanks," he said curtly to Mallory after he'd hung up, and before anyone had a chance to question him, he left the station.

Yvette was shivering on the sofa when he got back. Her jaw was clenched and her eyes were wild. It was all she could do to keep her teeth from chattering. A concerned Trigger had curled himself around her feet.

"Come here." He drew her into his arms and she fell against him. Her bony shoulders dug into his chest and her hair stank of stale smoke. He held her while she sobbed.

"What brought this on?" he asked, when she'd calmed down a bit.

"Becca made me talk about how I felt when it happened. How scared I was. And it all came rushing back." She spoke in short, staccato sentences, gasping for breath between each one. He rubbed her back. Becca had told him there might be a resurgence of emotion once she started to deal with what had happened. Yvette had locked it away and refused to talk about it for eight months, and now it was causing her to have anxiety attacks. She needed to get it out, talk about it, demystify it and put it into perspective.

"That's a good thing," he told her gently, hoping he was right. He knew nothing about psychotherapy or trauma counselling.

"How can it be a good thing if it makes me feel this way?"

"You're letting it out," he explained, repeating what Becca had told him. "It's part of the healing process."

She gave a shuddering sigh. "I don't feel like it's helping. I think it might be making it worse."

He took her head in his hands. "Give it a chance. Becca's very good at what she does." He smiled. "And I'm here for you too."

Trigger thumped his tail on the ground. "So is Trigger."

She fondled the dog's ears but couldn't muster a smile.

They made supper together in the kitchen and opened a bottle of wine. Yvette, who was on antidepressants, only had a small glass. Afterwards, Rob suggested they take Trigger for a walk around the block, but she refused. "I'm not ready, Robert."

He left her alone and walked Trigger by himself. The air was bitterly cold — in fact, he thought it might snow — but it cleared his head from the pressure he felt whenever Yvette had one of her attacks. He walked for much longer than he'd planned, and when he got back, Yvette had gone to bed. He left her to sleep — there was no point in going up, the sleeping tablets she took knocked her out — and made himself comfortable in the lounge with his laptop and the rest of the bottle of wine. He picked up where he'd left off this afternoon, browsing Patterson's phone logs.

The dental sales rep had made several work-related calls to customers he'd met in London prior to his death, including a dental practice in Hammersmith who were interested in buying an entire range in a certain brand. That must have been why he'd chosen the Pear Tree Hotel. Will, who'd analysed the calls earlier in the day, had written a side note saying that he'd spoken to the manager of the dental practice and they had been due to meet with Patterson on Monday morning to finalize the order. A meeting Patterson would never get to.

There was also an incoming call from a private number on the Wednesday evening, the day before his death. Will had highlighted it in yellow and written *NB* next to it. Rob realized he'd left the station before Will had had a chance to speak to him about the comment. He dialled his colleague and hoped he was still awake.

"Guv?" answered Will with more curiosity than tiredness. "Is everything okay?"

"Yeah, thanks, Will. I just wanted to ask you about the call you highlighted on Patterson's phone records."

"Oh, that. Yes, the call was made by a man called Kevin Mundy. He owns an online dental equipment store. He had an interview scheduled with Patterson the day he died."

Rob sat up, instantly more awake. "What time?"

"Thursday, 10.30 a.m."

That was close as dammit to their time of death. "Did you talk to him? What did he say?"

"He said he rocked up at the hotel and banged on Patterson's door, but there was no answer. He was going to ask the receptionist to call through, but she was nowhere to be seen, so he left. He figured Patterson had forgotten."

"Forgotten my arse. He was probably dead by then. Can we bring this guy in for questioning?"

"Sure, but he's got an alibi for the time of death. He went across the road to Starbucks and got a coffee. He said he flirted with one of the baristas there, and they're sure to remember him."

"Bring him in anyway," said Rob. "He may have seen something." Or someone.

CHAPTER 15

Doug couldn't concentrate. The forklift shuddered to a halt. His whole body ached with need. It had been several weeks since his last hit and the lure was strong.

"What's up?" the site manager called, noticing he'd stalled.

"Nothing."

"Well, get a move on. We don't have all day."

He started it up again and carried on loading the building material into the truck. Fucking idiot. If he didn't need this job so much, he'd smash the guy's head in. It wouldn't take much. The site manager was a bully, all talk and very little action. He'd known guys like him before. They acted tough but as soon as you challenged them, they backed right down. A small smile spread over his face as he imagined, just for a moment, what that would feel like.

Doug Bartlett had been a forklift operator since the middle of last year and he knew he had been lucky to get this job. Having spent eighteen months inside for armed robbery and aggravated assault, job offers were few and far between. Fortunately, the owner of the company had a son in the system and took pity on ex-cons trying to get back on their feet, and it sure as hell beat sleeping rough. His council flat wasn't much to look at, but it was warm and safe — well, as safe as a council flat in Southwark could be — and he didn't have to ask permission every time he needed a piss. More importantly, he was free to engage in his passion.

The thought made him break out in a sweat. He dumped the load and then glanced at his phone. Four thirty. Nearly time to knock off. He'd go home, shower, grab a bite to eat, then wait for his visitor. He'd made the call during his lunch hour and since then, he'd been counting down the hours.

He wiped the dust out of his eyes. It was freezing today, made worse by the wind chill, and every time he lifted a load of dirt, some of it blew back into his face. He could even taste it in his mouth. He made a note to buy one of those dust masks from the local chemist. He didn't want to get ill now that things were picking up.

Eventually, five o'clock arrived. Thank fuck for that.

He parked the forklift back at the site car park and clocked out. He didn't hang about and talk to the other guys — he didn't much like any of them. He knew they'd all go to the pub for a few beers and talk about stupid stuff, but he wasn't interested. He had something better to do.

Away from the site, he took off his dusty jacket and shoved it into his backpack. No one would sit next to him on the tube if he kept it on, not that he gave a fuck. He wanted to forget about work and focus on more fun stuff.

The icy wind blew right through him, but he didn't care. It felt good to be alive. It was warmer on the underground, which he took to Southwark Station. The area was bustling as the after-work crowd rushed to pick up groceries from Borough Market or went to meet their friends at the area's many trendy bars and pubs. His flat was several roads away from the market, in the less desirable area. Weren't all council blocks? He showered, then lay on his bed contemplating his evening.

Dinner was a doner kebab from the Turkish takeaway down the road. The food was great around here. Hell, compared to prison grub it was fucking gourmet. Doug ate at the long counter by the window, watching the people walk up and down the street. He saw some pretty girls and stared at them hard, imagining what he'd like to do to them.

He checked his phone. Not long now. He'd better get back.

He wiped his mouth on his sleeve and chucked the remnants of his kebab, including the packaging, in the bin, then walked out of the shop.

Soon. Soon he'd feel like himself again.

CHAPTER 16

Rob's mobile phone buzzed on the bedside table. He groaned, disentangled himself from Yvette's warm body and reached for the device. The time on the screen said 3.47. "Hello?"

A female voice said, "Sir, this is DC Ryan from Southwark Police Station. We have an incident that we thought you might be interested in."

"What incident?" And what was Southwark nick doing calling him in the middle of the night?

"A homicide, sir. A Caucasian male in his forties with multiple stab wounds."

Rob sat up straight in bed. Yvette shifted position beside him and gave a gentle moan.

"How many?"

"Excuse me?"

"How many stab wounds?"

"Oh—" She sounded flustered. "I'm not sure, sir. I wasn't there. I'm calling on behalf of my DS, Paul Cooper. He said to get you down there."

Rob sighed. This better not be a waste of time. "Can I have his number?"

"Yes, of course." She read it out.

"One minute."

He didn't have a bloody notepad or a pen nearby. He climbed out of bed and stumbled across the room to the doorway. He flicked on the hall light and made his way downstairs, rubbing the sleep from his eyes. In the kitchen, he found a pencil and a scrap of paper. "Fire away."

She read it out again, slower this time as if she were talking to a child. To be fair, it was four in the morning. He said he'd give Cooper a call and hung up. Trigger loped into the kitchen to find out what all the fuss was about.

The Southwark sergeant answered on the second ring. "Cooper." He had a real Londoner's accent, not unlike Mike's.

"This is DI Rob Miller from Putney MIT."

A pause. "All right. I was told to give you a bell 'cos I've got something you might want to see."

"Stab victim?"

"Yeah, it's a homicide with multiple stab wounds. He's a bloody mess, mate."

That was enough. "Give me the address," he barked. "I'll be there in half an hour."

* * *

The council block in Southwark was dark and gloomy. The street lamps did little to illuminate the hulking eight-storey brick building. He followed the flashing lights to the front where the south entrance had been cordoned off. Two police vehicles were parked diagonally in front of the building along with a SOCO van and an unmarked ambulance waiting to take the body away.

Rob parked the car and glanced up at the block of flats. Lines of glass windows, each with black metal frames, looked back at him, most of which were in darkness. At the south end, lights blazed on the fourth floor. He bet that was where the homicide had taken place. Above the block, the sky had turned a deep indigo as it does the hour before sunrise.

"DI Rob Miller, Putney MIT," he told the policeman guarding the darkened entrance. The officer shone a torch on his warrant card, then nodded and let him through the door. An icy blast whipped at his face as soon as he entered the stairwell. The vertical shaft was a natural wind tunnel. He reached for the railing and hung on as he climbed to the fourth floor.

It was even more frigid up here. Several police officers, their faces mottled by the cold, stood in the corridor informing any curious residents that they were to remain in their apartments. Two other policemen had secured the crime scene. Rob gave his name a second time and was handed the standard protective paper suit in plastic wrapping. He tore it open and pulled it on, along with the gloves and shoe protectors, then ducked under the tape into the flat.

Jesus, what a shithole. The carpet was so threadbare you could see the flooring below. Dust and God knows what else lurked in the corners and there was a substantial amount of mould creeping up the walls. The whole place smelled dank with an underlying odour of stale takeaways and urine. He shuddered and walked into the bedroom. Clothes were discarded over the floor like someone had just stepped out of them and left them there. Judging by the dust and the state of the windows, the place didn't look like it had ever been cleaned and there were visible damp stains under the wallpaper. But there was no body.

"In here," called a voice. Rob recognized it as belonging to the man he'd spoken to on the phone. He poked his head into the bathroom. It was a tiny cubicle only big enough for a toilet and a shower. "Cooper?"

"Yeah, you Miller?"

Rob nodded.

"I'll come out. You can't swing a cat in here." He shuffled out into the hallway, which wasn't much bigger, and shook Rob's hand. "Victim's name is Doug Bartlett according to his driver's licence. Someone's had a right go at him."

Rob stared past him into the bathroom. "Mind if I take a look?"

"Go ahead. I'll be over here." He nodded to the lounge.

Rob went in. A pathologist, a young woman in a head-scarf, was examining the body.

"Hi," he said. "DI Miller."

She gave him a nod. "Farah Ebrahim." He noticed she had a large camera slung around her neck.

A man lay on his side as if he'd tried to crawl into the foetal position, possibly to protect himself. There was blood everywhere — on the basin, spread out on the grimy tiles, on the rim of the toilet seat. His dirty wife-beater shirt was drenched with it.

"Christ," he muttered, taking it all in.

"Not a very dignified way to die," she said.

Rob peered around her and saw that the man was naked from the waist down. He'd obviously been going to the toilet when he'd been attacked.

Rob remembered seeing a pair of tracksuit pants, as well as discarded underwear, on the bedroom floor among the pile of clothes. He asked one of the SOCOs to bag the lot, just in case.

The victim was smaller than average for a man, around five foot nine with skinny, hairy legs. He had the start of a belly, which wasn't unusual for a man in his forties, and extremely dirty fingernails. The rest of him was similarly unimpressive.

His hands were calloused and etched with old scars. Rob was betting he worked in the construction industry, possibly as a brickie. "You going to take a sample of the dirt underneath his nails?" he asked, though they were so filthy it would most likely be impossible to tell whether he had any of the killer's DNA beneath them.

The pathologist gave him a *really?* look.

"Sorry." He backed off a little. This wasn't his crime scene. If he wanted the case, he'd have to request it via Detective Superintendent Lawrence, but given that it was the same MO as their killer, he didn't think it would be a problem. As it was, DS Cooper probably had his hands full. Southwark was the second most dangerous borough in London with one of the highest knife crime rates. He had his work cut out for him.

The pathologist lifted the dead man's top and inspected the puncture wounds.

"How many?" Rob asked.

"Twelve, at least." She leaned back on her knees to inspect his back. "More on this side, so maybe fifteen in total. I can't be sure at this stage, there's too much blood. Once I get him cleaned up, I'll have a clearer picture."

Fifteen. Rob exhaled slowly. Was the killer escalating, or was this victim of particular significance? There was no crime scene photographer, but the pathologist was taking photographs as she worked. In all fairness, it was the early hours of the morning and they were probably short-staffed.

"Any idea when he died?"

"Rigor mortis has set in," the pathologist replied. "So, eight to ten hours ago. I can't be more specific now, I'm afraid."

That would make the time of death between six and eight o'clock the night before.

"Had he had sex before he died?" Rob asked. The guy had it all hanging out, after all, and the bed wasn't made.

She shook her head. "It doesn't look like it, but as I said, I can't be specific until after the PM."

"Okay, thanks."

Rob walked around the apartment, taking his time. He asked the forensic officer if there were traces of semen on the bed, but he said no. Even so, the bedding had been taken away for further analysis.

He found DS Cooper on the phone in the lounge, standing with his back to the room, staring out of the window on to the concrete car park four storeys below. "I'll be home as soon as I can," he was saying into the phone.

Rob cleared his throat. Cooper turned around. "Sorry, the wife gets worried when I'm out too late."

Rob grunted. "I know the feeling."

Yvette hadn't said a word to him as he'd got dressed and left the house. She'd simply rolled over and gone back to sleep.

"Any sign that he had company?" Rob scrutinized the lounge. The old sofa was stained and grubby, and there was an armchair that looked like it belonged in the last century. The worn coffee table was cheap pine covered in ring marks, but there were no glasses or bottles anywhere. If Doug Bartlett had had a visitor, he hadn't offered them anything to drink.

"Not that we could find," Cooper said. "The shower had been used — there was water on the walls — so we think he washed and got dressed, then let his killer in. There's no sign of a break-in. And then, we're not sure. Maybe he went to the toilet, but why take his tracksuit pants and underwear off and leave them in the bedroom?"

"Maybe he was going to have sex?" said Rob, who couldn't think of why a man would walk around half-naked while there was someone else in the flat unless they were going to get it on. He also knew something Cooper didn't — that the perpetrator was a woman.

"In this dump?" Cooper shuddered. "It's not a very nice place to bring a lady, is it?"

"No, it's not." But some people didn't care about that. "Did you find a mobile phone on him?" Rob asked.

Cooper shook his head. "No."

"He must have had one." Who didn't these days? "The killer must have taken it."

"Why?" asked Cooper. He seemed puzzled, but he didn't have the advantage of knowing about the other cases.

"Because it may have had his or her number on it." He spoke loosely about the gender of the killer, not wanting to give away too much at this stage. They hadn't released that information yet.

"Aah." Cooper nodded, but his expression told Rob he had more questions than answers.

"Any witnesses?" Rob asked.

"My officers will do a door-to-door in the morning," the DS said. "Most of the other residents will be asleep now."

Rob would have preferred it done right away, but he didn't press the matter. Not his crime scene. If he could get this case transferred, he'd send his own team to do the house calls. "Will you keep me posted?"

"Yeah, sure." Cooper hesitated. "Is this similar to something you've got going on?"

"We have two victims with multiple stab wounds," Rob said. "It could be connected."

Cooper looked thoughtful. "As soon as our dispatch manager logged the call, it flagged an alert in the system to contact you. Do you think it's the same guy?"

Like him, Cooper had also assumed it was a man.

"It's possible," he said carefully. "The MO's the same. I'm going to talk to my boss to see if we can get the case transferred."

Cooper spread his hands. "Be my guest. I've got enough going on."

"Thanks, mate."

Rob shook his hand and left the crime scene. There wasn't much more he could do now, and he wanted to get home, shower and change, then get to the station early to talk to Lawrence. The sky glowed in the distance as he descended the stairs, not that it made any difference to the arctic temperature. He nodded to the officer on the ground floor and headed to his car.

Before pulling out of the parking spot, he looked up at the unattractive building one last time. Why here? What did this guy have in common with Yousef and Patterson? Tony had said it could be the type of person that the killer was going after, rather than the person himself. But as far as Rob could see, the three victims couldn't be more different. Yousef was a drug dealer, Patterson a sales rep and family man, and now Bartlett, who was . . . ? What? As soon as he got control of the case, he would find out.

His skin prickled as he drove out of the car park like it does when someone is said to be walking over your grave. Three victims, all with the same MO. It looked like they officially had a serial killer on their hands.

CHAPTER 17

"You've got to be shitting me," bellowed Lawrence after Rob had briefed him later that morning. Several officers glanced nervously towards the office.

Mallory shuffled from foot to foot, but Rob stood his ground. "It's the same MO. Fifteen puncture wounds this time, covering the victim's back and stomach." He left out the bit about Bartlett being in the toilet at the time of death. "Sir, this is our case. I want to send some of our officers over there to do house visits. Someone might have seen something."

Lawrence frowned. "Are you sure, Rob? Southwark is a little bit of a departure for our West London killer, isn't it?"

"Yeah, but it's definitely her, there's no doubt about it. That's three murders now." Rob gave him a pointed look.

Lawrence held up a hand. "Don't say it. Don't bloody say it." Not saying it wasn't going to make it any less true.

"Say what?" asked Mallory.

Rob shook his head.

Lawrence gave a dramatic sigh. "Okay, Rob. You win. I'll get on the phone and let them know. From now on, the case is yours. Get those officers out there. I want this thing tied up ASAP. I've had enough now. We can't have this woman running around wreaking havoc. Let's hope to God the press don't get wind of it. We can't have them linking this to the other two stabbings."

"Yes, sir." Rob gave a curt nod.

"What was that all about?" Mallory asked on the way out.

"Serial killer," said Rob, looking over his shoulder at his DI. "Lawrence is allergic to the phrase."

Mallory chuckled. "I should have thought he'd be used to it by now."

As soon as everyone was in, Rob called a meeting. He'd googled Doug Bartlett but had come up empty-handed. Bartlett was, however, on the police criminal database.

Rob faced his team in the incident room. "The victim, Doug Bartlett has form. He spent eighteen months inside due to armed robbery and assault but was released last July. We need to get the details of that case. Let's find out who he assaulted and why. This could be a retaliation." Not that he thought it likely given the two previous murders.

"Also — and I have no idea if this is relevant — he was going to the toilet when he was attacked." Heads bobbed as everyone turned their eyes to the front.

"Seriously, guv?" said Mike.

"Yep. He was found on the bathroom floor, naked from the waist down. There were fifteen puncture wounds — more than either of our other victims."

"Was it sexually motivated?" asked DS Jenny Bird.

Rob shrugged. "It doesn't appear to be, but we'll know more after the post-mortem. He was walking around naked, however, so maybe they were about to have sex when she attacked him."

"Do you think our killer could be a sex worker?" Jenny asked. Jo had suggested the same thing. "He could have arranged for her to come over, willingly let her in, then been caught unawares when she went for him."

"It would explain why Bartlett had his pants off," said Mike.

"And why Yousef offered her a drink," Mallory mused.

Rob narrowed his eyes. "What about Patterson? He wasn't the type to hire a prostitute. He was married with kids."

"But he was a travelling salesman. He was away from home, his wife would never know." Mike warmed to his theory. "Who's to say he hadn't done that sort of thing before?"

Rob fell silent for a moment. He pondered this new theory. It made sense on several levels, but on others it didn't add up. "I didn't see any calls to unknown numbers on his phone records. I doubt he had a prepaid SIM, he wasn't the type. He had two phone contracts, one for himself and the other for his wife. He was a good guy. Didn't have so much as a parking ticket."

Mike shrugged.

"Okay, let's consider that angle," Rob said. You never knew. It was worth following up. They didn't have much to go on. "Jenny, you and Mike follow it up. Check if any of the neighbours noticed a strange woman on the premises the evening he died."

"Maybe Forensics will find something," said Mallory hopefully.

Rob raised an eyebrow. "You should have seen the state of his flat. I doubt they'll find anything useful in that squalor. Besides, our killer is forensically aware. She hasn't left anything behind yet."

"They all make mistakes eventually," Mallory said.

Rob pasted on a grim smile. "Let's hope so."

* * *

"Oh my God. You're not serious?" Yvette echoed Lawrence's sentiment from earlier that day. It was late, he was tired, and the last thing he felt like was a flaming row, but he could see his wife was gearing up for one.

"It's not like before," he told her, keeping his voice even. He knew where she was going with this. "This time it's a woman, and the victims are all male. You're not in any danger."

But she'd pulled her dressing gown tight around her slim frame and was jutting her head out. "How do you know it's a woman?"

Rob regretted telling her that. The DSI would be incredibly pissed off if he found out. "DNA found at one of the crime scenes."

"But you don't know for sure? You can't know for sure." Her voice rose several notches.

"No, we don't know for sure, but we're pretty certain it's a female killer."

Yvette looked like she was trying to push herself back into the wall. "What if this woman comes after you?" she said.

"She won't. She doesn't even know I'm in charge of the case."

"It's in the papers. All she has to do is look."

"But we haven't released any information on the killer. Nowhere does it say we're looking for a woman — so please don't tell anyone," he added, as a precaution.

Her eyes blazed and for a moment she looked like the old Yvette. "Of course I won't. I don't talk about your cases. You never tell me anything, anyway."

"I'm telling you now."

She pouted and reached into her pocket for her cigarettes. She lit one, took a drag and exhaled. "I'm scared, Rob. I don't like this. What if she finds out you're hunting her and comes after you?"

"She won't." Rob sat down on a kitchen chair. God, he was tired. He'd spent most of the afternoon looking into Doug Bartlett's background. He'd been arrested as a kid for mugging an old man, then he'd progressed to burglary and assault, followed by his period of incarceration, and for the last six months he'd been working for a construction company as a forklift driver, among other things. Tomorrow morning he was going to speak to Bartlett's boss. "You're overreacting."

That was it. Yvette gave him a cold look, tossed her hair back and stormed upstairs. Rob leaned back and sighed. He knew she was frightened, but there wasn't much he could do about it other than reassure her nothing was going to happen. Last year had been a one-off, an anomaly, an unfortunate incident. He caught lots of criminals — they didn't all come after him, or his wife. Wearily, he got a beer out of the fridge and went to sit in the lounge. There was no dinner. Yvette hadn't cooked. He'd make himself a sandwich later.

He was just resting his head back on the headrest when his phone buzzed. It was DS Bird.

"Hi, Jenny."

"Guv, you're not going to believe this."

"What?" He could do with some good news round about now.

"I was conducting the door-to-door at Bartlett's block this evening and one of the residents, a Mrs Henderson, saw a woman in a trench coat and high heels enter the building just before six o'clock yesterday evening."

Rob sat up straight. "Is she sure it wasn't another resident?"

"She's sure. She'd never seen her before."

"Did she give a description? Did she look like a sex worker?" He fired off the questions, his pulse kicking up a notch.

"Medium height, dark hair, slim build," Jenny replied. "She couldn't see her very well because the light at the south entrance was out."

Yes, it was. He remembered the police officer having to use a torch. "Was Mrs Henderson outside, then?"

"Sort of. She was in the corridor having a smoke. She lives on the first floor. Being curious, she waited until the woman had gone up the stairs, then watched to see where she stopped."

"Fourth floor?" guessed Rob.

"Bingo."

"Okay, great work." His voice was breathy. "Let's get any CCTV footage sent over. I want to ID this woman as soon as possible."

"Yes, guv."

She hung up and Rob took a long pull on his beer. Finally, they had a lead.

CHAPTER 18

Glen O'Connor was a stocky Irishman with a weather-beaten face and pale, watchful blue eyes. He was from Ballymena in Northern Ireland and had started the construction company twenty years ago when he'd first come to England. It was now a fairly large enterprise, and they had some big contracts. At the moment, they were clearing ground for a new shopping complex.

"Aye, Doug's been working for us since last July," he said. "Why do you ask?"

"Doug's dead." Rob figured it was better to come right out with it. He'd got the impression this guy would appreciate the directness.

"Dead?" Glen's eyes widened, then narrowed again. "How'd he die?"

"He was murdered."

There was a silence as Rob let this sink in.

Glen sighed. "You know he was inside, right?"

Rob nodded. "Yeah. Eighteen months."

"I gave him a job because I felt sorry for him." He glanced down and his jaw tensed. "My lad went through a bad phase a couple of years back and did some time too. He battled to get a job afterwards."

119

"That was nice of you," Rob said. Glen O'Connor seemed a decent bloke. "Can I just ask, was Doug acting strangely at all these last few days? Was he quieter than usual? More aggressive?"

O'Connor shrugged. "Not that I noticed, but you might be better off having a word with his line manager. I didn't know him that well."

"Who might that be?" Rob asked.

O'Connor pointed to a tall guy yelling at a man driving a digger. "That's Tomas, over there."

"Can you call him in?"

"Sure, take a seat. I'll get him on his mobile." O'Connor disappeared into his office and closed the door.

Instead of sitting down, Rob stood by the window and watched as Tomas answered his phone, then looked up at the site manager's office. He said something to the man in the digger, then strode up the small dirt mound towards them.

"I'm DI Miller," Rob said, giving the man a once-over. He was taller up close and lean, with a hard expression on his narrow face. "I want to talk to you about Doug Bartlett."

"What's Doug done?" asked Tomas straight away. He had a thick, Eastern European accent.

"What makes you think he's done anything?"

Tomas shrugged. "He's not here and you are."

Fair point.

"Doug was killed last night." Rob watched the line manager for a reaction. His eyebrows rose, but he didn't look all that surprised.

"I'm sorry to hear that. What happened?"

"He was stabbed."

The eyebrows lifted higher, but he didn't reply.

"Did you notice anything different about Doug these last few days?" pressed Rob.

The manager thought for a moment, then shook his head. "No, he was always a grumpy sod."

It was strange hearing such an English term delivered with an accent. Tomas had obviously picked that one up off his co-workers. "Did everybody think that?"

He nodded. "He never came to the pub with us at the end of a shift. It was like he was too good for us, or he had something better to do."

"Did he ever say where he was going?"

Another shrug.

"But he was a good worker?"

"He worked hard, like all of us." Tomas gave him a hard stare. "We didn't know him."

What he was effectively saying was his death had nothing to do with any of them.

"Nobody here had a grudge against him? He didn't have an argument or a fight with anyone?"

A slight hesitation. "No."

"You sure?"

Tomas sighed. "A couple of weeks ago he had an argument with Bill, but it was nothing serious."

"Bill?"

"Yeah, Bill's over there. His wife came to fetch him one day and he said Doug was giving her strange looks. Bill's pretty possessive over his missus."

"Really?" Rob glanced out of the window. Bill was the big guy with thick, chunky arms operating the digger. "Can I speak to him?"

Tomas hesitated. Rob guessed he didn't want Bill to know he'd ratted on him. Rob compromised. "Okay, I'll ask your boss to get him."

Tomas nodded, relieved. "Thanks, mate." He went back to work.

O'Connor put on a hard hat and went to call Bill.

The big guy entered the office, making it seem small by comparison. He was easily six foot four with a belly and huge hands and feet. He looked strong, too. Rob introduced himself and showed Bill his warrant card.

"I used to be in the military," Bill said. "Great times."

Rob could believe it. The digger driver looked like he could handle himself on the battlefield, and under one partly rolled sleeve, Rob could make out a tattoo. Rob wouldn't have wanted to pick a fight with him. "Which regiment?" he asked.

"Paras."

Like his boss. "I need to ask you about an altercation you had a few weeks back with Doug Bartlett."

"Doug? Oh yeah, he was eyeing up my missus."

"What happened?"

"Nothing. I told him to stop it, and he did. Making her feel real uncomfortable, he was."

"You didn't hit him?"

"Nah. Not worth it, little runt like him."

Everyone was probably a little runt compared to Big Bill. Rob had to strain his neck to talk to him, and he was six foot himself.

"Okay, thanks. That's all."

"Is Doug in trouble?" asked Bill.

"Doug's dead," Rob told him.

Bill seemed genuinely surprised. "Who killed him?"

"That's what I'm trying to find out," said Rob with a grimace.

Bill straightened to his full height, which was impressive, and stuck out his barrel chest. "Well, it ain't got nothing to do with me."

Rob believed him, but he had to ask. "Where were you on Wednesday evening between six and eight?"

Bill's eyes narrowed. "I told you, I didn't have anything to do with Doug."

"Then you won't mind giving me your alibi."

A pause. "I took my wife to the cinema. And before you ask, we saw *Emma*, the new Jane Austen adaptation. Then we went out for a curry."

At Rob's surprised look, he shrugged. "She likes all those old-fashioned movies."

He must really love his wife, thought Rob. "Okay, well thanks for talking to me. I'll let you get back to work now."

Bill nodded and left the office, glancing over his shoulder as he made his way back to the digger.

CHAPTER 19

"It turns out our victim, Doug Bartlett, was not well liked by his work colleagues. 'Grumpy sod' was the term used," Rob told his team when he got back to the station. They had all piled into the incident room and were standing around the boardroom table.

"Did any of them have a motive to kill him?" Mallory asked.

"No, it doesn't look like it. I spoke to a couple of his colleagues. No one liked him, but no one disliked him either. He had a minor altercation with the digger driver a few weeks ago, but that was resolved. They all said his behaviour seemed normal leading up to the attack. This case is exactly like the others — the victim wasn't expecting it. It caught him by surprise when it happened."

"There *is* CCTV outside Bartlett's block." Jenny came in, pocketing her mobile phone. "I've asked the council to send it over ASAP."

"Great, thanks, Jenny. Keep me posted. We need an ID on this woman. If you can get a clear frame, we might be able to run it through facial rec." Facial recognition software wasn't new, but it was only just being rolled out across the force. Just last week he'd downloaded an app to his phone that enabled him to identify suspects in real time. If she was on the criminal database, they'd find a match.

"Will do."

"Her DNA wasn't on file, so it's unlikely her face is either," reminded Mallory.

Rob gave him a sideways glance. "There's always a chance."

"If she's a sex worker, how do we go about tracking her down?" Jenny asked.

"It would help if we knew where she worked," replied Rob.

Will cleared his throat. Rob remembered he'd done a stint in Vice a couple of years back. Except it wasn't called the Vice Squad anymore. It had been renamed Human Exploitation and Organised Crime Command, or SCD9 for short. He gave him a nod.

"The first thing we have to figure out is whether she's working the streets or is an escort," Will said. Everyone turned to face him. "The street girls pick up punters randomly and it's all down to chance. The escorts work from home or through an agency. They do call-outs and make home visits. Because our victims were all killed at home or in a hotel, I'd say she's the latter."

"Right, so how does that help us?" asked Rob.

"If she's freelance, she's bound to have a website or at the very least a dedicated phone line or email address so clients can contact her. If she works for an agency, they'll have a website with the profiles of all the girls on it, but a telephone operator will take the bookings."

"She'd have to be a freelancer to get away with this, surely?" Rob remarked. "An escort would have to answer to someone. They can't go around killing off their customers."

Mallory snorted. "It's not very good for business."

"We don't have a phone number or an email." Rob ran a hand through his hair in frustration. None of the victim's personal phones had been found at the crime scenes. Patterson's records had been easy enough to get hold of, but he was in the clear. "Patterson didn't make any calls to unknown numbers," he said. "And we can't access the other victims' records since they were pay-as-you-go."

"What about their emails?" asked Will. "Have we checked those?"

"Forensics sent through a report," Rob acknowledged.

"I'll get on it," offered Mallory.

"There's something else," added Will. "Escorts usually stick to a specific area. Most of them don't have their own cars, so they take public transport. Yousef lived in Hounslow, which is a lot further out than Southwark and Hammersmith. It doesn't add up."

"If she purposely chose these men," said Rob, "we've got to find out why. Let's dig into their personal lives and see if we can find something that connects them. Everybody get on this, except those who are looking for Bartlett's late-night visitor on CCTV. There must be a common thread." A thought struck him. "If this woman is an escort, you said she's unlikely to have a vehicle?"

"That's usually the case," said Will.

"Are we wasting our time looking for cars that turned into Yousef's street?"

"Maybe not," said Will, hedging his bets. "You never know, she may be the exception."

Rob nodded to Jeff and Mike. "Okay, let's keep on with that line of enquiry anyway, just in case. And while you're at it, see if any of the same vehicles pop up at the other locations."

"Yes, guv," said Mike.

"Now, what do we know about Doug Bartlett's priors?"

Jenny spoke up. "He broke into an elderly man's house two years ago and assaulted him, leaving him tied up in the kitchen, before robbing the place. It turns out he'd done some landscaping work for him earlier in the month."

"When he cased the place," added Rob.

"Yes, and there was also an alleged assault against a woman the year before, but she dropped the charges."

"Now that sounds suspicious," said Rob. "Who was she?"

"A Christy Blackman."

"Let's get her details. I want to pay her a visit."

Jenny didn't ask why, she simply nodded and began tapping away on her tablet. "I've sent it to you," she said a few moments later.

"I've just thought of something," said Will. "There's a website for sex workers called SAAFE. It's a forum where women can post warnings about potentially dangerous clients, time wasters and scam artists. It also offers advice and information to sex workers. It might be worth having a look to see if anything's been posted about these killings?"

"Do it," said Rob.

* * *

Rob took a delighted Jenny with him to visit Christy Blackman who, he felt, might be more inclined to talk to a female officer. Mallory was a great detective, but he wasn't particularly warm or empathetic.

Christy lived in a functional apartment block in Vauxhall. It was one of the many new builds that had gone up in recent years. Construction was ongoing in the area and the chilly blue skyline was intersected with cranes.

Jenny followed him up a flight of stairs and they walked along an enclosed corridor to flat twenty-three. Thank God it wasn't a freezing wind tunnel like in Bartlett's block. In the narrow gaps between buildings Rob could make out the chilly grey Thames flowing rapidly past, its surface ragged and uneven thanks to the gusty wind. It was nearly six o'clock in the evening so Christy should be home by now, assuming she was gainfully employed.

Rob pushed the buzzer. They waited, listening to the low-level growl and occasional *thunk* from the construction sites around them. Rob rang a second time, and they heard footsteps on a wooden floor. The door opened.

"Can I help you?" The woman standing inside was an attractive blonde in her late twenties. Average height, she had a body to rival Yvette's and platinum hair down to her waist. Her face was expertly made-up with dark eyes, lots of mascara and bright pink lips. Rob stared at her in the dim light. Those eyelashes couldn't possibly be real.

"Are you Christy Blackman?" he asked.

"Who wants to know?"

He held up his warrant card. "I'm DI Miller and this is DS Bird. Can we come in, please?"

She hesitated. "Actually, this isn't a good time. I'm about to go out."

He squared his shoulders. "This won't take long."

She glanced from him to Jenny, who offered a small smile, and back at him, then sighed. "Okay, but let's make it quick. I'm late for an appointment."

Rob thought he knew what type of appointment that was.

They walked into a surprisingly clean apartment with inexpensive but tasteful furniture. "Take a seat." She gestured to the cream leather sofa. Rob sat down with Jenny beside him. It was soft and they sank in further than he'd expected. He leaned forward to compensate.

"What's this about?" she asked somewhat defensively. Her eyelashes were so long they reminded him of a peacock's.

"Do you know this man?" Rob held up a photograph of Doug Bartlett taken at the crime scene. His skin was tinged with grey and his eyes were shut — it was clear he was dead.

She gasped. "What happened to him?"

"Did you know him?" pressed Rob.

She shook her head, suddenly frightened. "No, never seen him before."

"Except you filed a complaint against him in 2017." Rob frowned. "For assault?"

She stuck out her lower lip and her eyes darted to the floor.

Jenny shuffled towards the edge of the sofa. "Christy, we aren't here because of what you do for a living. That man was murdered and we're looking for anyone who might have information about him."

Christy's gaze rose slowly to Jenny's face. "Murdered?"

"Yes. I promise you, we don't care about anything other than finding the person who did this." She took the photo from Rob and held it up.

Christy studied it, gnawing on her lip. "I saw him once. He was a customer."

Rob exhaled. Jenny continued with the line of questioning. "Did you know his name?"

"He said it was Doug."

She nodded. "That's great, thanks. Now, what can you tell us about Doug?"

The platinum blonde stared sullenly at the photograph.

"Was he a nice man?" Jenny prompted.

Christy shook her head. "No, he wasn't."

"What makes you say that?"

"He tried to make me have sex without a condom on and when I refused, he got pretty rough."

"Did he hurt you?" asked Jenny.

Christy nodded. "Yeah, he held me down and left bruises on my arms and legs. Prick."

Jenny shook her head. "I'm sorry you had to go through that, Christy. Did you report him?"

"I tried." She gave a throaty laugh. "But the coppers gave me a hard time, so I dropped the charges. I just wanted to get out of there. But I did warn the other girls about him."

"How'd you do that?"

"On a website."

"Was that the SAAFE website?" she asked.

Christy nodded. "It's where all the girls post warnings about the rough ones or the ones who don't pay."

"Did this man pay you what he owed?"

Again, she shook her head. "No, he didn't. He said I hadn't done what he wanted so he wasn't going to pay me. When I told him we had an agreement, he pushed me on to the bed and told me to shut up. He said he'd hurt me if I wasn't careful." She shrugged. "So, I shut up."

Rob took a deep breath. Jesus. What these girls had to go through.

"Thanks for being so honest with us, Christy," said Jenny, in her soft voice. "I've just got a few more questions. Is that okay?"

Christy nodded. Rob noticed she had talons for nails, painted a bright fuchsia. She inspected them now as she waited for the next question.

"How did Doug contact you? Was it via a website or by telephone, or by some other means?"

"I'm an independent contractor," she said with pride. "I used to work for an escort agency, but I went out on my own last year. Best decision I ever made."

"Working for yourself is always the best option, isn't it?" said Jenny as if they were talking about bookkeeping or interior design, not prostitution. Rob knew she was empathizing with the subject, finding common ground. She was good at it too.

Christy gave a little nod. "The agency took a big cut, but then I didn't have to do any of my own marketing or anything. Now I'm in charge of everything."

"Where do you advertise?" Jenny asked.

"On punter websites, through word of mouth, that sort of thing." She was being purposefully vague. It was a crime to solicit sex after all.

"Do you have a contact number for Doug?" Jenny asked.

"I did have."

Rob felt a shot of adrenalin surge through his veins.

"But I'm not sure I still do." His heart dropped.

"Could you check for us?" enquired Jenny.

Christy reached into her handbag and pulled out the latest model of iPhone. She scrolled through the numbers, her pink talons clicking on the screen. Eventually, she shrugged. "No. I must have deleted it."

Rob let out a low groan.

"It was a long time ago and I was never going to see him again."

"I understand," said Jenny.

Rob sat up straighter as a thought occurred to him. "Christy, did you post his phone number on the SAAFE website?"

She perked up. "Yes, of course. That's what we do to warn the other girls."

"What's your username?" he asked. When she frowned, he added, "It's so we can trace the number you posted on there."

She didn't have to give him any information, strictly speaking. If she refused, he'd just get a warrant, but he was hoping Jenny had softened her up enough so that she'd offer it up voluntarily. He was right.

"PinkFlamingo556." She blinked several times, her long lashes sweeping against her cheekbones.

"Thank you," said Rob. "You've been a tremendous help, Christy. I mean that."

She smiled for the first time. Rob got the impression it wasn't often she got complimented.

"He deserved this, you know." She nodded towards the photograph. "I bet it was a pimp who did him in. He probably beat up some poor girl and this was what they did to him. Can't say I'm sorry."

Rob didn't reply. Jenny thanked her again and they left the flat. Christy left right after them, heading to her next client.

CHAPTER 20

"If his number is on that website, anyone could have contacted him," said Rob once they were back at the station. "I'll bet Christy wasn't the only woman he roughed up."

"Do you think our killer is targeting violent men?" Jenny had her tablet open and was trawling the SAAFE forum in search of the warning posted by PinkFlamingo556.

"It's a possibility," Rob replied. Tony had said the killer could be going after a type. "Check if Yousef's or Patterson's name is mentioned on that site."

Mallory was shaking his head. "I can't see Patterson as someone who assaults women."

Rob agreed. "Patterson is the one victim that doesn't fit. Yousef was a drug dealer, he exploited kids and vulnerable adults to distribute crack and heroin into the Home Counties. He wasn't a nice bloke. It's conceivable that he hired escorts. Bartlett had a history of violence. He'd been in prison for assault and we know he used prostitutes. But Patterson . . . ?" He let his sentence fade.

"I double-checked Patterson's laptop," said Mallory. "And according to his browser history, he's never visited any dodgy sites. He's squeaky clean."

"The killer must have had something else against him then," mused Rob.

Mallory stroked his chin. "Like what? A bad sales deal? A faulty dental drill?"

Rob shook his head. Patterson was a mystery, the missing link in the chain.

"Will, can you get a list of escort agencies operating in the London area? Let's contact them and find out if Yousef was one of their clients."

"I doubt they'll give us that kind of information without a warrant," he said. "I remember how tight-lipped they are from my time in Vice. We couldn't get a thing out of them. If it came out that they give away their customers' info to the cops, they wouldn't be in business very long."

Rob sighed. "Okay, but get the list anyway. We may need to get warrants if it comes to it."

* * *

Jeff came in, looking flushed. "Guv, we've found something. Come and have a look at this."

Rob followed him into the warren where Mike was sitting in front of a large screen showing black-and-white CCTV images of the street outside Bartlett's council block in Southwark. The ugly, bulky building looked even more oppressive in monotone.

"We've found this woman arriving at the block at 6.27 p.m. the night Bartlett was murdered." Mike pointed to a dark figure approaching the block. She was wearing a short skirt, high heels and a trench coat, which was tightly wrapped around her. She had dark hair and was looking down, so the camera didn't pick up her face, only shadows.

"That's her, right?" said Jeff, slightly out of breath.

Rob nodded. "That's her, but we can't see her face. Do you have anything clearer? Anything we can run through facial rec?"

Mike grimaced and moved the video on a bit. "Not really. Here, she looks to the side and we can see her cheek, but the rest of her face is still in darkness."

Damn it. They were so close. They had the woman arriving on camera, but it was impossible to see who she was. All they knew was she was medium height, slender, dark-haired and had great legs. At least it confirmed what the first-floor resident at Bartlett's block had witnessed.

Rob's phone buzzed in his pocket. He ignored it, his mind on the CCTV. "How are you getting on with those vehicles at Yousef's?" he asked Mike.

"Yeah, we're getting there. We've whittled it down to twenty-seven possibles now," he said. "It's taking a while to contact all the owners. Most of them are happy to talk to us over the phone, but for anyone who isn't or who sounds suspicious, we send a PC to check them out. So far, everyone's been accounted for."

"Okay, keep me updated."

"Will do, guv."

* * *

"Guv." Jenny grabbed his attention as he emerged from the warren. He walked over to her desk.

"What have you found?"

"There are two references on the SAAFE website about a potentially dangerous man called Adam," she said.

It took Rob a moment to make the link. "As in Aadam Yousef?"

"Maybe." Her cheeks were flushed with excitement. "Look, it's here under 'Warnings and Wasters'." She indicated some text on the screen.

Arabic man. Over six foot. Calls himself Adam. Called late evening and wanted submissive GFE. Picked me up at Hounslow station in a BMW. Looked like he had money, but afterwards, refused to pay and when I tried to leave, got violent. Phone number xxxxxxxxx328.

"What's submissive GFE?" Rob asked.

"I'm not sure I want to know," Jenny replied.

"It's an acronym for Girlfriend Experience," said Will, coming over. "It basically means kissing and cuddling. It's one of the most expensive services, actually."

Jenny stared at him.

"Kissing is very personal," he added with a shrug.

Rob felt his phone buzz again. Whoever it was would have to wait.

"Is that the only one?" he asked.

"There are a few comments below — see?"

Rob checked the replies to the post.

Sounds like the same guy who got physical with me. Hounslow. Arabic. Name's Adam. He looks rich but doesn't pay.

I know this guy. Did the same to me. Broke a tooth when I tried to leave.

"Christ," muttered Rob. "Why do they do it?"

"The money's good," said Will. "Many of these girls are supporting kids, they need flexible hours and decent pay."

"But at what price?" murmured Rob.

Jenny took a shaky breath. "Do you think this could be our guy?"

"It's possible," said Rob. "Contact the site admin and get those protected mobile phone numbers for Adam and Doug. I'll contact the phone company and see if we can get hold of their call logs. We might even be able to trace them to the killer." But that was a very long shot.

* * *

Armed with the phone numbers, Rob went to see Lawrence, who was still in his bubble. It was dark outside and the rest of the team had knocked off for the night. As soon as he had requested the call logs and the trace, he would be out of here too. Yvette had called several times today, but he hadn't been able to answer. He didn't admit that he was scared she'd call him home again, and he couldn't leave. The case was hotting up and he was the senior investigating officer. How would it look if he dashed off every time his wife had a wobble?

Was that mean? He sighed, pushing the guilt aside. He'd pick up something nice on the way home and they could eat together and maybe watch a movie on Netflix or something.

"Still here, sir?" He knocked on the glass, but as usual, the door was ajar.

"Come in, Rob. I've been meaning to ask you for an update." He closed his laptop and took off his glasses. "How's it going?"

"I think we're finally getting somewhere." Rob sank into the chair opposite Lawrence.

"Oh, yes?"

"Yeah." He patted the folder in his lap. "We've managed to find a link between two of the victims. They were both listed on a forum used predominantly by sex workers to report violent and dangerous men."

The Superintendent's eyes widened slightly.

"DS Bird got hold of the site administrators, who gave us the men's phone numbers. We'll cross-reference their call logs to see if they contacted the same woman the day before or the day of their deaths."

"You think our killer is a prostitute?"

"Yes, sir. Someone with a grudge against violent men."

"You said two of the victims were on this forum?"

Rob shrugged. "Patterson, the second victim, doesn't appear to have engaged a sex worker. There was nothing in his emails or call records to connect him to the others."

"Why was he targeted, then?"

"Honestly, sir, I don't know. We're still putting the pieces together. But Yousef and Bartlett were both listed on this site. I'd like to request a warrant to access their phone records."

Lawrence nodded. "Of course, go ahead."

"Thanks." Rob got up to leave.

"How's Yvette? I believe Becca's been to see her."

Rob turned to face him. "Yes, Becca's been a few times now. I think it's dredging up some painful memories for Yvette, but that's to be expected."

"Glad to hear she's working through it." The DSI got to his feet. "Go home, Rob. It's been a long day."

"Yes, sir."

Rob put through the warrant request, then packed up. Lawrence was still in his office when he left the squad room.

* * *

"Hi, honey, I'm home," sang Rob as he let himself in, his arms filled with takeaway bags from Yvette's favourite Indian restaurant. They did a tasty saag paneer that she loved.

Trigger bounced around at his feet, inordinately pleased to see him. He fondled the dog's ears, then put the packages in the kitchen. "Yvette? I've bought dinner."

There was no reply.

"Where is she, Trigs?" He poked his head into the lounge. There was a dent in the sofa where she usually sat curled up, her legs beneath her. The television was off. It was gone eight thirty. Yvette never missed an episode of *Coronation Street*.

Mildly alarmed, Rob climbed the stairs and peered into their bedroom. Also deserted. Where had she gone? He knew for a fact she wouldn't have left the house on her own accord. He pulled out his phone and rang her. It went to voicemail.

He ran downstairs and back into the kitchen. "Yvette?" he yelled at the empty house. Could she have gone out? If so, where?

He looked at the three missed calls he'd received today. What if something had happened to her? Heart thumping, he opened the sliding doors into the garden. Trigger immediately darted out as if to say, *Are we going walkies?*

"In a sec, Trigger."

He walked back into the house looking for clues. Trigger's bowl was empty, but that didn't necessarily mean she hadn't fed him. The exuberant Labrador wolfed down his food faster than you could prepare it. He opened a tin of dog food and emptied it into the bowl with some kibble. Trigger fell on it like a ravenous hyena.

Frowning, he scrolled through his phone for her sister's number. It rang several times before a feminine voice with the same lyrical quality as Yvette's answered.

"Hello?"

"Hi, Naomi? This is Rob. Is Yvette there?"

There was a pause, then Naomi replied. "*Oui*, one moment."

Rob exhaled in a long whoosh. Thank God. The line fell silent and nearly a full minute later, Yvette's voice said, "Hello, Robert." She only called him that when she was mad.

"Jesus, Yvette. Why didn't you tell me you were going out? I got home to an empty house and I was worried. Are you okay?"

"I am now."

"Look, I'm sorry I couldn't speak to you today, I'm in the middle of a case and it's been really gathering pace today."

"I had an anxiety attack. I couldn't stay there by myself, so I called Naomi."

"That's okay. You did the right thing. I just wish you'd let me know, that's all."

"I would have done if you'd answered your phone."

"You could have sent me a text."

A pause. "I'm going to stay here for a few days."

"Are you sure? I won't be working all weekend."

"Yes, you will."

He didn't bother to correct her. Now they were making headway in the investigation, he wouldn't be able to stay away, and Yvette knew that. Most of his team would be working too. When they had an active investigation, free time went out of the window. Once the case was over, they'd have time off to rest and recuperate. That was just the way it was.

"No, I think I need to be around people for a bit. I don't want to be alone with my thoughts."

Rob could understand that. She was alone at home all day while he was at work. "Okay, sweetheart. I'm sorry I couldn't be there for you today. I'll come and fetch you on Sunday, okay?"

"Okay."

"I love you."

Another pause. "Love you too." Then the line went dead. Rob studied the mound of Indian food on the kitchen table. At least he'd worked up an appetite during the day.

"I guess it's just you and me, Trigger."

CHAPTER 21

The River Thames shimmered beneath the cobalt-blue sky, while the sun shone weakly overhead. Trigger loped happily beside him, darting off every few metres to chase a duck or pick up a stick, his tail a continuous blur. Rob watched as an eight-man rowing boat glided past, taking advantage of the good weather gap, their strong arms working in unison. They moved quickly and within seconds had rounded a bend in the river and disappeared.

On the way home, Rob stopped at the local grocers and bought the paper, along with some eggs and bacon. He made a hearty breakfast, read the paper — there was no mention of Doug Bartlett's murder — and, feeling revitalized, set off for work. Being a Saturday, the squad room was quieter than normal but his team would come in, even if it was only for part of the day. Lawrence's office would stay empty, though. The Superintendent didn't work weekends — he didn't need to. That was one of the perks of being in charge.

Rob logged on to his computer and took care of the first order of business. The warrant had been approved. He wasted no time getting on to the phone companies to request the call records for Aadam Yousef and Doug Bartlett. Once they had the telephone numbers, getting hold of the logs was easy. Both O2 and Vodafone agreed to send the records over as a matter of urgency. The big operators were used to working with law enforcement, particularly now a lot of organized crime was conducted via mobile phone.

The coffee machine in the waiting room gargled away as Rob contemplated the connection between the two victims. Was it possible Yousef and Bartlett had been targeted because they beat up women? Was their killer someone who had had enough and decided to take matters into their own hands? While he waited for the rest of his team to arrive, he rang Tony and ran this past him.

The criminal profiler was in agreement. "It would explain the frenzied nature of the attack, the multiple puncture wounds and the wily manner in which she gained entrance. I think you're on the right track, mate."

Had the killer found "Adam" and "Doug" on the forum? Was that her hunting ground? But there was no sign of "Dennis" or "Den" on the site. Of course, he could have used a fake name, but Rob didn't think he'd be on there. For one, he didn't live in London, and two, he simply wasn't the type.

Mallory was first to arrive, followed by Mike and then Jeff, who was eating a McDonald's Egg McMuffin.

"Hiya," greeted Jenny, her earphones in. She was casually dressed in leggings and a jumper. They all relaxed a bit when they worked on the weekend. The dress code fell by the wayside. Rob was wearing jeans and a navy blue hoodie with *SURVIVE* written across the front. It was some designer label, thick and good quality, but he couldn't remember which one. Yvette had bought it for him at Harrods last year.

Will came in rubbing his eyes, carrying a grande coffee from Starbucks.

"Heavy night?" asked Rob with a grin.

Will grimaced. "Something like that."

By ten o'clock, the whole team was in and the air buzzed with anticipation. This was the part of the investigation that Rob loved, the bit where they connected the dots that brought them ever closer to their mysterious female killer. The hunt.

The phone records came in shortly before midday. Mike took a break from the CCTV viewing and did something cool with a spreadsheet that enabled them to identify the calls that appeared on both men's records. There was only one.

"Bingo!" Mike scribbled the number on a Post-it note and handed it to Rob. "There's your killer."

Could it really be that simple? Rob's pulse throbbed in his neck as he took the Post-it. He stared at the digits written there, Mallory peering over his shoulder. "Let's run this number through the system and see if it flags anything."

Mallory got right on it. He didn't need to write the number down.

Rob contemplated ringing it, but he didn't want to spook their suspect. If she got wind that the police were after her, she'd disappear faster than a speeding bullet and then they might never catch her.

"It's unlisted," said Mallory, a short while later.

Of course it was. "A sex worker wouldn't have a traceable phone," he muttered.

"We could call, pretending to be a punter," suggested Will. "Make her an offer she can't refuse, then nab her when she arrives."

Rob considered this. "It's too risky." But he had another idea. "Why don't we set up a dummy profile on the SAAFE forum, warning others about a particularly violent punter? If she's hunting for victims on the forum, she'll find the feed soon enough."

Will nodded enthusiastically. "Great idea, guv. I'll set it up. With a bit of luck, she'll fall right into our trap."

Rob wasn't going to count on it. They didn't have any concrete evidence that this was their murderer yet. A couple of phone numbers on a forum wouldn't hold up in court. Even the fact that the suspect had dialled both victims' phone numbers would be viewed as circumstantial. "Okay, go ahead, but I don't want to act on this just yet. We need to ID the caller, first."

"Gotcha." Will's fingers flew over the keyboard as he got to work.

Rob called Lawrence at home and got permission to extend their existing warrant to include this latest phone number. It was with giffgaff, a satellite service provider that piggybacked off the main networks, so it was a rather more complicated procedure getting hold of the right person to request the call records, especially on a Saturday. Eventually, Rob explained what he wanted and the woman on the other side agreed to send through the logs as soon as she could.

"I'll run the number by SCD9," Will said over his shoulder. "They might have it on record somewhere. You never know."

"It's worth a shot."

Will copied the number down and picked up the phone. He still had a few contacts in Scotland Yard's SCD9 unit and since serious crime didn't come to a halt at the weekend, there was always someone on duty.

* * *

There were no other CCTV sightings of the woman in the trench coat and heels at any of the other murder scenes. Rob gazed at the still of her outside Bartlett's place and wondered what her story was. She'd obviously been assaulted or abused by a punter in the past — an occupational hazard, he imagined — but it still didn't give her the right to take the law into her own hands and go around stabbing people.

Rob took a cigarette break and went outside to call Yvette, but she didn't pick up. She was pissed off at him, he knew that, and to be fair, he probably deserved it. But realistically, he couldn't leave work every time she had a panic attack. Perhaps it was best she stayed with her sister for a while. At least that way she'd have the support she needed.

He drew deeply on his cigarette and tried not to think about how if it hadn't been for him, she wouldn't be in this mess to begin with. He stomped out his cigarette butt and went back to the squad room.

"I've got something, guv," said Will as soon as he walked in.

Rob raised his eyebrows. "Give it to me."

"My contact at SCD9 ran that mobile phone number through their database and got a hit. It belongs to an escort agency in Central London called Daring Divas."

"That's great! Good work, Will."

He glowed with pride. Rob didn't dish out too many compliments.

"So, our killer *is* an escort," Rob said slowly. "Didn't the agency notice her clients turning up dead?"

"Why would they?" said Will. "The way it works is the client calls in and makes a booking, or books via the website. The sex worker attends the appointment, gets paid and hands the commission over to the agency. There's no follow-through to check customer service. If the client never calls the agency again, they'll assume he's not interested. Not dead."

Rob contemplated this. "And we've done a good job at keeping these deaths away from the mainstream media."

"Even if they were mentioned in the press, none of the punters ever use their own name, so the agency still wouldn't make the connection."

"Okay. Let's go pay this agency a visit." Rob grabbed his jacket off the back of his chair. "Thanks, Will. Mallory, you're with me."

* * *

Daring Divas had a small administrative office near Leicester Square in Central London. It was next to a seedy nightclub called Galaxy that would be pumping in a few hours' time, but right now, at 4 p.m. on a Saturday afternoon, was deserted. The front was covered by a steel roller door, and without the backlighting, even the name looked flat and dull.

On the other side of the escort agency was a newsagent. A crowd of youths had gathered outside and were sharing a box of cigarettes. They didn't look up as Rob and Mallory walked past.

"Good area for business." Mallory glanced up at the nightclub sign. "Right in the centre of London's West End."

"Not easy to spot unless you know it's here," said Rob. The door was painted a glossy black and there was a smart buzzer and a grated microphone on the wall beside it. Apart from that, there were no identifying features, no plaque on the wall, no sign above the door, not even a label beneath the buzzer.

He pushed the button and a moment later a throaty female voice said, "Can I help you?"

Rob looked up and saw a small camera hidden behind a satellite dish erected below the second-storey window. It looked like it was part of the mechanism of the dish, but its bulbous glass eye pointing at the front door gave it away.

He held up his card. "I'm from the police. I need to ask you a few questions." He didn't have a warrant for this visit, so the woman was under no obligation to let him in.

"What's it in connection with?" the voice enquired.

"One of your customers."

"We don't give out information on our customers," the voice replied. "We have a confidentiality agreement."

"I understand, but this is about a customer who was murdered last week." Rob put his mouth close to the microphone beneath the buzzer. "It's a homicide enquiry. We're not with the Vice Squad."

A short pause. "Come in."

The door clicked open. They pushed it inwards and entered a manky corridor with threadbare carpeting and outdated wallpaper on the walls. Rob crinkled his nose at the musty smell. They climbed the flight of stairs directly ahead of them to the first floor. On the landing, the décor was different.

The walls were painted a startling white, the floor was polished parquet and smart black lettering on the glass door read *Daring Divas Escort Agency*. The effect was classy and professional.

Rob pushed a second buzzer and was granted access. He swung the glass door open and walked across gleaming floorboards to the front desk, Mallory at his heels. Behind the counter sat a young woman in a fluffy pink jumper. Rob showed her his card, as did Mallory.

Her eyes widened. "W—What can I do for you?" Different voice.

"Can we speak to the manager?"

A door at the back opened and a middle-aged blonde (dyed) in a dress two sizes too small came out. "You'd better come through," she said in what Rob gauged was an Essex accent.

They followed her into a back office. It was small but tidy and contained a large desk, two visitors' chairs and a side table upon which sat a printer and, beneath, a giant shredding machine. Shredders always made Rob suspicious, even though most companies used them to destroy unwanted personal documentation. The woman gestured for them to sit down.

"Thank you for seeing us," he said, starting out with some goodwill. After all, she could have refused them entry or just not answered the bell.

She lowered herself into the chair behind the desk and studied them. "You're not from Vice?"

"No. We're from the Putney Major Investigation Team. We're investigating a murder."

She gave a slow nod.

"And you are?" asked Rob.

She tilted her head back. "You can call me Francine."

Not her real name, then. "Well, thanks again, Francine."

Before he could say any more, she cut in, "You understand I can't divulge information about my clients." She pursed her lips. "It wouldn't be good for business."

Up close, she had smooth skin and crystal-clear blue eyes. She was possibly younger than he'd first put her at. Regardless of her age, however, he got the impression she was far more astute than her appearance suggested.

"Actually, it's two of your clients we need to talk to you about." Rob took Yousef's and Bartlett's photographs out of his pocket and lay them on the desk in front of her.

She stared at the grey, lifeless faces for a long time. "I've never seen either of these men before."

"I understand," said Rob. "Their names are Aadam Yousef and Doug Bartlett. They were both killed in the last two weeks. I need to check if they were clients of yours."

She was already shaking her head. "Our punters don't use their real names."

"We think Doug did, and Aadam may have called himself Adam."

She pursed her lips. "What makes you think they're our clients?"

"They both made calls to this agency in the days before they died."

The penny dropped and a flush creeped into her cheeks. "And you think one of my girls had something to do with their deaths?"

Rob met her gaze head-on. He didn't reply — he didn't need to.

"I can assure you, none of my girls were involved in this," she snapped. "I would have known."

"Would you?" said Rob. "If you were paid your commission, how would you know the punter was dead?"

She fell silent. The only sound was the gentle hum of her laptop, which was open in front of her. Eventually, she said, "I can check our booking system."

"Thank you." Rob exhaled quietly. She was cooperating. Mallory met his gaze and gave a small nod. She typed something on the keyboard then waited while it searched. A whole minute passed before she raised her head again.

"I can confirm that we have a Doug and an Adam on our books, but I'm afraid I can't give you any more details than that."

"Which days did they make bookings?" enquired Mallory.

She shook her head.

"Was it in the last month?"

Her eyes flickered to the screen.

"Am I right?"

She gave a slight nod. "But I'm not giving you the names of the girls."

Rob sat upright. "Girls? They saw two different girls?"

Francine shut her laptop with a definitive snap. "If you want anything else, you'll have to come back with a warrant." She knew her rights. There wouldn't be any point in pressing her for more information. The steely glint in her eyes told him she wouldn't budge.

"Okay." He stood up. "You've been very helpful, Francine. If we need anything else, we'll come back with the proper authorization." Mallory seemed vaguely surprised at his acquiescence but got up all the same.

Francine showed them out. The receptionist was on the telephone. "I'm afraid Monalisa isn't available tonight, but I can offer you Chiquita instead."

"You didn't want to push her, guv?" Mallory asked.

Leicester Square had got even busier while they'd been inside. Theatregoers, tourists and late-afternoon shoppers crowded the pavements and spilled on to the roads. Cars tooted while mopeds zigzagged through the packed streets.

"It wouldn't do any good. She wasn't going to give us the names of her girls. We'll have to come back with a warrant or find some other way of getting that information."

They made their way to the car and drove back to the station.

"Yousef and Bartlett saw two different girls," Rob pondered. "I wasn't expecting that."

"If it was them," Mallory pointed out. "Adam and Doug are pretty common names."

"True, but what are the chances of them both calling the escort agency in the last month?"

Mallory shrugged. "I guess so. Still, we can't be sure it's them."

"Not until we get hold of the escorts who met with them." Rob deftly manoeuvred the undercover police car through the throngs of traffic. He suddenly thought of his empty house and took his foot off the gas. Why rush? There was no real reason to go home yet. Yvette was at her sister's for the whole weekend. Then he remembered Trigger waiting patiently, or rather impatiently, for him, and stepped on the pedal again. His canine friend would be sure to be hungry by now, though Rob had left a gap in the sliding door to the garden so the Labrador could get in and out during the day. He didn't think it was fair to keep him locked up all the time and it was pretty cold outside despite the blue sky, so he'd compromised. Yvette would have had a fit, but he was fairly confident the house would be okay. Richmond was a safe area and both his neighbours were home since it was the weekend.

"If it's two different girls, which one of them is our murderer?" asked Mallory, as they crawled along in back-to-back traffic through Earl's Court.

"And why did she target Dennis Patterson?" added Rob. A man who had no conceivable history of assault or engaging escorts. He sighed. There were too many questions and not enough answers. "Let's wait until Monday. I'll speak to the boss and see if I can get a warrant for the agency. We need to talk to those escorts."

* * *

The rest of the weekend was quiet. He rang Yvette, offering to collect her from her sister's, but she declined.

"There's no point in me coming home when you're going to be at work next week anyway."

"I miss you," he told her over the phone.

"Now you know how I feel," she replied stubbornly. He heard her inhale and knew she was smoking.

He sighed. "This is my job. You can't expect me to stay at home and not work. At some point you're going to have to focus on getting your life back."

That was the wrong thing to say. "What do you think I'm doing?" she shrieked. "I even agreed to see your bloody counsellor, for all the good it's doing me."

Rob didn't want to get into an argument over the phone, so he apologized. "Okay, stay there until you feel able to come home. Just know that I love you." His words sounded flat to his own ears and she didn't return the sentiment. They hung up after that.

Trigger whined and put his head on his knee. "I know, Trigs," he'd said, stroking the dog's ears. "I miss her too."

CHAPTER 22

"I can get you a warrant for the escort agency, Rob," the DSI said on Monday morning. "But I'd advise against it."

"Why's that?"

"I spoke to Bryson over at SCD9," said Lawrence. "And Daring Divas is one of the better agencies around. The girls are clean, they're well looked-after, and the woman who runs it often passes on useful information to the unit. It wouldn't look good if you sent a bunch of uniformed officers in there, confiscating equipment and searching the premises."

Rob sat back in his chair and studied his boss. "So, what you're saying is Francine is a police informant."

"Unofficially, yes." The Superintendent tapped his pen on the desk. "She's useful to Bryson's unit. She knows everything that happens in the West End and has provided valuable information over the years. In return, they leave her alone."

"And you don't want us interfering."

"Bryson did ask nicely. Apparently this woman has links to organized crime gangs in the area. Her husband's family, I believe."

Rob ran a hand through his hair. He knew there was more to her than had met the eye. Damn it. They were getting close, he could feel it.

"How else are we going to move forward? We need to speak to those escorts. They may have valuable information that could help us solve this case." His voice rose in pitch and volume. "One of them might even be our killer."

Lawrence pursed his lips. "What about using one of the other escorts or the telephone operator? Anyone who can look up the information for you."

"We don't know the names of any of the employees or the escorts." He thought for a moment. "I suppose we could put one of our officers in there. They could pretend to be a sex worker, maybe get to know some of the other escorts or take a peek at the booking system."

Lawrence considered this. "It's an option."

"Although, it's not ideal," admitted Rob. "It would take time, time we don't have. We need that information now, before our killer strikes again."

"I'm not keen to go in all guns blazing," said the Superintendent. "Sending in an undercover officer looks to be our best option at this point. Any suggestions?"

At that moment, there was a knock on the glass door.

"Sorry to interrupt. I thought I'd pop in and see how you're getting on."

Both men glanced up to find Jo standing at the door. She was wearing a tight skirt coupled with a starched white shirt tucked in at the waist. Her legs were stockinged and on her feet were a pair of navy high heels, which made her legs appear endless.

When neither man said anything, Jo asked, "Is something wrong?"

Lawrence glanced at Rob, who gave a little nod.

"Why don't you come in and take a seat?" the DSI said. "There's something we'd like to run by you."

* * *

"Are you insane?" Jo gawked at them in disbelief. "It's not even my case."

"You'd be doing us a favour," said Rob.

Lawrence nodded. "I've read your file, you've done undercover work before. This should be a doddle for you."

"I went undercover at a law firm," she said. "Not an escort agency."

"We just need some information from their booking system," Rob explained. "It wouldn't involve anything dangerous."

"Is that even admissible?" she asked.

"It doesn't have to be," countered the Superintendent. "We just need the names, something to go on."

Jo sighed. "Isn't there anybody in SCD9 who can do it?"

"Probably, but we want to keep this close to our chest," said Rob. "You understand the case, you've seen one of the crime scenes. You know what this woman is capable of."

Jo fell silent.

"Come on, it won't take long. You just have to show up, have an interview with the owner, Francine, and get rid of the receptionist for a few moments while you hack in to the system."

"Why can't you just bribe her?" said Jo. To be fair, it wasn't a bad idea.

"We may have to if this doesn't work," Rob said. "But it's worth a shot, don't you think?"

"How do I hack in to the system?"

Rob had been thinking about this. "We'll arrange for a package to be delivered by an awkward courier, so the receptionist will have to leave the desk to sign for it. While she's away from her desk, you search for the names. Chances are she won't lock her computer just to receive a package."

"It's risky. She might."

"If she does, then we've had it," said Lawrence. "We might be able to give you a thumb drive to insert, which will enable us to clone the hard drive, but that's violating all sorts of privacy laws."

"It might be worth it as a plan B," Rob said. "We'd have access to that information if we got a warrant anyway."

"True." The Superintendent pursed his lips.

Jo sighed. "My boss is never going to sanction this."

"I'll have a word with him." Lawrence gave her a reassuring nod.

Jo looked doubtful. "Okay, talk to him first, then let me know, but just for the record, he's not going to go for it."

* * *

Two hours later, they had the green light for the undercover work.

"I don't know how Lawrence talked Pearson into it," Jo grumbled. "He's not usually such a pushover."

Rob grinned. "The man knows how to get what he wants."

"Clearly." She blew a stray hair off her face. They were sitting in the police canteen, eating a sandwich and discussing the case. "I can't believe I'm doing this."

"You'll be okay," said Rob, his mouth full. "I have faith in you."

She shot him a sideways glance. "Easy for you to say. You're not the one who has to dress up as a prostitute and hack in to a computer."

"Okay, let's talk about timing." Rob finished chewing. "How about tomorrow afternoon? I don't think they're open during the mornings. You can visit the office in Leicester Square and apply for a job. You'll have to come up with a convincing cover story."

"I need more time to prep," she said. "They'll want to see glamour shots."

"Time is of the essence here."

"I know that, but if this is going to work, I have to look like the real deal. I can't just waltz in off the street with some selfies of myself in a bikini. They'll never hire me. I'm going to need a professional photographer to take some quality shots in a staged environment, like a hotel room."

"We have a photographer who can help with that."

"No offence, but I think I'll hire a private photographer. I'm not having the local SOCO gawking at me in my lingerie."

Rob laughed. "Okay, no problem. Arrange it and bill the department. The DSI will sort it out."

"I'll need underwear, too," she said. "Somehow I don't think anything I've got is going to cut it."

"I wouldn't be so sure," said Rob with a naughty grin. He'd seen her in her underwear once before and it had worked for him.

She swatted him with her napkin. "Enough of that, thank you. Let's move on."

He laughed. "Okay, get what you need and set up the photo shoot for tomorrow. We've got to move on this."

She shook her head. "This is crazy. If any of these photographs make it on to that website, I'm screwed. I'll never be able to look my colleagues in the eye again."

"You won't be there long enough for them to load your pictures on to the website," he said. "You'll have to move fast. We'll help by delivering the parcel to the premises five minutes after you arrive. The timing is everything. That way, the receptionist will be away from her desk for a few minutes, and you'll have time to either look up the information or clone the hard drive."

She exhaled. "Gotcha."

* * *

"Jesus," spluttered Rob when he saw the photographs the following evening. Jo had called him to say they were done and she had the shots. He had met her at a pub in Waterloo, near to where she lived, for dinner. Away from the prying eyes of the station.

"I take it you approve?" She gave him a sly glance.

"Hell, yeah." It was hard not to. In the first photograph she was wearing a pink lace bodysuit and bending forward, showing off her cleavage to maximum effect. In the second, she was wearing a black sports bra, minimal make-up other than lip gloss and her hair mussed up like she'd tumbled straight out of bed. A mental image of her waking up in his bed in a similar state flashed through his mind. He swallowed hard. In the third picture, she was wearing a white shirt, unbuttoned and open at the front, exposing an indecent amount of cleavage. Her lips were painted pillar-box red and she wore a pair of black-rimmed glasses. It was evocative and sexy. There were a few more images but he didn't trust himself to look. He handed them back to her, aware his hand was trembling ever so slightly. "They're perfect. I'd hire you."

She smiled and slotted them back into the manila A4 envelope that they'd come in and put them on the seat next to her. "I'm sure."

"Honestly, if I didn't know better, I'd think you were a real pro."

That made her laugh. "Thanks. I think." She took a sip of her beer. "So long as they work, that's all I'm concerned about. I don't want the woman, Francine, to see through me the first moment I'm there. You said she was pretty savvy."

"She is, yeah. The important part is to make sure you're there at least fifteen minutes early. She's unlikely to be ready for you straight away. That way, it'll give you time to get to the computer once the receptionist is called away."

Jo nodded. "I'll give it my best shot."

He smiled, determined to suppress his body's reaction to her photographs. "I know you will."

CHAPTER 23

Jo walked into the Daring Divas office with just the right amount of swagger. She didn't want to overdo it, be too stereotypical, but at the same time, she needed to make an impression. *Hire me*, her look had to say. *I can get the men going.*

The push-up bra under her tight red T-shirt made her breasts appear full and perky, and at least a size or two bigger than they were. The new denim jeans clung to her like a second skin and showed off her long legs to their best advantage. At least her colleagues wouldn't see her like this. She'd worked hard to get where she was, and she didn't want to be promoted for the wrong reasons.

It was overcast and drizzly today, so she'd worn a knee-length padded coat over her outfit, similar to what she imagined working girls would wear when on public transport, but she took it off as soon as she entered the heated interior of the agency.

The young woman behind the reception desk looked up. "You're early," she said. "Francine was expecting you at three."

"I know," said Jo in a breathy voice she'd been practising for this assignment. "I didn't want to risk being late in this weather."

"You come far?" asked the girl.

"Brixton," Jo replied. "But there's engineering works on the Victoria line near Stockwell."

The girl nodded.

Jo glanced at the door leading to the manager's office. "I can wait."

"You'll have to. She's not here."

Excellent. Jo took a seat and fired off a text message to Rob letting him know the coast was clear.

The telephone rang. Jo listened as the girl took a booking. "Zahara. Eight o'clock. What do you want?" she asked. There was a pause. "CBT will be fifty quid extra." Jo didn't know what that was, but she suspected it had nothing to do with cognitive behavioural therapy.

The girl tapped away on the computer. "Okay. That will be £300 in total. It's cash in hand."

Come on. Ring the bell, dammit. Now was the perfect time.

The girl hung up the phone and smiled at Jo. "He's a new one. Could tell he was nervous."

"Do you get a lot of new ones?" she asked.

The girl shook her head. "Nah. Most are regulars and have their favourites. The girls prefer it that way. They like to know what they're in for."

"Do they ever have bad ones?" Jo asked.

The girl shrugged. "Comes with the territory, innit. If they rough up the girls we blacklist them, and if it's bad we report them to the police."

"That's good to know." Jo gave a relieved smile.

The girl looked her over. "You new to this?"

Jo shuffled in her seat. "Kind of. I've been out of it for a while. Had a bad experience."

Before the girl could reply, the doorbell rang.

This is it.

The receptionist glanced at the video feed. "Hello?"

"Delivery," came the reply.

"Come on up."

"I can't leave my bike out here," said the delivery man. "Can you come down?"

The receptionist sighed, then said, "One sec." She rolled her eyes at Jo. "I'll be right back."

Jo watched as she opened the glass door and disappeared down the stairs. It was now or never. She jumped up and ran around the back of the reception desk. The girl hadn't logged out of the computer. Thank God.

Jo tabbed through the open windows on the screen until she came to the booking system. It was on the page confirming Zahara's appointment. She clicked on *Clients* and scrolled down until she came to Adam. Luckily, he was fairly near the top.

She clicked on his latest booking. He'd asked for a home visit from Amber on Monday 27 January at 2 p.m. That was it!

Clicking on Amber's name took her to the girl's portfolio page. Nothing there listed her contact details. Crap. She went back to the beginning and looked for the section that stored employee details.

The receptionist was arguing with the delivery driver downstairs.

Breaking into a sweat, Jo searched for Amber's details. There was no physical address, just a PO box and a phone number. Jo took a snapshot of the screen on her phone.

She heard the door downstairs close. Adrenalin buzzing in her ears, she went back to *Clients* and scrolled down to the D's. She clicked on Doug's booking details. Nothing recent. The last booking was 15 December. That wasn't right. By all accounts, he should have hired an escort on 5 February, the night he was killed.

Footsteps on the staircase. There was no time to do anything else. She returned to the home page and hoped the receptionist wouldn't notice it wasn't where she left it. Nothing she could do about that. She whipped back around the desk just as the girl pushed open the door.

"What are you doing?" she asked, pausing in the doorway.

"I was looking for a loo, but you don't seem to have one."

The girl relaxed. "Oh, it's upstairs. You have to go this way."

"Thanks." Jo darted through the double doors and up the threadbare staircase. Safe in the tiny cubicle with the door locked, she called Rob. "I've got the details," she hissed.

"Great work. What did you find?"

"Yousef did make a booking for the day he died," she said. "But there was nothing for Doug."

"Nothing?" She heard confusion in his voice.

"No. Sorry. Last call-out was the fifteenth of December."

"That doesn't make sense. We know he had someone in the flat with him the day he died."

"I know. Listen, I'm going to try to sneak out of here. You don't need me to go through with the interview now, do you?"

"Yeah, that's fine." Rob sounded distracted like he'd been caught off guard. Well, it wasn't her fault. She'd done her bit and now she wanted to go home, take a shower and clean this gunk off her face.

She was on her way downstairs when she remembered she'd left the envelope with her photographs on the sofa in the waiting room. Shit. For a moment she contemplated leaving them there, but she couldn't risk those photographs ending up online. It could potentially mean the end of her career. With a sigh, she knocked on the glass doors. Maybe she could retrieve the envelope and then tell the receptionist she'd changed her mind.

Unfortunately, Francine chose that moment to come up the stairs.

"Hiya," she said in a cheerful voice. "You must be the new girl come for the interview?"

"That's right." Jo put on her breathy northern accent and forced a smile.

"Well, come on through," said Francine. "Everything okay, Mary?"

After all the exotic names on the database, Mary sounded extremely dull. The receptionist nodded. "Yes, took a few more bookings while you were out."

"Good. Good."

Francine sauntered into her office and called Jo. "Come on through, love. Let's have a little chat and you can tell me all about yourself."

Jo groaned internally. It seemed like she'd have to go through with this interview whether she liked it or not."

* * *

"Thank God," Rob exclaimed as Jo rounded the corner half an hour later. "What happened? When we spoke, you said you were on your way out."

He'd been pacing up and down the pavement beside the car, smoking one cigarette after the other, keeping a tight eye on the time. If she'd been any longer, he'd have been hard-pressed not to go inside and look for her.

"I'm sorry. Francine came back and I had to go through with the interview."

"You did?" He studied her for a moment then broke into a relieved smile. "How was it? Did you get the job?"

Jo punched him on the arm. "It's not funny. She asked me what my specialities were. Thank goodness I brushed up on some of the terminology before I left."

"What are your specialities?" he wanted to know.

"None of your business."

He laughed. "Did she buy your story?"

Jo nodded. "They have a vacancy and it's mine if I want it."

"What did you say?"

"I said, 'That's great.' What else could I say? I couldn't change my mind at the last minute."

Jo looked amazing. He knew she'd be feeling like a tart, but to him she just looked like she was going to a bar or a nightclub. Half of the young women he saw out these days were dressed exactly like Jo was right now, although she wouldn't see it that way. Those tight jeans really emphasized her legs, and that clinging T-shirt . . . God help him. He took a steadying breath. "Well, you got the information, that's all that counts. Now we have a name."

"Amber isn't much to go on. Hopefully you can trace her real name from the PO box or phone number."

"Phone's probably a burner," said Rob. "But if she has a PO box her real details must be on file. I'll get on to the post office in the morning. You did great."

Jo eyed him sullenly. "I feel dirty."

He chuckled. "Fancy a drink?"

She hesitated. "Don't you have to get home to Yvette?"

He didn't meet her eye. "She's staying with her sister at the moment."

Jo didn't comment. "In that case, I'd love a drink."

"Great."

They left the car on the double yellows and walked to the Coach and Arms, a traditional English pub off Haymarket.

"What are you drinking?" Rob asked, stopping at the bar.

"Chardonnay, thanks."

He ordered while Jo found them a table. When he got back with the drinks, she was looking at the paper she'd scribbled Amber's details down on. "It's strange there was no booking for Doug Bartlett."

"Very. In fact, I can't understand it. Francine said they were both on the system, so I just assumed they'd both hired an escort the day they died." He put the drinks down and took a seat opposite her.

"Could Doug have hired her off the books?" Jo reached for her wine. "Maybe if he was a regular, they decided to cut out the agency."

"Possibly, but according to his records, he called the agency the day he died. Why would he do that and not book an appointment, then negotiate with the escort separately?"

"I don't know." Jo stared into her glass. "Maybe he didn't have her number?"

"I doubt they would have given it to him."

Jo took a sip of her wine. "What time was Yousef killed?"

"Between 4 and 8 p.m." said Rob. "Why?"

She nodded at the note she'd made. "His appointment was for two o'clock."

Rob's stomach sank.

"Would Amber have stayed there the whole time?" Jo gazed at him with wide eyes.

"No, it's unlikely. You're sure of the time?"

"Positive."

He sighed. "I don't know what the going rates are, but I'd imagine a two-or-more-hour appointment would cost a fair bit. But then, Yousef had the money."

"I guess so." She didn't sound convinced. Well, neither was he.

Then he remembered something. "Yousef's body showed no evidence of sexual intercourse. He didn't have sex before he died."

Jo frowned. "Now I'm really confused. If Amber killed him, she'd have been with him for over two hours. What were they doing if they weren't having sex?"

Rob felt the tenuous link they had on this case dissolving. "Maybe Yousef was into something else, some weird fetish or something. Or maybe they were just hanging out. Will mentioned a Girlfriend Experience — just kissing and cuddling."

Her dimple flashed. "I suppose that's possible."

They were silent for a moment, each sipping their drinks.

"What if he showered?" said Jo "Wouldn't that wash away any traces of sex?"

Rob contemplated this for a moment. That was something they hadn't considered. "It might have done. Let me ask the pathologist." He pulled out his phone and called Liz Kramer, who was on her way home.

"You'd better not be sending me to a crime scene, Rob," she said as soon as she picked up. By the hollow tone of her voice, he could tell she was using her hands-free kit.

He chuckled. "No, you're okay, Liz. Just a quick question."

"Fire away."

"Is it possible Aadam Yousef, our first victim, showered before he was killed?"

A pause. They could hear the indicator ticking in the background. "He may have done. His hair wasn't wet, but that doesn't mean he didn't shower."

"So, he could have had sex before he died but it didn't show up because he'd cleaned himself?"

"Yes, a shower with soap would wash away any trace of semen and other bodily fluids," she confirmed.

Rob thanked her and hung up. Jo was staring at him expectantly.

"You're right," he said, his pulse ticking up a notch. "He could have showered after they had sex. Then come back downstairs and poured them both a drink — and that's when the killer struck."

Jo studied him. "It's possible, but why would she wait until after he'd showered? Why didn't she just kill him before they had sex? Let's face it, if you're going to murder someone, you may as well do it before you sleep with them, right?"

She had a point.

Jo continued, "And say, for argument's sake, she did sleep with him first, how could she have known he was going to take a shower?"

Rob stared blankly at her. "You're right. It doesn't add up. She couldn't have known."

"Unless he was one of her regulars?" suggested Jo. "Maybe that was one of his quirks. He liked to shower immediately after sex." She gave a little shrug.

"There are too many variables." Rob sighed and leaned back in his chair. "Too many things that don't add up. Like why did Doug call and not make a booking? Who was the woman on the CCTV if she wasn't one of the girls from the agency? Why was Doug half-naked? And why was Patterson, the sales rep, targeted at all? We have a thin connection between Yousef and Bartlett, but it's tenuous at best. The CPS would laugh us out of court."

Jo pushed the piece of paper over to him. "Maybe Amber can shed some light."

Rob put his hand on it. "Let's bloody hope so."

CHAPTER 24

After a couple more drinks, Rob announced he had to go. "Trigger is waiting for me at home."

"It's like having a child," chuckled Jo. He admired the way her eyes glittered when she laughed.

"He keeps me company."

A cold blast hit them as they walked outside. It was dark already, but no less busy. A mist hung over the street, illuminated yellow by the street lamps. Throngs of people marched up and down the pavements through the murky glow.

"How long is Yvette away for?"

He shrugged. "No idea. She doesn't like being alone while I'm at work, and since I have a job to do . . ."

"Is she no better?" asked Jo.

"Not really. Becca's giving her some support, but she's still extremely agoraphobic. She won't leave the house and jumps at every little thing. She's convinced the person we're hunting is going to come for me, like the Stalker did."

Jo frowned. "I'm sorry to hear that. It must be very hard."

"Yeah, it's a completely irrational fear. I wish there was something I could do, but apart from being with her constantly, which is obviously out of the question, there isn't anything. I feel so helpless."

Jo put a hand on his arm. "She'll pull through. It'll take some time, but she'll get there."

"I hope so."

Jo hesitated, then pulled him into a hug. He held her close, absorbing her warmth. For a moment all was right with the world.

"I'd better get home." He backed away.

She nodded. "Keep me posted."

"I will, and thanks for today. I appreciate the risk you took."

She grinned. "It was fun. I always enjoy working with you, Rob."

The problem was, so did he.

* * *

Amber's real name was Ingrid Harris and she lived in Camberwell, a supposedly up-and-coming borough in South London. As Rob drove through the litter-strewn streets, all he could see were looming council blocks, red-brick terraced houses that looked like cardboard cut-outs, and small parades of shops containing a newsagent, an off-licence and, of course, a pub. Groups of youths in hoodies accumulated on street corners, some on bikes and others on foot, mostly up to no good. It was ten in the morning — why weren't they at school?

"I wouldn't want to live here," said Mallory, echoing his thoughts.

They passed an ambulance flying in the opposite direction, its siren screeching through the mid-morning air. It was another cold, drizzly day and the wipers were on, clearing the windscreen when it became slick with rain.

"What's the postcode?" asked Rob.

Mallory relayed it from memory and Rob entered it into the satnav. The blue line led them further down the road, then left into a long, suburban street, and right into what looked like another council block, although this one was in better condition than the others. It had a landscaped garden out front with a small children's play area, although it was deserted on account of the weather. Rob parked on the road outside. Bad things happened to police vehicles in council blocks, and even though theirs was unmarked the trouble-makers always spotted them.

"Flat nineteen," said Mallory. "Canbury House."

The complex was broken up into three different blocks. Canbury House was in the middle. They entered through a pedestrian walkway and jogged through the rain, past the playground and across the concrete car park to the entrance. Rob shook out his jacket, then buzzed number nineteen.

A tinny voice said, "Yeah?"

"It's the police," said Rob. "We need to ask you a few questions."

Silence. Rob thought she'd gone and was about to buzz again when the voice said, "Come in."

Surprised, he glanced at Mallory. That didn't usually happen, especially with people who liked to fly under the radar. Mallory shrugged. He wasn't complaining.

They followed the signs to the first floor and found number nineteen at the end of a draughty corridor. The door was already open and a young woman stood there in a towelling robe. Her strawberry-blonde hair was piled up in a makeshift bun and her skin was devoid of make-up. Rob realized that she probably worked nights and they must have woken her up. She looked tired, with soft purple shadows beneath her eyes. He put her age at around thirty, give or take.

"Sorry to disturb you, Miss Harris," he began, watching her expression. "We'd like to ask you some questions about Aadam Yousef, one of Amber's customers."

She paused, unsure of what to say. The red bulb from inside the apartment made her hair glow with a pink aura. Eventually she asked, "Who?"

"Amber. Your alter ego."

"No, which customer." It seemed she was going to coop-erate. Good.

He smiled. "Aadam Yousef, but you probably know him as Adam."

Mallory showed her the picture of Yousef. She cringed. "Shit. What happened to him?"

"We were hoping you could tell us." Rob jostled forward so she had no choice but to step back inside the apartment. "Do you mind if we come in?"

Reluctantly, she beckoned them inside. They followed her down a small passage into the living area. It was comfortably decorated in bright colours with fluffy cushions on the sofa and a knitted turquoise throw on the armchair. The blinds were raised and the rain pattered down on the windowpanes. She gestured for them to sit down.

Rob picked up a heart-shaped pillow and handed it to Mallory, before sitting down. Mallory hesitated, then sat beside his boss, tucking the cushion in the crease beside him. Ingrid perched on the edge of the old armchair, which creaked disapprovingly.

"He's dead, isn't he?" Her eyes were fixed on the photograph in Mallory's hand.

Rob nodded. "Yes, and we think you might have been the last person to see him alive."

She stiffened. "I didn't kill him, if that's what you're asking."

"We didn't say you did," said Rob, who had been secretly hoping she had done. It would have made life so much easier. But faced with this girly thirty-year-old in her pink nightgown and bare feet, he wasn't convinced she was the cold-blooded killer they were after.

"Could you tell us about the last time you saw him?" he asked, in a gentle, non-threatening voice.

She bit her lip. Admitting she was at his house would be construed as soliciting and she could get arrested. He put her mind at rest. "We're homicide detectives, Miss Harris. We're not concerned with why you were there."

Her shoulders dropped as she visibly relaxed. "Okay, well I got there at two o'clock. That was the time of our . . . appointment."

"Had you visited him before?" Rob asked.

She shook her head. "No, this was my first time with Adam. You were right, that's what he called himself."

They both nodded.

"He offered me a drink, which I refused." She arched an eyebrow. "You can't be too careful."

Christ, Rob thought with a shudder. He was immensely glad he didn't have daughters. He wouldn't get a wink of sleep. "What then?"

"We went upstairs." She gazed at them pointedly. They got the message.

"And afterwards?" asked Rob. "Did he pay you?"

"Yes, he did, although he liked it rough, if you get my drift. Some of them do. They like to show you who's boss."

He thought he saw her shudder. "Did he hurt you?" he asked.

She shook her head. "Nothing I couldn't handle. Anyway, afterwards I took my money and left."

"How did you get to his house?" said Mallory.

"I took the train. He's a bit far out, in Hounslow, but I'd heard from the other girls that he paid well, so I figured it would be worth it."

"And did he? Pay well?"

"Yeah, he likes the add-ons, so it all adds up. Not really my cup of tea, but beggars can't be choosers, eh?" She giggled.

Rob cringed inwardly. What kind of life was this? Ingrid was young enough to get married, have kids and live a normal life. What was she doing selling herself to men who liked to show them who's boss? He sighed and reminded himself it wasn't his place to judge.

"What time did you leave?" asked Mallory.

"Three. I had another client at five, so I took an Uber. The tube can be a bitch after schools kick out."

Jesus. Two appointments back to back. No wonder she looked knackered.

"And he was in good health when you left him?"

She met his gaze. "Yeah, he was fine. Nothing wrong with him. He even had a smile on his face."

"Can anyone vouch for you?" said Mallory.

"The Uber driver," she said. "You wanna check my phone?"

"Please, if you don't mind," said Rob.

She disappeared, presumably to the bedroom, but came back a moment later holding a rose-gold iPhone. "I'll just pull it up for you."

She pressed the screen a couple of times and then handed the phone over to him. He was looking at her Uber app. The last one was 3.07 p.m. on Monday 27 January. Just like she'd said.

He took a screenshot of the page and handed the phone back to her. "Would you mind sending that to me?" Her eyes narrowed. "It clears you from our investigation," he added.

"Oh, in that case, sure." He gave her his number and she WhatsApped it to him.

"How about these men?" Mallory took two more photographs out of his jacket pocket and held them up. The first was of Dennis Patterson, the second Doug Bartlett. "Do you know either of them?"

She studied the shots for a long time, then shook her head. "No, I don't know them."

"Not customers?" asked Rob.

She gave him a hard look. "No. I'd tell you if they were. I've been straight up with you." She fidgeted. "Is that all?"

"One more thing," he said. She groaned, but he ignored her. "Did you notice anyone else outside when you left Adam's house? Anyone standing in the shadows or waiting in a car, that sort of thing?"

She thought for a moment. "Nah, sorry. I didn't see no one, but then I wasn't really looking."

This had not gone the way he'd expected. Instead of finding their killer, they'd met with yet another dead end. Yousef had been alive and well when Ingrid had left him. He was pretty sure the Uber driver would vouch for her. She wasn't their killer.

CHAPTER 25

Sure enough, the Uber driver confirmed Ingrid's alibi. He'd picked her up at seven minutes past three and taken her home to Camberwell. "Sweet girl," he'd called her.

"So, the escort is in the clear?" enquired Lawrence later that day. Rob was standing with him beside the coffee machine outside the squad room. There was no one else around.

"It looks that way." Rob sighed. The coffee machine gurgled. "And she's never met Patterson or Bartlett before."

"Could she be lying?"

"I don't think so. She didn't lie about knowing Yousef. And she took a long look at their photos. I really don't think she knew them."

The Superintendent took his mug out of the machine. It had *My daddy catches bad guys* written on the side. Rob put his down and pushed the button. It spluttered to life.

"Where does that leave us?" asked Lawrence.

"No closer to finding the killer, sir." Rob leaned against the wall, hands in his pockets. He felt like a school kid who'd been caught doing something wrong. Except he hadn't. He'd followed the trail of evidence and done everything right, yet it had still led nowhere.

"I suppose it has occurred to you that the killer might not be an escort."

"Yes, but both Yousef and Bartlett were customers of Daring Divas escort agency. That's the only link we have, so it would stand to reason that it was someone connected with the agency."

"But Patterson wasn't?"

"No."

"I admit, it seems like a hell of a coincidence."

There was a pause while Rob reached for his coffee. The machine burbled to a stop. "Who else has access to the agency booking system?" asked the DSI.

Rob thought back. "Francine, of course. Then there are the telephone operators who take the bookings."

"Could it be one of them?"

"It could," Rob said. "But in order to question them, I'm going to need that warrant you didn't want to give me."

Lawrence sighed. "Okay, let me have a word with Bryson and I'll get back to you."

Rob nodded. "Both Yousef and Bartlett are on that website."

The Superintendent, who was about to turn around and go back into the squad room, halted. "The forum site?"

"Yeah. But if that's how the killer is targeting them, it could be anyone." Rob thought about the fake profile Will had set up. "There *is* one way we could test that theory."

The Superintendent raised his eyebrows.

"Will, I mean DS Freemont, has set up a bogus profile on the forum, pretending to be an escort. He could post a warning about a punter who enjoys beating up women — we'll make him look really bad — and then we wait to see if anyone requests the guy's details."

"You think that'll work?"

"I don't know, but it's worth a shot. If that is how the killer is finding them, she might want to teach this guy a lesson too."

Lawrence pondered this for a moment, then gave a curt nod. "Okay, run with it, but in the meantime, I'll get you that warrant. Enough pissing around now, we need to clear everybody from the agency first."

"Yes, sir."

* * *

Rob and Mallory were back at Daring Divas. It had gone five o'clock and since they'd been there, the phone hadn't stopped ringing. Instead of the young woman who was there before, another lady sat behind the reception. She was older, in her forties, with curly brown hair and a pinched expression. Still, she smiled politely when they walked in.

"We're here to see Francine," Rob told her.

The woman buzzed her manager, who came out of her office. "Come this way, officers."

The receptionist's smile faltered.

Francine shut the door and gestured for them to take a seat. She sat down and crossed her legs in front of her. "Now, what is it you want to know?"

"Thanks for cooperating."

She scoffed. "Save me the bullshit, detective. It's not like I had a choice."

They hadn't got a warrant after all. Bryson had called Francine and told her to play ball or else she'd have the police crawling all over the building. This was preferable to ruining her business.

"Could you give us the names of the escorts who saw those two men I mentioned last time?"

"Remind me who they were?"

"Adam and Doug," said Mallory.

She tapped away on her laptop. "Amber saw Adam on Monday the twenty-seventh of January and Guadalupe saw Doug on the fifteenth of December last year."

"Is that the last time Doug booked one of your girls?" asked Rob, just to be sure.

She nodded, her eyes on the screen. "Yeah."

"That's strange, because we've got proof that Doug called here on the fifth of February, the day he died. Why would he do that if he wasn't hiring one of your girls?"

Francine looked genuinely surprised. "Really? There's nothing in the system that says he made a booking that day. Maybe he changed his mind."

"Maybe," said Rob. "Except a woman was seen going up to his flat on Wednesday evening."

Mallory slid the photo taken from the CCTV camera across the desk to her. "Do you recognize this woman?"

She picked it up and studied it. Rob noticed she had long, perfectly manicured nails. "This could be anyone. I can't see her face." The woman had wavy, shoulder-length brown hair, but apart from that you couldn't make out her features.

"But no one springs to mind?" he asked.

"No." She pushed the photograph back at Mallory.

"Francine, who else has access to your booking system?"

She thought for a moment. "Me, Mary, Ruth, Angie and Issy. They're my telephone operators."

"Who is on duty now?" he asked.

"That's Ruth," Francine said. "She's been with me for years. Mary works every weekday, ten till six, then Ruth takes over for the night shift. We close our lines at one in the morning. Angie does the weekend day shift and Issy the evening shift."

"How long have they been with you?" Rob asked.

"Mary's been here just under a year. She started as an escort but couldn't cut it, so I gave her a job on the phone lines. Angie's been here a bit longer, maybe two years and Issy's quite new. She started a couple of months ago. Why?"

"We're going to need to talk to them," he said.

Francine sighed. "You realize after this they'll probably quit and I'll have to hire new staff."

"I'm sorry about that," said Rob sincerely. "But this is a murder investigation. Apart from you, they were the only ones with access to the system."

"Are you saying one of them killed these men?" Her gaze turned hard and her voice brittle.

"That's what we need to find out."

"Where were you between four and eight o'clock on the twenty-seventh of January?" asked Mallory.

"How am I supposed to know?" she snapped. Mallory looked taken aback.

"How about Thursday the thirtieth of January?" asked Rob.

Francine stared at them as if they were mad. "I don't know. The dates mean nothing to me. I'll have to look in my calendar." She picked up her phone, which was lying face down on the desk and flicked through the calendar function. "On Monday the twenty-seventh I was here at the office until seven. That's right, I remember now, I met my husband for dinner."

"What about the other dates?" asked Rob.

"Thursday the thirtieth of January . . . What time did you say?"

"Late evening."

"I was at home. My husband will vouch for me."

"And finally, Wednesday the fifth of February."

She flicked the page to February. "I was at a party that night," she said smugly. "My sister-in-law's fiftieth. There are about a hundred people who saw me there."

Rob sighed. "Okay, Francine. Could you give me the contact details for all four of your telephone operators as well as Guadalupe, the girl who saw Doug in December?" It might be worth questioning her too. He was done with traipsing around town, from now on Uniform could pick the lot of them up and bring them in for questioning.

"If you insist," she said. "But don't take Ruth until tomorrow, she's on all evening and I can't do without her."

"I'm not going back to the station now," said Rob. "We'll pick them all up tomorrow."

They waited for her to look up the information.

"Do you know of any girls who've been assaulted by punters?" Rob asked.

Francine's gaze darkened. "It happens from time to time. We blacklist those bastards. If it's really bad, we encourage the girls to contact the police, although hardly any of them do."

"Could you give me a list of their names?" he asked.

"You think one of my girls could be doing this to get back at these guys?"

She was shrewd, Rob gave her that much. "Maybe. It's a line of enquiry we're following. The nature of the attacks are such that they are likely to be revenge killings."

Francine studied him. "I can't see any of my girls killing anyone, but I'll make you a list of those who I know have been treated badly. Shall I email it over or do you want to wait?"

"We'll wait." Rob leaned back in his chair and crossed his arms.

Mallory got up. "I'll go talk to Ruth."

Francine printed out the contact details for all four telephone operators as well as Guadalupe. Then she thought for a moment, typed some more on her laptop and printed out five additional names. "These are only the ones who required hospitalization," she said.

Rob whistled. "And they're still working for you?"

She shrugged. "What else are they gonna do? It's much harder to feed a family being a checkout girl at Tesco."

And therein lies the problem, thought Rob. He thanked Francine and they left, Ruth staring daggers after them.

CHAPTER 26

"The telephone operators are here," panted Mallory. He'd run down the road from the station, and passed them in the lobby. Unlike Rob, Mallory didn't live close by in Richmond. He commuted from Clapham Junction every morning, but it was only a ten-minute train journey when all ran according to plan. Today they'd been delayed. "All except Mary who's on duty at the agency."

Rob nodded. "Let's arrange for her to come in this evening after she knocks off."

He grabbed a cup of coffee, then went downstairs to the two interview rooms on the ground floor. It was more than enough for a small station. Ruth and Angie each occupied a room, while Issy waited in a holding area. He'd asked a delighted Jenny to accompany him again. She'd proven herself to be extremely adept last time.

"Let's interrogate Ruth first," Rob suggested. "She was there last night when we questioned Francine."

As expected, Ruth wasn't particularly forthcoming. She exuded a deep-seated distrust of the police, which made questioning her difficult.

"Could you state your full name for the record, please?"

"Ruth Danes."

"And Ruth, how long have you worked for Daring Divas Escort Agency?"

Ruth scowled at them as if they'd said a bad word. "Nearly five years."

"You know the business well?"

Another glare, and a nod.

"Were you on duty when Adam or Doug made their appointments?" They already knew from Francine that it was Mary who had taken Adam's booking.

"No."

"But you did book Doug in with Guadalupe on the fifteenth of December last year, didn't you?"

She narrowed her eyes. "I can't remember that long ago."

"Here's a printout of the booking." Jenny slid a piece of paper across the table towards her. "See, that's your name at the bottom."

She shrugged. "I must have done, then."

"Do you know Doug Bartlett?" Rob asked.

She stared at him. "Why would I know him? He's a punter."

"No reason. We just have to ask these things."

She huffed and stared down at her hands.

"Could you tell us where you were at these dates and times?" He passed another piece of paper to her listing the dates and times of the three murders.

She frowned. "How am I supposed to remember?"

"Please try," Jenny said with a smile. "It will help to clear you from our investigation."

Ruth glanced at the female sergeant, then sighed and picked up the piece of paper. Her hands were rough and wrinkled and spoke of a hard life. She gazed at it for a long moment. Eventually she said, "The twenty-seventh was a Monday, so I was at work. I do the evening shift which means I get in at five and leave at one in the morning."

Rob nodded. "What about the other two dates?"

"I don't remember exactly, but Thursdays I'm usually at home, although I might have gone out to do some shopping. On Wednesday the fifth I was working in the evening."

"Here?"

She nodded. "I ain't been off sick in months."

"Thank you." Rob made a note in the file in front of him.

"Can I go now?"

"Just one more thing and this is a bit sensitive. Have you ever been a sex worker yourself?"

She inhaled sharply and for a moment it looked like she might get mad, but then her shoulders sagged and she nodded. "A long time ago."

Rob nodded. "What made you stop?"

She shrugged. "I got too old. So, I did a secretarial course and got office work after that."

Rob consulted his file, then he looked up. "Ruth, is it true that you were so badly beaten by a customer that you had to be hospitalized?" He'd done some research into the four women last night. Yvette still hadn't been in touch and Rob had to assume she wouldn't be coming home in the near future.

Ruth swallowed, her eyes hard. "Like I said, it was a long time ago."

Jenny said softly. "Would you mind telling us what happened?"

A pause. "I worked in King's Cross, picking up punters from nearby pubs and bars. It was a bad time for me. I was hooked on . . . Well, anyway, I'm clean now, this was years ago."

Jenny nodded encouragingly.

"This Nigerian guy, a big bastard, took me to his van. He was a delivery driver, I think. I got in the back and he . . . Well, he was rough and huge, he damaged me down there. When I tried to push him away, he hit me. I screamed and he went fucking crazy. He punched me over and over until I blacked out. Then he dumped me in an alleyway. The next thing I knew, I woke up in hospital. It was a week before I could walk again."

Rob stared at her. The more he learned about the sex industry the more he wondered why anyone would want to work in it. Sex workers were so vulnerable, and no matter how liberated women were these days, they often didn't have the strength to fight off an angry man. That was a fact. "You're lucky you weren't killed."

"He hurt me so badly I couldn't have children."

Jenny whispered, "I'm so sorry, Ruth."

She shrugged. "That's life on the streets for you."

"Still, it's a terrible thing to have happened. Did you report him?"

"I tried, but I didn't know anything about him. He said his name was Don, but he could have been lying. I didn't have his car registration number or anything like that, so the cops couldn't do anything about it."

"Did you quit after that?" said Jenny.

Ruth nodded, her face expressionless. She was a hard woman, and Rob could understand why. "Do you feel angry about what happened?"

Ruth gave him a look that said, *What do you think?* "I look out for other girls now," she said. "I give them advice and help them if they get into trouble."

"How do you do that?"

"Forums and stuff."

Rob raised his eyebrows. "Do you ever go on the SAAFE forum?"

She frowned. "Yeah, I'm a senior member. I've been on there since they started, five years ago — about the same time I started here. Before that, there was no place where women could warn each other of the bad ones or the scam artists."

Rob met Jenny's gaze. Ruth would have direct access to the telephone numbers of punters who had been warned against. That's opportunity. And she had a deep-seated anger towards violent men. One had damaged her so badly it had altered the course of her life. That's motive. Was she the revenge killer?

"She was at work during two of the murders," Jenny pointed out as they left the interview room. "It can't be her."

"She fits the profile," he murmured.

You can be certain of one thing — this was a frenzied attack committed by someone fuelled by rage.

"There must be a lot of women who fit that profile," said Jenny. She had a point.

Before they'd concluded the interview, they asked Ruth's permission to take a DNA swab. To their surprise, she'd agreed.

"A guilty woman would have refused," Jenny said.

"True, but maybe she thought she'd been careful. Out of all three murders, we only found a smidgeon of DNA under one of Patterson's fingernails. Other than that, there was no trace."

"Ruth has an alibi for two of the three murders," Jenny pointed out. "She was working at the agency on the evenings of the twenty-seventh and the fifth."

"Hmm, look into that, will you? We need proof. She could have redirected the phone line to her mobile or popped out for an hour or so during the evening. Who would have known?"

Jenny nodded. "I'll get right on it."

"Thanks, Jenny, and by the way, you were great in there."

Jenny beamed.

* * *

"I like her for it," Rob told Mallory at lunch time. They were sitting in the canteen eating sausage rolls fresh from the oven. "She's had a terrible time of it, but she's a hard woman — you can see it in her eyes. Plus, she had means, motive and, quite possibly, opportunity."

"That doesn't make her a killer," Mallory pointed out.

Unfortunately, he was right. There wasn't enough to convict her. The other interviews hadn't offered much in the way of leads either.

Angie worked the weekend day shifts as she was at home looking after the kids during the week. Her husband, who owned a small hardware store in Peckham Rye, took over the childminding duties on the weekends so she could work. They needed two salaries to make ends meet. Children were expensive.

Rob wouldn't know. He wondered how Yvette felt about children now. With everything that had happened, maybe she'd had a change of heart. Rob still wasn't sure where he stood on the subject. At first he'd agreed with her — kids were such a big commitment, they took over your whole life — but lately he'd been thinking more and more maybe he would like to have a family. He could picture himself taking the kids to the park on weekends, Trigger in tow, and having family barbecues and beach holidays. Anyway, it was point-less thinking about it now. Yvette wasn't even at home yet. It was a conversation they'd have when the time was right.

His heart felt heavy as he turned his attention back to the investigation. They still had a long way to go.

All three men had been murdered during the week, so interviewing Angie and Issy were just formalities, but he had to be sure. They had access to the booking system, after all, which made them suspects.

Issy started work at five o'clock on Saturday and Sunday. She had only been at the agency for a few months and was still getting to grips with the system and the terminology. "I don't know what half them things are," she confided in the interview. "I just follow the price list. I found it a bit shock-ing at first, but now I'm all right with it."

Rob could imagine it being a shock to someone who wasn't familiar with it. Neither Angie nor Issy had worked in the sex industry before. They were purely admin staff. They had no apparent grudge against men or the trade in general.

Both were young and only too happy to have a flexible job that left their weeks free. Issy worked as a shop assistant Monday to Friday. "Mornings only," she told them. "'Cos I'm studying, innit."

"What are you studying?" Jenny asked kindly.

"Reflexology," she told them with a serene grin. "I want to have my own business one day."

Rob wished her well, he really did. Everyone should have a chance to do something they loved.

After that, he got Jenny to write up the interviews and met Mallory for lunch to fill him in.

"There's only Mary left," said Mallory. "She's coming in after six this evening. I've arranged for a squad car to pick her up at the agency after her shift."

They were just finishing up when Rob's phone rang. He answered it with a curt, "DI Miller."

To his surprise it was Angie's soft voice on the line. "I remembered something unusual that happened," she said. "It might be nothing, but it's to do with that hotel where that man was murdered."

Rob was suddenly listening hard. "What is it?" In her interview he'd asked her if she'd known any of the three men. She'd insisted she hadn't, and Rob had believed her.

"There *was* a booking for the Thursday before last, at that same hotel. It wasn't the man you asked me about, though, it was someone else. I think his name was Lewis."

"Why didn't you mention this before?" he snapped.

"I only just remembered. I'm on the bus on my way home."

"Who did he book?" rasped Rob, aware that Mallory was watching him closely.

"Well, that's the thing, sir. The escort never turned up. He rang me to complain that weekend," she continued. "I thought he was trying to get a freebie. Well, there was nothing I could do. I didn't take the original booking."

Rob's breath caught in his throat. "She never arrived for the appointment?"

"No, he said he waited all morning, but she didn't come. Eventually, he gave up and went out. Right pissed off he was."

"Who was the girl?" Rob asked.

"Amber."

CHAPTER 27

"Jesus Christ, she was bloody there!" Rob paced up and down the squad room. "She was in the same hotel as the second victim on the day he died."

His team had gathered around to see what he was ranting about.

"That's too much of a coincidence," remarked Jenny, who'd just got off the phone to Francine. "It must be related."

"Damn right it's related."

"But she didn't know him," pointed out Mallory. "We showed her the photographs, remember?"

Rob ran a hand through his hair. "She must have been lying." He recalled the strawberry-blonde hair, the towelling robe, the face devoid of make-up. She was a damn good liar.

"Maybe Amber and Ruth were in it together," Mallory suggested.

Rob stopped pacing and stared at him. "It's possible. Let's bring her in right now. Send a squad car to pick her up. It won't hurt to scare her a little." Mallory reached for the phone.

Lawrence bellowed across the floor. "Rob, my office."

Rob strode in, feeling highly agitated. He'd sat face to face with Ingrid and been taken in by her sob story, when all the time she'd been playing him.

"Update."

Rob got him up to speed, ending with Angie's latest revelation.

"Get her in here now," barked the Superintendent. "Find out why she lied. Also, it might be worth talking to the staff at the hotel again. Maybe someone saw something. A cleaner, perhaps."

He had a point. They'd spoken to the receptionist, but not the cleaning staff. The receptionist had found the body and no one had been into Patterson's room since the day before, so there hadn't been any need. But Lawrence was right, someone may have seen something. "I'll get DC Manner and DC Clarke to follow up," he said. They deserved a change from viewing endless rounds of CCTV footage in the warren. "I've sent out an alert for Ingrid, which is Amber's real name."

"I need you to give a press release this afternoon," Lawrence informed him, moving on. He wasn't interested in names, he just wanted the perpetrator caught.

Rob ground his teeth. He hated speaking to the media. It was always an ordeal, no matter how often you did it. Fielding a million questions, unable to give any real answers, while trying to restore the public's faith in law enforcement. Not an easy job in the current climate.

The Superintendent threw a newspaper on the desk in front of him. "We need to do some damage control. Look at this tosh."

Rob glanced down at the headline. *Revenge Killer on West London Murder Spree.*

"Christ, how'd they find out?" He grabbed the paper off the desk and scanned the first paragraph. All three of their victims were mentioned, along with the brutal nature of each attack.

"They always do eventually," intoned Lawrence. He was not impressed. "They've linked Yousef's, Patterson's and Bartlett's murders. They're talking about a serial killer. They've even suggested it might be a woman! How the fuck do they know that?"

Rob went cold.

No, surely not. She wouldn't do that to him. But then, she was the only person he'd told, and she was currently very pissed off with him. It might not be her, he rationalized, hoping for the best. His entire team also knew. Any one of them could have leaked it to the press or told a friend or a family member who'd mentioned it to a willing journalist. Hell, even Jo could have inadvertently mentioned it to one of her colleagues at the National Crime Agency. That's how these things went.

"I don't know, sir."

He needed to speak to Yvette.

"Well, regardless, Vicky wants to have a word, so go see her now. The conference is at four outside the building, so make sure you're prepared. We have to be seen to be on top of this."

* * *

Vicky Bainbridge, their press liaison officer, was based on the second floor with the other administrative departments. It was only the murder squad who were on the top floor.

Rob knocked on the door and a throaty feminine voice called out, "Come in."

He went in and smiled. "Vicky, how are you?"

They didn't bump into each other very often, but when they did Vicky always had a friendly, bordering on flirty, smile for him. Rob liked her. She was a confident, attractive woman who knew how to handle the press. Something he was clueless at.

"Good, Rob. It's nice to see you." She gave him a little hug. "Please, take a seat. Let's go through what you're going to say."

Rob sat down. He had no clue what he was going to say, so he started with the basics. Twenty minutes later they had his "speech" outlined, and happily, it ticked all the right boxes — assertive, showed they had the investigation under control, allayed the public's fears about a serial killer.

"And strictly no questions at the end," Vicky told him. "This isn't an appeal, this is a statement updating the public on the status of the investigation. Don't get suckered into saying anything more."

Rob nodded. "I've got it. Thanks, Vicky. See you at four?"

She nodded. "Of course."

* * *

The next couple of hours flew by. An ecstatic Mike and Jeff were dispatched to the Pear Tree Hotel to interview every available staff member, including the outsourced cleaning service and kitchen staff. They'd been told to collect statements from anyone who was on the premises on Thursday 30 January. "Check everyone," Rob had told them.

Guadalupe, the escort who'd been with Doug in December was brought in. She'd been away for a couple of days because it was half-term and her eight-year-old son was off school. Rob had interviewed her himself, because he hadn't envisaged she'd have much to contribute to the investigation. It was simply a matter of dotting the i's and crossing the t's.

Guadalupe was a stunning Afro-Caribbean woman in her late twenties. She had poise and style and could have easily been a model. Rob wondered if she'd still look so great in ten years' time. He resisted the urge to advise her to leave the industry and do something else, anything else, to get away from selling herself for sex. It wasn't his place.

Her real name was Sharon Leonard and she lived in a flat in Fitzrovia with her mother and son. She was an exotic dancer and picked up some extra work as an escort. "It's not a full-time thing," she'd explained. "I don't get no maintenance from Mikey's dad, so I have to do it."

If only Tesco paid more, thought Rob.

Guadalupe, or rather Sharon, told him Doug was "pretty rough" but "all right". He liked to assert his dominance, but he wasn't a big guy, "if you get my drift," so it wasn't painful, and he never slapped the girls around. He preferred to hold them down instead.

Sounded like a real charmer.

She didn't recognize Yousef or Patterson. Rob watched her eyes as she studied the pictures and could tell she was shocked by their lifeless expressions. He was pretty sure she wasn't lying to him. Not like Amber.

* * *

Rob finally got hold of Yvette. He'd tried to call her several times the last few hours, but each time it had diverted to voicemail.

"Darling, I've been trying to get hold of you," he said. "There's something I need to ask you." It was freezing outside on the pavement. The air was heavy with cold like it was going to snow. He could feel it pressing down on him, seeping into his collar and up his sleeves. He turned his back on the wind, which didn't make much difference.

She snorted gently and he could imagine her pouty face. "I've been busy."

"Busy doing what?"

"Helping Naomi." Her sister ran a small cooking school from her house in Southfields, he recalled. He was surprised. Yvette had never shown any interest in cooking before. She was more of a canapés-and-cocktails kind of girl. Her diet was limited to salad, soup and cigarettes.

"That's great." At least she was doing something constructive and not mooching around. "How are you feeling?"

"Better than being at home," she said, which meant she was staying put for the time being. It was probably for the best, anyway. The case was hotting up, and this way he would be free to work the long hours it would take to catch this person.

"I miss you," he said. The wind whistled around the detached brick building. He hunched over.

"What do you want, Rob?" Her voice was soft but the bitterness was still there. He sighed. Married eight months and already his wife had moved out. Was he really that bad a husband?

"You remember what I told you the other day, about the killer being a woman?"

"Yes?"

"Did you tell anyone?"

A heavy pause. "I may have mentioned it at dinner the other night."

Shit. He kicked the wall with his boot.

"Sweetheart, I told you it was a secret. It's in all the papers today." What the hell was he going to tell Lawrence and the others? That he was the leak? He cringed and shook his head.

"I think people should know, for their safety."

He sighed. "Except now the killer knows too, which makes it that much harder for me to catch her." Why couldn't she understand that?

"*Je suis désolée.* I didn't realize it was such a big secret. Naomi and Harrison had friends over for dinner and we were talking about you. I didn't know they were going to tell anybody." She did sound sincere. Perhaps she really hadn't realized.

"It's okay, don't worry about it. What's done is done." It was his fault for mentioning it to her in the first place. The blame lay with him. He wondered what they'd been talking about at dinner. It couldn't have been good. It was a wonder his ears weren't burning.

"Any idea when you'll be home?" he asked.

"When you catch this killer," she stated. "I don't feel safe there by myself knowing that psycho is out there."

I'm doing my best, he wanted to yell. She made it sound like it was his fault a serial killer was on the loose.

"Are you still seeing Becca?" he asked wearily.

"Yes, she came yesterday."

"Good. I'm proud of you." That was something at least. "I've got to go now. I'll call you later."

"Sure. Bye, Rob."

CHAPTER 28

Rob glared at the sea of reporters outside the police building. Their voices seemed to merge into one continuous chant.

"Do you have any leads?"

"Is there a serial killer out there?"

"What are you doing to catch this person?"

"Is it true you're looking for a female murderer?"

The questions flew at him from all angles. Luckily, he'd got his speech out of the way, assuring the public that they were doing everything possible to catch the killer. He thanked them all for coming, although he doubted if anyone heard him, and darted back inside the building. No wonder Lawrence delegated the press statements to him.

"Bloody hell," he murmured to Vicky who'd stayed by his side for moral support. "I'm glad that's over."

"You did well." She smiled alluringly. "Let me buy you a coffee to celebrate."

He grimaced and squeezed her arm. "Actually, do you mind if we take a rain check? I've got to prepare for an interrogation."

"Sure, no problem." A flicker of disappointment crossed her face, but she hid it with her lip-gloss smile. "Take care,

Rob." She headed for the elevator, leaving him alone in the silent foyer.

The duty sergeant gave him a nod as he walked towards the stairwell. Now he was alone, his ears were ringing, a high-pitched sound that permeated his brain. The pressure was on. They had to catch this killer before she struck again. If they didn't, it would be *his* head on the block. The last thing he needed was for the National Crime Agency to waltz in and take over the investigation, but that's exactly what would happen if they didn't find a lead soon. Lawrence was already fielding calls from Scotland Yard, who were worried the Putney murder squad were out of their depth. He gritted his teeth as he climbed the stairs to the third floor. He'd show them.

* * *

Shortly after six, Rob, accompanied by Jenny, went to interview Mary. They greeted her cordially and offered her a cup of tea, but she declined. The interrogation room was cold and sterile with blank walls that seemed to close in on you. In the middle was a steel table and four chairs, bolted to the ground. There was nothing to look at other than the cameras positioned in the two opposing corners to catch the suspect from a side and front angle.

A recorder sat on the table, its red light flashing ominously, indicating the interview was in session. Mary sat upright, her thin arms folded in front of her. Despite being in her late twenties, she appeared almost childlike as she watched them with wide eyes.

Rob got down to business. "Can you state your name for the recording?"

"Mary Larson." He could hear the tension in her voice.

He tried to allay her fears. "Mary, you're here because we need to ask you some questions about the men that were murdered. You have been cautioned but you're not under arrest. You also have the right to a solicitor, should you wish to have one present."

She shrugged. "I don't need one. I haven't done anything wrong."

Rob smiled at her. He knew she'd waived her right. The duty sergeant informed all persons of interest about their rights before they were interrogated. Suited him fine. "Okay, let's get started." He nodded at Jenny, who positioned three photographs on the table in front of her. "Do you recognize any of these men?"

She glanced down, then shook her head. "Are they the ones who were killed?"

"Yes. Take a good look."

She did so, her eyes flitting from the first to the second and then to the third, before re-settling on him. "I don't know them."

"Mary, Francine told us that before you were a telephone operator, you were a sex worker. Is that right?"

Mary seemed surprised by the sudden change in direction, but she nodded. "For a short while, yes, although I didn't have any bookings. I couldn't go through with it. When I cancelled, I thought Francine was going to fire me, but she didn't."

"She hired you instead?" said Rob.

Mary nodded.

"That was nice of her." This from Jenny.

Mary managed a weak smile. "She was very kind to me."

"How long ago was that?" asked Rob.

Mary thought for a moment. "It must have been about a year ago."

"What did you do before that?" Rob asked.

She pursed her lips. "Waitressing, bar work, promotional stuff, that sort of thing."

"Was there a reason why you didn't go through with it?" asked Jenny, catching her off guard again.

She blinked. "What do you mean?"

"Well, did you have a bad experience with a man in the past, something that made you decide not to go through with it?"

"Oh, I see. No, nothing like that. In fact, I had a very happy childhood. It was only when my father passed away that I decided to get into the escort business. My mother and I needed the money, or we'd lose the house." She dropped her head. "We ended up losing it anyway because I couldn't make the mortgage repayments. Office admin doesn't pay as well as prostitution."

"I'm sorry to hear that," Jenny said.

"Where is your mother now?" asked Rob.

"She's in semi-sheltered housing near Reading." She didn't elaborate. That would be easy enough to check.

"Mary, did you make Amber's booking on the twenty-seventh of January with a man called Adam?" Rob pointed to Yousef's photograph.

"Yes, I did, but I didn't know who he was."

"That's okay. Do you remember speaking to him on the phone?"

"Yes, he's used us before. Not Amber, but other girls. He doesn't like using the same girl more than once."

"That's unusual, isn't it?" asked Jenny. "Don't the punters like to stick to their favourite escorts?"

"Sometimes." She shrugged again. "I don't know. He wasn't like that."

"Did you also make a booking for Amber at the Pear Tree Hotel on the thirtieth of January?"

She thought for a moment. "Was that the prank caller?"

"Prank caller?" Rob stared at her.

"Yeah, Amber got to this guy's hotel room and he told her to piss off. He said he hadn't called anyone."

"You think it was a joke?"

She nodded. "It happens a lot. People think it's funny to waste the escort's time. Sometimes kids do it to prank their friends, that sort of thing."

"I see." *Some prank*, he thought.

"Okay, what about Doug Bartlett?" He nodded to the third photograph.

Mary frowned. "I don't remember that name."

"Are you sure? According to his phone records he rang the agency at 12.39 p.m. on Wednesday the fifth of February, the day he died."

She pursed her lips and shrugged. "I'm sorry, I don't remember talking to him. Could he have used a different name?"

"It's possible," said Rob. He studied a printout of the agency's system log for that day. There were no appointments booked between 12 and 1 p.m.

Rob gazed at the paper in his hand. "The call lasted over three minutes. If it wasn't you he spoke to, then who was it?"

"I don't know, maybe Francine? I do take a lunch break, you know." Her gaze was steady and slightly accusatory. He sighed. They were getting nowhere. Mary had no reason to kill these men, she hadn't been sexually assaulted in the past and she had no history of actual sex work. Frustrated, he pushed his chair back, got up and exited the room, leaving Jenny to tie up the interview.

CHAPTER 29

Ken Billows was having fun. He gazed down at the smooth, slender back gyrating in front of him and ran his hand down the spine, ending with a whack to the buttocks. The woman beneath him whimpered. He hit her again, harder this time. The room filled with a resounding *smack!*

"Hey!" she complained, breaking his rhythm. "Easy."

"Shut up," he growled. She was bent over the bed in front of him while he pounded into her from behind. This was one of his favourite positions. It was so satisfying watching her pale butt jiggle as he thrust into her. He gripped her hips to give himself more leverage. Soon the mist began to descend, obscuring his vision.

"Oh, yeah!" he moaned, not realizing or caring that the woman underneath him was gritting her teeth, willing it to be over. He increased his tempo until the sensations overwhelmed him and, with a guttural yell, rammed into her one last time before securing his release. The woman collapsed on to the bed. He pulled out and strode towards the bathroom, leaving her to sort herself out.

When he got back, she was fully dressed and waiting for him, an annoyed expression on her face. "Time to pay up."

He sneered and considered not paying, but he'd be banned from using the agency again if he didn't. He enjoyed the girls at Daring Divas, they were a classy bunch, and clean, which was more than he could say for most of the hookers he picked up. The problem with agency girls was that you couldn't rough them up too much. More's the pity. He loved making them cry out in pain, seeing the fear in their eyes, but that dark secret he kept to himself. If he wanted to hire them, he had to play by the rules.

Every now and then he did indulge in his darker passion. When the urge was too strong and couldn't be denied. When the escorts at the agency weren't enough. But that wasn't too often, and he was always careful. With what he liked to do to women, there were always consequences.

He scoffed and fished in his jeans pocket for his wad of cash. He threw three fifties on the bed. "There you go."

The woman, Brooklynn her name was, picked it up and pocketed it without a word, then breezed past him and out the door. He had a sudden urge to slap her silly face, make her pay for her cocky attitude, but he held back. Now wasn't the time.

He strolled back into the living room and turned on the TV. Some American cop show was on that he quite enjoyed. He grabbed a beer out of the fridge and sat down in his underwear to watch. He was halfway through the programme when the doorbell rang. Who could that be? He wasn't expecting anyone. He debated not answering it, but then it rang again.

"Coming!" He strode into the bedroom and pulled on a pair of sweatpants and a T-shirt. When he got to the door, he peered through the peephole and saw a pretty brunette standing there. Not bad.

He opened it, a smile on his lips. Perhaps he could entice her in. He was ready for round two and this time he wouldn't be so gentle. "Hey, sweetheart, what can I do for you?"

A piercing pain wiped the smile off his lips.

He glanced down and saw blood seeping through his shirt. "What the fuck, bitch?" Grabbing her arm, he pulled her inside. Whoever she was, she'd just made a monstrous fucking mistake. Didn't she know who she was dealing with? If she wanted pain, he would show her pain. He was an expert at it. Enraged, he took a swipe at her, but a second burning slice to his abdomen caused him to catch his breath.

"Shit." The fight went out of him. Instead, he clutched his stomach, trying to stem the flow of blood, but it kept on coming. He needed something thicker, a towel — and a doctor. Except the fucking bitch was coming after him with the knife. He stumbled away from her into the lounge, clasping his wounds, feeling the blood gush from beneath his fingers. He didn't know stab wounds could hurt so much.

"Ugh." He collapsed on to the living room floor. He stared at the woman who'd stabbed him. "Who are you? Why are you doing this to me?"

"Think of me as an avenging angel," she sneered and raised her hand again.

"No!" He twisted away from her on to his stomach, but the knife hit him in the lower back. "Stop," he cried. His back was on fire. "Please, don't do this."

The knife fell again, piercing a kidney. The pain knocked the breath from his lungs. Tears filled his eyes, blurring his vision. Again and again the knife fell, puncturing his organs, tearing into his muscles and slicing through soft tissue. Mercifully, after the fifth or sixth blow, Ken felt the pain subside and the darkness settle in. Usually he didn't like the dark, it reminded him of the cupboard under the stairs where he'd been locked as a boy, but right now he welcomed it. Bring on the peaceful dark. Anything to stop the pain radiating through his body.

Soon, all he could feel was the soft carpet beneath his cheek and a strange floating sensation as the life drained out of him.

CHAPTER 30

It was Trigger who woke him up. The Labrador bounded on to the bed and shoved his wet snout in Rob's face.

"Ugh, go away." But he opened his eyes and that's when he heard it. His phone was vibrating on the bedside table next to him. He'd forgotten to switch the sound back on before he went to bed. During the day, a discreet buzz in his pocket was enough, but at night, if it wasn't on full volume, he was liable to sleep right through it. Tonight being a case in point.

Groggily, he reached for it. It was quarter to twelve. He'd only been asleep an hour. It was a withheld number. The only people who called from withheld numbers in the middle of the night were law enforcement.

"Miller."

Trigger lay down on the floor next to the bed and stared up at him with wide eyes.

"Sir, we've had a call from Kensington Police Station. They've got a stab victim. You asked to be notified," came a female voice.

"Yes, uh, thanks. Is it multiple stab wounds?" He held his breath waiting for her answer.

"I believe so, sir."

"Thank you. Please send me the address. I'm leaving now."

"Of course."

The line went dead. A few seconds later a text message came through containing the crime scene address. Rob recognized it as just off Cromwell Road in South Kensington. Before he'd met Yvette, he'd dated a girl who lived behind the Natural History Museum. It seemed like a lifetime ago now, but he liked South Ken. It was a vibey area with many excellent bars and restaurants.

He forwarded the message to Mallory and pulled on his trousers, nearly tripping over the dog in the process. Trigger, who thought they were going for an impromptu midnight stroll, leaped to his paws. "No, not tonight, Trigs. Sorry, mate. I've got a crime scene to get to." He was well aware he'd started talking out loud to his dog.

He patted Trigger's head and pulled on a T-shirt and a tracksuit top. He pocketed his phone, put on his trainers and ran down the stairs. He felt bad leaving Trigger, who gazed at him with sad eyes as he shut the door. That dog certainly knew how to make him feel guilty, but then, he'd learned from the best.

The drive to South Kensington took a little under twenty minutes. Traffic was surprisingly light for a Friday night, but then the arctic wind was still howling, and it had rained earlier, which meant your usual partygoers had opted for a pizza in front of Netflix instead of going out.

The victim's apartment block was situated in a quiet side street called Glenville Place. It was a shiny new build, at least ten storeys high, constructed with lots of chrome and glass. There was no designated parking, as was often the case in London, so he parked on the street behind two police vehicles, their lights flashing silently, casting eerie blue reflections off the building. He didn't spot a SOCO van or an ambulance. Perhaps they had yet to arrive. Mallory's Toyota Prius wasn't here either.

He opened the glove compartment and took out a pair of latex gloves and shoe protectors, stuffing them into his jacket pocket.

"Hiya, mate." He greeted the uniformed police officer on duty at the front entrance, a rectangular glass box with sliding doors that were fixed open. "DI Miller from Putney MIT."

The man nodded. "Seventh floor. Easy how you go."

"Thanks." Rob entered the freezing cold lobby and pressed the button for the elevator. Seven floors were too far to run up when you didn't have to. The lift only took a moment to open, and soon he was travelling up to the crime scene. He wondered what he'd find. Would this be like all the others. Or worse?

The lift opened and he stepped out on to an eerily quiet landing. No curious neighbours? That must be a first. "Where is everybody?" he asked the police officer at the door.

"The rest of the floor is unoccupied," he told Rob. "They're still selling off the units."

Convenient for the killer, thought Rob. *Less so for the police as there are no witnesses.*

He gave his name as he pulled on his shoe protectors and gloves. The officer wrote it down and stood aside so he could enter the apartment.

Rob found he was holding his breath. The other three crime scenes had been fairly shocking, but the killer was escalating as she progressed. What would he find here?

The first thing that he noticed was the blood spatter on the cream-coloured carpet just inside the door — the point of impact. The killer had struck straight away. No small talk, no *Come in. Would you like a drink?* He followed it like a trail of breadcrumbs to the living room, a larger-than-expected space containing cheap, functional furniture most likely from IKEA. Lying in the centre was the body of a man. He was prostrate on the carpet, which was now a deep red thanks to his dramatic blood loss. His back was covered in puncture wounds, a myriad of dark seeping holes where he'd been stabbed to death.

Rob's breath caught in his throat. *It was her.*

A middle-aged man in a crumpled suit stood staring down at the body. He too was wearing shoe protectors and gloves. He glanced up as Rob entered. "DI Miller?"

Miller nodded. "Yeah, and you are?"

"DI Rooney. Kensington CID." The two men shook hands. The Kensington detective nodded to the victim. "You seen this before?"

Thanks to the media attention, everybody knew that Putney MIT was investigating the revenge killings, as they'd become known. He nodded. "It looks like our killer. Same MO. Who's the victim?"

"Flat's registered to a Mr Ken Billows. He's just moved in by the looks of things. Most of his belongings are still in boxes in the spare room."

The name meant nothing to Rob. He wondered if Billows was also a client of Daring Divas. Where the hell was Mallory?

"SOCO are on their way," Rooney said. "I'm waiting for them to arrive before I inspect the body."

"Good call." Rob didn't go too close either. "It looks like the initial attack took place at the front door. There's blood in the passage."

"Yeah. I'd say the victim was stabbed there, then stumbled into the living room and collapsed on the carpet. I reckon the first stab wound was to his stomach. He's got blood all over his hands and he wouldn't have been able to reach the ones on his back."

Rob studied Rooney more closely. His face was almost as wrinkled as his jacket, with deep creases around his eyes, but Rob knew appearances could be deceiving.

"Who discovered the body?" he asked. There didn't seem to be anybody else around other than the handful of uniformed officers and DI Rooney. Even the floor was deserted.

"The security guard," Rooney said. "He's downstairs in one of the police vehicles being treated for shock." He gave a half-smile.

"I'll go and have a word." Rob scanned the room. It didn't appear disturbed. He was willing to bet the victim had stumbled in here and died where he'd fallen, after which the perpetrator had left without touching anything. It was unlikely they'd find any DNA at the scene.

The living room merged into a small kitchen with granite countertops and pale-grey units. It was stylish and functional. The only appliances visible were a kettle and toaster, both chrome and probably new. It looked like the victim had been making a fresh start by moving in here. Rob studied the sink, but while it was wet, like it had been used recently, he couldn't see any blood. Forensics would need their UV light again. He checked the bathroom, but that was clear too.

"Find anything?" Rooney had been watching him.

"Nope. We'll have to wait for the crime scene guys to get here. I don't think there's much we can do until then and I don't want to contaminate the scene more than necessary."

Rooney nodded. "I'll wait outside."

Rob left him talking to the officer at the front door and took the stairs down to the ground floor. The narrow stairwell smelled strongly of fresh paint and Rob was glad to get out into the open, even if the icy wind did make his eyes water. There was definitely snow on the way.

"Where's the security guard who found the body?"

The officer guarding the entrance pointed him in the right direction. More police vehicles had arrived and officers were in the process of cordoning off the street. A SOCO van pulled up, out of which emerged two blue-clad scene-of-crime officers and a white-clad pathologist. They entered the building fully suited-up, sombre expressions on their wary faces. They knew what was coming.

Rob rapped on the window of a police van and a face turned towards him.

"Are you the guard who found the body?" Rob enquired after he'd opened the car door.

The man nodded and held out a beefy hand. "Yeah, who are you?"

"DI Rob Miller, Putney Major Investigation Team. Can we have a quick chat?"

"Sure."

Rob marched round the vehicle and got in. The heating had been on and the car was warm. "What's your name?"

"Albert."

"Albert who?"

"Adebayo."

"Nigerian?"

The man nodded. "I've been here four years."

Rob gave him the once-over. The guy was stocky and built like a boxer, toned and powerful. His nose looked like it had been broken a time or two as well. Rob bet he packed one hell of a punch. He wore a branded security uniform and a black fleece with a logo on the pocket. *Prism Security Services*. As far as he could see, the man had no weapon on him.

"Talk me through how you discovered the body?"

Albert took a deep breath. "I was doing my rounds. I usually check all the floors a little after 11 p.m. A lot of the apartments are still vacant, so I've been told to look out for vagrants or squatters."

Made sense. "Go on."

"I was on the seventh floor when I saw Mr Billows's front door was open. When I got closer, I saw the blood on the floor and I knew something terrible had happened."

"What did you do next?"

"I went to see if he was okay." Rob glanced at the security guard's feet. They'd have to take his DNA and boot prints to eliminate him from the crime scene.

"He was lying in the lounge, face down, covered in blood." He looked down at his hands and Rob noticed they were clenched tightly together in his lap. Albert might be a tough guy, but the sight of the blood-soaked body had given him a shock.

"So, you called the emergency services?"

"Yeah, man. I dialled 999 straight away."

Rob patted him on the shoulder. "Okay, thanks, mate. One more thing. Don't go anywhere until the forensic guys have taken a DNA swab and your shoes."

* * *

Rob pulled on a full forensic paper suit, shoe protectors and gloves before entering the apartment a second time. He was pleased to see Rooney had done the same. The forensic officers were hard at work processing the crime scene and bagging anything of relevance. They knew what to look for — personal items with which to identify the body, shoes, watch, wallet, DNA samples, anything that would help them separate his forensic footprint from that of his killer's.

Rob introduced himself. He didn't know this patholo-gist, or any of the SOCO team, but then Kensington wasn't his neck of the woods.

"Any idea of time of death?" he asked the young man bending over the body.

The pathologist glanced up. "He's still warm and rigor has yet to set in. I'd say death occurred no more than three or four hours ago."

Late evening, around 9 p.m. He mentally went through his suspects' whereabouts. Ruth would be on duty at the agency, which ruled her out. They still hadn't been able to locate Amber, which was suspicious in itself. According to Francine, she'd taken the night off, despite it being a Friday and one of the busiest days of the week. It was beginning to look like she'd done a runner. Had she been here tonight? Was this her work?

Mallory, also kitted up, entered the room. "Hi, guv, sorry I'm late. Didn't see your message until just now."

Rob waved it off and got straight to business. There were a couple of things playing on his mind. "We need to check if Ruth is on duty at the agency," he said, thinking out loud. "And whether this guy, Ken Billows, hired an escort tonight."

Mallory glanced at the dead body, then nodded. "I'll call her now." He walked back out again, phone to his ear.

* * *

"I count twenty-five stab wounds on his back," the pathologist was saying to Rooney, "and possibly more on his stomach."

He turned the victim over and inspected his abdomen. "Yep, two on his front."

"Those must be the initial ones." Rob looked around the living room. "Find a mobile phone anywhere?" he asked one of the scene-of-crime officers.

"No, sir," came the reply. "And the landline hasn't been installed yet."

As before, the attacker must have taken it with her.

"We have something in the bedroom," called a voice from down the hall.

Rob and Rooney went into the bedroom. A scene-of-crime officer was shining a black light on to the bed. The duvet was on the floor and the sheets were rumpled. It looked like someone had slept in it fairly recently.

"Semen all over the bed." The officer moved the light around and Rob saw the luminous telltale signs. Plenty of it.

"Fuck me," muttered Rooney, appropriately.

"Any sign of who he was with?" Rob glanced at the side pedestal that had a lamp, a beer bottle and a packet of cigarettes on it.

"There might be some female DNA on the sheets," SOCO said.

"Make sure you bag the bottle and the smokes." Rob nodded at the bedside table. The officer nodded and got to work. He opened his case and began swabbing the sheets for preliminary samples before wrapping the whole thing in a plastic bag. More tests would be run at the lab.

"I don't get it," he said to Rooney as they watched the SOCOs process the scene. "Why was he stabbed at the front door?"

"She slept with him then killed him," said Rooney. "Nice lady."

No, it didn't add up. The blood spatter indicated he was stabbed at the front door first, then he'd moved into the lounge.

"Maybe it wasn't her?"

"Huh?" Rooney glanced at him. "You saying this wasn't your killer?"

"No, it's her all right. What I'm saying is maybe it wasn't the woman he slept with who killed him."

"You mean he had two female visitors?"

Rob rubbed his temple. His head was beginning to hurt. "Maybe."

Was it possible that this victim hadn't been killed by his lover? If someone else had stabbed him while the woman had been here, it meant they might have a witness. "We have to find out who he slept with — she may have seen something. That is our top priority."

Mallory charged back into the flat. "Guv, Billows *did* hire an escort tonight. Ruth has just confirmed it. Her name was Brooklynn and her booking was from seven till eight. I've got the address."

Rob thumped him on the back. "Great work, mate. Let's go."

CHAPTER 31

Brooklynn lived in a tiny row of mews houses in Fulham. It was a dark, moonless night and the only sound came from the restless wind as it tousled trees and sent rubbish bins flying across the street. A lone fox prowled along the pavement in search of food, its onyx eyes flashing through the blackness.

"Bit spooky with this wind," muttered Mallory as they crossed the road and approached number five.

"I wonder how she affords this." Rob studied the well-maintained bungalow with its white exterior and green-shuttered windows. The recycling bins were stacked outside the front door, and the roses and lavender bushes were pruned for the winter. Someone obviously took care of the place.

There was a small Ford Escort parked outside on the street in front of the house, but the road sign said free parking after midday, so it could have belonged to anyone. Rob rang the doorbell. It was nearly two in the morning.

They waited a few minutes. Rob rang a second time. Eventually, they heard footsteps coming down the hall. A sleepy voice called out, "Who is it?"

"The police. Open up, ma'am."

A pause, then a shuffle and the sound of the chain being lifted off the latch. The handle turned and the door opened a crack. "Can I see some ID, officers?"

If Rob was surprised, he didn't show it. He held up his warrant card, as did Mallory. "I'm DI Rob Miller and this is DS Mallory from the Putney Major Investigation Team."

She peered through the crack, then nodded and opened the door. Rob found himself facing a middle-aged woman with greying hair standing in her nightgown. "What's this about?"

"Do you know Bernadette King?" asked Mallory, who had got Brooklynn's real name from Ruth.

The woman nodded. "That's my daughter. What do you want with her?"

"Is she here?" asked Rob.

"Yes, she's asleep upstairs."

"Can you wake her, please? We need to speak with her." He kept his voice firm, official.

The woman nodded and turned to go upstairs, but before she reached the first step, a pale face peered down from the banisters. "What's happening, Nana?"

"Nothing, sweetie, go back to bed."

"Who are they?" The face belonged to a boy of about six dressed in Spiderman pyjamas.

"Just some gentlemen who want to speak to Mummy." She gave them an imploring look, then climbed the stairs. A few moments later, a tall, dark-haired woman with a bemused expression came down. She had pulled a loose jumper over her pyjamas and her feet were bare. She looked very young. "Can I help you?"

"Bernadette?" asked Rob.

She nodded.

He moved in. "Bernadette King, I'm arresting you on suspicion of the murder of Ken Billows."

* * *

In the police interview room, Bernadette, or Brooklynn as she was known on the Daring Divas website, looked fragile. She was an attractive woman, beautiful even, with strong cheekbones and slanting olive eyes, which at the moment were clouded with fear.

Across from her sat Rob and Mallory, both wearing serious expressions. They'd gone for the hard-line approach to try and scare her into confessing what she knew. It often worked best with timid suspects. She was tired and still disconcerted after being woken from her bed and dragged down to the station without time to change. They'd issued her with a police tracksuit, which she looked surprisingly good in.

"Were you at Ken Billows's flat tonight in Kensington?" began Rob. He decided not to ask her if she knew him, because it was quite obvious by the booking that she did. He didn't want to give her time to formulate a lie.

She nodded, her eyes huge as she gazed at him.

"What time was that?"

"B—Between seven and eight," she stammered, gripping her hands tightly together on the table. Rob glanced at them and tried to imagine them wielding the knife that had stabbed Billows to death. He couldn't. Still, that didn't mean she didn't do it.

"Why were you there?"

She hesitated, afraid to speak, afraid of what it might mean.

"Did Brooklynn have an appointment?" enquired Mallory, in a slightly less aggressive tone. They'd questioned enough suspects together to know how to play off each other.

She nodded again, tears filling her eyes.

Rob took a deep breath. "Mr Billows was found dead this evening at his apartment." He showed her a photograph of the body taken at the crime scene. Billows was lying face down in a puddle of his own blood.

Bernadette's hand flew to her mouth.

"Did you do this?" Rob glared at her.

"No! Of course not. I just had sex with him. He was fine when I left — I swear." She was shaking now, clutching at the table like it was a lifeline.

"Is that all?" Rob persisted. "You didn't stab him because he was too rough with you?"

"What? No." She was crying now.

"Did he hurt you? Is that why you killed him?"

She shook her head, tears pouring down her face. Rob glanced at Mallory, who gave a little shake of his head. Rob was inclined to agree.

"Okay, Bernadette," he said more gently. "Why don't you talk me through the evening?"

She sobbed. "I have a child at home. He's everything to me. If you put me away, I don't know what he'd do."

"Bernadette, look at me."

She glanced up through her tears.

How could someone so young be a sex worker? What a waste of a life. He leaned forward. "If you didn't kill Mr Billows, then you don't have anything to worry about, but you were at his house on the night he died, so can you see how this looks?"

She nodded, her lip trembling.

"You were probably the last person to see him alive."

She bit her lip to keep it still.

"So, tell us what you know, and we'll take it from there."

"Okay." She wiped her eyes on her sleeve and took a shaky breath. "I got to his place at seven. It was a bit scary like, being in a big block that was only half-full."

"He told you that, did he?"

She nodded. "Anyway, I went in and we . . . well, you know. For a moment, I thought he wasn't going to pay me, but he did. Then, I left."

"He paid you in full?"

"Yes."

"How much was that?"

"£150."

Rob didn't want to know what that was for. He turned his attention back to the events of the evening. "Did he walk you to the door?"

"Yes, he saw me out and I left."

"There was no one else around? No one in the corridor or outside the block?"

"I saw a security guard," she said, "but I don't think he saw me."

She made sure he didn't see her, more like. "And you're sure you didn't see anyone else?"

"No." Another sob escaped her. "I'm sorry, I didn't."

"How did you get home?"

"I took the bus. There's one from South Kensington to Fulham."

"What time did you get back?"

"Around half past eight. Just in time to tuck my son up."

Rob glanced at Mallory, who nodded. He'd follow up with the mother and son. The police were searching her house, looking for evidence of blood spatter on her clothing and shoes, and of course, any sign of the murder weapon.

"Does your mother know what you do for a living?" Mallory asked.

Bernadette recoiled. "God, no. She thinks I work in a pub. I'm saving to put myself through college. I want to be a lawyer."

Rob was at a loss for words. Was this what it had come to? Girls selling themselves to pay tuition fees? Christ.

"You mean this is only a temporary gig for you?" Mallory again.

"Yes, of course. I'm saving so much more than I would waitressing. Another few months and I'll have enough for my undergraduate degree. It would have taken me years in a pub."

"There are student loans for that sort of thing," pointed out Rob.

She gave him a look that said, *Seriously?* "I'll be paying that back for years afterwards. No thanks."

"It's a safer option than what you're doing."

She blinked at him and he decided to shut up. This was her decision. If she wanted to put her life on the line to pay for university, then that was up to her.

"Okay, Bernadette. Thanks for speaking with us. We aren't charging you right this minute, but we're going to hold you until we've finished searching your house. Then you'll be free to go home." Provided they found nothing.

She dropped her head in her hands and sobbed in relief. Rob felt bad for giving her such a hard time.

* * *

They headed back up to the deserted squad room.

"Any news on Ingrid?" Rob asked Mallory. He flicked the switch at the door and the floor was bathed in a harsh, fluorescent light.

"Nothing as of yet. We have all units looking out for her. She can't get far."

"Do you think she did this?" Rob sank into his chair. God, he was tired. The adrenalin of the last few hours was wearing off and he suddenly felt like if he put his head on his desk, he'd sleep for a week.

"She's our most likely suspect," Mallory said. He perched on the end of the desk. "Ruth was at the agency all evening, and it looks like this girl's in the clear. I can't see her slaughtering a client when she's got a young one at home."

"She wants to be a lawyer." Rob shook his head.

"I hope they never find out about her past life."

Mallory had a point. She'd be disbarred faster than you could say, "Objection, Your Honour," if it was revealed she used to be a sex worker. Perhaps that's something he ought to mention to her when he released her.

True enough, the house search didn't turn up anything. The clothes she'd worn that night were strewn on her bedroom floor and contained no traces of blood. Neither did her stilettos, which were found beside the bed.

Rob released her, but only after she'd given them a DNA swab to match that found on the bed. He made sure to point out how detrimental her current job would be to her future career. That gave her pause, and he could tell she hadn't thought it through. He hoped it made a difference, but somehow, he doubted it would.

CHAPTER 32

It was gone eleven before Rob made it into the station. He'd slept like the dead from the moment he'd fallen into bed at six that morning until a frantic Trigger had woken him up at ten. Feeling bad, he took the dog for a quick walk, then showered, dressed and grabbed a couple of croissants and a coffee on the way to work. The high street was already springing to life with Saturday shoppers and walkers heading for the river. The wind had dropped and a fine layer of frost crunched underfoot. Still no snow.

He'd given the team the rest of the weekend off so there was no one there other than himself, Mallory and Will, who was monitoring the fake online profile they'd set up on the SAAFE forum. Mike had left a note on his desk saying they'd talked to everyone at the Pear Tree Hotel and no one had noticed anything untoward. The way things were going, Rob wasn't surprised. The hotel didn't have a CCTV camera and the one on the street outside had been down due to an electrical fault. Bloody typical.

Will's alias was a sex worker called Elementa. Her warning read: *Violent Boundary Pusher. Mid 30s. English. West Kensington. Calls himself Peter or Pete. Relatively good-looking. Don't be fooled. Removed condom while we were doing doggy. When I asked*

him to put it back on, he said no. I told him to leave and he got physical.
Hit me a couple of times before leaving without paying. Watch out for
this guy. Number is 0759538****.

The description was vague enough that it could be anyone, and West Kensington was right in the middle of their target zone. It was close to South Kensington with good transport links to the rest of the city but slightly dodgier.

"Any hits so far?" Rob asked, wiping crumbs from his mouth. The squad room was so peaceful on the weekends. No ringing phones, no whirring of the printer or beeping of computers. Just the soft tick of the wall clock and the distant hum of the traffic outside on the high street.

"No, only a couple of comments like, 'I think I know this guy,' or 'This could be the same guy I saw last week.' Obviously, he isn't, since the dude is a figment of my imagination." Will chuckled. "But I used a legit pay-as-you-go phone number."

"Keep going," replied Rob. "You never know. Someone might get in touch and ask for his contact information. In the meantime, trawl the forum for our latest victim, Ken Billows. Look for any references to him. We know he's a client of the Daring Divas agency, but that in itself isn't reason enough to kill him."

"Sure. I'll get right on it."

Rob switched on his computer and settled back into his chair, waiting for it to boot up. He'd just achieved a semi-state of calm when Mallory leaped up, phone still attached to his ear. "We've located Ingrid!"

"Where?" Rob jumped, knocking over his coffee, but he grabbed the cup just in time. Thank God it still had the plastic lid on.

"She's just got home, apparently she was at her boyfriend's house."

"Boyfriend? Shit."

"They're bringing her in."

* * *

"Why didn't you tell us you knew Dennis Patterson?" Rob asked Ingrid. They were back in the interview room and he was tired of being Mr Nice Guy.

"I *don't* know him," Ingrid insisted, her eyes flickering over the photograph lying in front of her on the steel table. She was dressed in jeans and a sweatshirt, her strawberry-blonde hair was pulled back in a ponytail and she had a faint smudge of eyeliner beneath her eyes.

"You had a booking at the Pear Tree Hotel the day he died."

She thought back. "Oh yeah. But that was a dud. I rocked up and knocked on this geezer's door. He told me he hadn't called a whore — he was quite rude, actually — and told me to piss off." Her eyes widened. "Is that him?" She touched the picture.

Rob nodded. Mallory said nothing.

Her voice rose a few notches in pitch. "I didn't know! I swear, the guy I met didn't look anything like this dead guy."

Death had a way of bloating and distorting facial features. He paused, puckering his lips contemplatively. She *could* be telling the truth. A healthy, upright man would look decidedly different from one who'd been dead over twenty-four hours and suffered traumatic blood loss. He decided to give her the benefit of the doubt. For now.

He rubbed his forehead. "Okay, let's start from the beginning. You had an appointment with a client at the hotel. Any idea what his name was?"

"Lewis, I think. Mary made the booking, ask her."

"And when you knocked on the door, this guy answered?" He prodded the photo with his finger.

"Yes." Her gaze was clear and a little defiant. "Like I already said, I didn't know it was him at the time."

"You sure you got the right room?"

"Yeah, I even called the agency to double-check. I thought there might have been a mix-up."

"What did you do then?"

"I left. There wasn't anything else to do. I couldn't go around knocking on doors asking if anyone had ordered a blow job, could I?"

Mallory smothered a snort.

"What time did you leave?" Rob tried to stay focused, although something was playing at the edge of his mind.

She tilted her head to the side. "It must have been around noon. He was an early appointment. I usually like those 'cos it means I can take the night off, but this guy just wasted my time."

They let her go shortly after that. Rob was beginning to think she really hadn't recognized Patterson from the photograph, and there was nothing solid they could hold her on.

Rob pushed open the doors to the squad room. "Something she said got me thinking," he mused. "What if Mary got the room wrong?"

Mallory broke his stride. "You mean she sent the escort to the incorrect suite?"

Rob nodded. "It's possible, isn't it? I know she thought it was a prank, but what if she misheard the caller or entered the wrong number into the system?"

Mallory's face lit up. "It wasn't a prank. Someone else called the agency to book the appointment."

Rob felt a surge of adrenalin shoot through him. "Get the names of all the guests who stayed at the hotel that night and see if there's a Lewis registered. One of them hired an escort and later called to complain that she hadn't rocked up." He knew it was a long shot — but maybe, just maybe, the punter had checked in under the same name he'd used to call the agency.

"No luck," said Mallory, a short while later. "I checked the hotel guest list and there's no Lewis registered. I bet that wasn't his real name."

"Hardly surprising." Rob sighed, but he hadn't given up hope. He was sure they were on the right track. "Listen, I've been thinking that Patterson's murder could be a case of mistaken identity. If the killer thought Lewis was in room eight, she would have gone there to murder him, except it was Patterson's room and he hadn't hired an escort. The thing is, the killer wouldn't have known that. She would have assumed Patterson was Lewis and that's why she stabbed him."

Mallory's expression turned incredulous. "You mean it was an accident?"

Rob held his hands out. "Why not?"

The DI shook his head. "The poor sod would have had no idea why he was attacked."

Rob inhaled sharply. "This means the killer *is* getting their information from the agency booking system. It has to be someone connected with Daring Divas."

But who?

Will, who'd been listening in, held up a finger. "Not necessarily."

Both Rob and Mallory turned to face him.

"There's a Lewis on the SAAFE forum too," he explained. "There are several warnings about him. Check this out." He scrolled to a post from a user called Roxygirl69.

Calls himself Lewis, Lou, Louie. Mid 30s. Comes across all charismatic at first. Don't be fooled, he's a convicted criminal (done prison time) for beating up escorts and women. Found out later from police. Has many numbers.

Will glanced up. "As you can see, she lists several mobile phone numbers but as per the site protocol, the last four digits are blacked out. You have to contact the user directly to get the full number."

Rob frowned. "If he's a convicted felon, we should have a record. Let's find out who this guy really is. He sounds like a piece of work."

"He might also be in danger." Mallory sank into his chair. "By now the killer must know she made a mistake. What if she goes after him again?"

Rob blinked a couple of times. "Shit. We'd better find out where he is and put a unit on him, just in case."

"On it," said Will. "I'll also contact Roxygirl69 and get the phone numbers from her. I doubt any of them are registered, but we might be able to trace him that way."

"Ask her if anyone else has enquired after him." Rob snapped his fingers. "If our killer hunts on the forum, she would have got in touch with this Roxygirl to get a number for Lewis. Same goes for the other victims."

"Yes, guv."

"If that's the case, it could have been Lewis himself who gave out the wrong room number?" Mallory extrapolated. "Or the killer misheard. Either way, she got the wrong guy."

The atmosphere in the room suddenly became charged. Rob felt his skin prickling like it did when a lead panned out. Things were finally starting to make sense. Finally, they'd solved the anomaly that was Dennis Patterson.

"It's crazy to think the killer murdered Patterson by mistake," Will murmured, turning back to his keyboard.

Rob couldn't agree more. "She thought she was killing Lewis, a convicted woman-beater, meanwhile he was next door, waiting for a blow job that never came."

Mallory swivelled around to face his desk. "How unlucky can you get?"

"Or lucky," said Rob. "Depends from whose perspective you're looking at it."

* * *

Sick of office coffee and in need of a break — paperwork always gave him a headache — Rob went to get an espresso from Caffè Nero in the high street and call Yvette.

He and Mallory had spent the last few hours documenting every move they'd made in their quest to find the killer. That was the worst part of the job, writing up reports and filing statements, mapping their every move so that nothing could be questioned in court, should they ever reach a point where they could prosecute.

Except that would require actually having a suspect in custody, Rob thought grimly. At the moment, all they had was a hazy image of a woman with dark hair in a trench coat.

Yvette, not surprisingly, didn't pick up. Annoyed and unwilling to leave the sanctuary of the café just yet, he dialled Jo's number. She answered with an upbeat, "Rob, how nice to hear your voice."

"What you up to?" He smiled at her response. Was she out with friends? Maybe she had a life and wasn't working on her weekend.

"Not much," she replied. "I've just got back from Borough Market and now I'm making some lunch and catching up on paperwork. We arrested several more suspects in the county lines gang, so there's a shitload of paperwork to catch up on."

"Yeah, I know the feeling." He was secretly pleased she wasn't out enjoying herself.

"How about you? You at work?"

"How'd you guess?" he asked.

"I know you." He sensed her smile. "Are you using me as an excuse for a smoke break?"

He grinned. She always managed to put a smile on his face. "More like I'm using my smoke break as an excuse to call you."

She laughed. "That works too."

"Do you want to meet up later?" The words were out before he'd had time to think about them.

A slight hesitation. "Sure. Why not? It is Saturday, after all."

"Great. Same place as before?" Waterloo was twenty minutes away if he caught the fast train.

"Yep, eight o'clock suit you?"

"Perfect."

"See you then."

Rob hung up and gazed into his coffee for a long moment. *She's just a friend*, he told himself. There was no harm in meeting a friend for a drink on a Saturday night, was there? It wasn't like he had anything else to do. Ignoring the tug of guilt, he downed what was left of his coffee and headed back to the squad room.

CHAPTER 33

"I can't find any reference to Ken Billows on the forum," said Will with his mouth full. He was eating a Big Mac at his desk.

"Another anomaly." Rob rested his head on the back of his chair. Just when he thought he had a handle on this case, something popped up to throw a spanner in the works. First Dennis Patterson had been the odd man out. A decent family man. No reference to the agency or the SAAFE forum. Then they'd solved that mystery and narrowed it down to an agency connection, but then ex-con Lewis appeared on the forum, which cast that theory in doubt. Now, when it looked like the forum was definitely the killer's hunting ground, Ken Billows was nowhere to be found on it. Back to square one.

"He could have used a different name," Mallory pointed out. He was holding a cup of tea. Unlike most cops, Mallory didn't like coffee. He was a tea drinker.

"It's possible," agreed Will. "That's the problem when you're dealing with punters. There are heaps of warnings on here. Any one of them could be about Billows."

"Did we look up Lewis's criminal record?" asked Rob, changing tack.

Mallory nodded. "Yeah, I was getting to that. Reginald Lewis, or Reggie as he was known by his mates, was arrested for beating up a sex worker last April. He did six months for assault. A year before that he was cautioned for domestic abuse — his girlfriend issued a restraining order against him. And the year before that, he was brought in for questioning with regard to another incident with an escort, but she didn't press charges."

"Can I see a photo?"

Mallory handed him a mugshot of Reginald Lewis.

"I can't believe the murderer mistook Patterson for this guy." Rob flicked the picture.

"Obviously no one mentioned he was a big, bald black dude," replied Mallory.

Lewis's hard, scornful eyes stared out from the picture. Funny how that had made the difference between life and death.

* * *

"Yes!" Will sat up in his chair and punched the air. "Finally."

Rob and Mallory turned to face him. "You got something?" asked Rob.

The DS pointed excitedly to the computer. "Icequeen has messaged asking for Peter's number. She said she reckons she met this guy last night. A complete bastard. Same thing. Removed the condom. Wouldn't pay. Hit her across the face." He looked away from the screen. "To think there are actually guys out there that do this."

"Give her the number," said Rob without hesitation.

Will glanced at him. "What if she calls?"

"I'll take the pay-as-you-go phone. I'll be Peter."

Both Mallory and Will stared at him. Rob could understand their hesitation. They had no plan. This had been a spur of the moment thing, a just-in-case scenario. None of them had actually expected it to work. Even now, they couldn't be sure this Icequeen was their killer. It could be a genuine enquiry by a woman who'd been assaulted and wanted to make sure it was the same guy before she went to the cops.

"It might not be her," he said. "But if it is, we can't let this opportunity go."

"How will you catch her?" asked Will. He hadn't responded to the query yet. His hands remained poised above the keyboard.

"If she's the killer and she's set her sights on Peter, she'll want to set up a meeting."

"It'll have to be in West Kensington," said Mallory. "That's what we put in the original post."

Rob nodded. "We'll cross that bridge when we come to it. Right now, it's still a long shot." He didn't want to get his hopes up. Not yet. If and when she rang him, he'd start getting excited. Until then, they carried on as normal.

"I'll give it an hour." Will relaxed his fingers. "I don't want to make her suspicious by responding too quickly."

"Good point." Rob went back to his desk. "I'll take that phone home with me for the rest of the weekend, and I'll let you know if she calls."

"Guv, we're going to have to run this past the Superintendent," said Mallory, always the voice of caution. "You can't go and meet her by yourself."

His DS was right, he couldn't do that. It needed to be a planned operation with backup, possibly even armed police. The problem was, they didn't have any concrete evidence that it was her, and he wasn't sure the Superintendent would dedicate resources to a project that might never happen.

"I'll speak to him," he said. Then to Will, "Why did you choose West Kensington?"

"I live there," replied the DS.

Rob smiled at him.

Will's eyes widened. "No way," he said.

* * *

"It's a good plan," Jo agreed that night at the pub in Waterloo. They were sharing a bottle of red and sitting in worn armchairs near the fire. Slow jazz was playing in the background and with every bar Rob felt a little of the pressure in his back and shoulders dissipate.

"Lawrence wasn't so sure. It took a lot of persuading to get him to go along with it, but in the end, he relented. I think he knows this could be our one shot at catching this woman."

"Is that it?" Jo's gaze fell to the scratched Samsung lying on the table.

"Yeah." He patted it reverently. "It's on full volume, too, so I don't miss it." It was fairly busy in the pub, but the noise level wasn't too bad. It shouldn't be a problem to hear if it rang.

"What if she wants to meet tonight or tomorrow?" asked Jo. "Then what?"

Rob frowned. "Will has a place in West Kensington that we can use at short notice. Although, I don't want to give her the address unless I'm absolutely sure she's going to show up."

"You could arrange to meet her at the tube station," suggested Jo. "Then take her to Will's place. I've heard some girls do that rather than going straight to a punter's house. It gives them time to suss him out and change their mind if the guy doesn't seem legit, you know?"

Rob nodded slowly. "What if she clocks me, then changes her mind? It would be better if she came straight to the apartment. Less chance of her backing out."

Jo sipped her wine. Her blonde hair glowed in the fire-light. "What about a motel or an Airbnb?"

"A motel has the risk of cameras and security staff, not to mention the other guests, and what Airbnb owner is going to want a killer in their apartment? I want to make this as easy for her as possible."

"And I suppose you've thought through what you're going to do if she attacks you?" Her clear blue eyes focused on his.

He shrugged. "Unlike the other victims, I'll be expecting it. I'll wear a vest, so my torso is protected, but I want to catch her with the knife in her hand, before she has time to attack."

"A vest is a good idea." Jo cradled her glass. "I wouldn't want anything to happen to you."

He smiled. "It won't."

She nodded, but the worry was still etched on her face. He resisted the urge to reach for her hand. "Besides, she might not call at all. It could be a false lead. The real killer could be someone linked to the escort agency rather than the forum. We still don't know for sure."

Jo pursed her lips. "I was thinking . . . The killer might not be someone who's been abused, she might be a close relative of someone who was abused. If they'd lost someone, that would make them equally mad, wouldn't it?"

Rob gazed at her for a long moment, his eyes narrowed. "That's an interesting point. We've been looking for someone who had a bad experience with a punter in the past. We've been following up on a list Francine gave us of girls who've been hospitalized, brutal sexual assaults, that sort of thing, but we haven't — I haven't — thought about the relatives of the victims."

"You should check it out."

Rob fired off a message to Mallory telling him they needed to get the team to follow up on all their main suspects first thing Monday morning. That included the four telephone operators, the escorts booked by the victims and Francine. *We need to look for family members of abused or assaulted sex workers*, he said in his text.

"It could be a mother or a daughter of one of the escorts." Rob pocketed his phone. He thought of the lady who'd opened the door at Brooklynn's house. They'd have to recheck everyone.

"It sounds like you've got some work to do." Jo finished her glass of wine. "Maybe I should leave you to it."

"It can wait until Monday." Rob refilled her glass. He was already on his second. "The team deserves a break, they've worked hard this week, and there isn't much we can do tonight."

"Haven't we all?" She reached for her glass and sighed contentedly. "This is really nice, Rob. We should do it more often." She studied his face. "How are things with Yvette?"

He shrugged. "She's still at her sister's." He wondered if she was ever coming home. He hadn't rung her again, but then she hadn't called him either. It seemed they were maintaining radio silence.

"Any idea when she'll be back?" There was no edge to her voice, she was genuinely interested.

"After this case, I suspect." He glanced at Jo curled up in the armchair, her hair framing her face, her lips stained red from the wine. "The thing is, I'm not sure I want her to."

It was the first time he'd admitted it, even to himself, and he immediately felt guilty. He tried to find the words to explain how he felt. "She's my wife," he said, "and I love her, but I can't help thinking she'd be better off with someone else."

"You can't mean that?" Jo gasped. "After everything you've been through?"

Rob sighed. "Yvette hated my job even before we got married. That's why she left me the first time. She couldn't handle the erratic hours, the phone calls in the middle of the night, the constant worry. You know what it's like."

Jo gave a sad nod. "Why do you think I'm still single?"

"Perhaps it's time we put this whole sordid mess behind us and moved on. Made a fresh start of it. Just living with me reminds her of what happened, I think that's part of the problem. My job causes her untold anxiety. She's waiting for a killer to come knocking at the door."

Jo let him talk and the more he did, the more he realized he'd come to a decision. "I honestly think it's for the best," he said. He looked down at his wine glass. "I don't make her happy. I never did."

Jo leaned forward and put her hand on his arm. "I'm sorry, Rob."

He gave her an embarrassed grin. "I didn't mean to harp on like this. My personal life is not your problem."

"We're friends, Rob. You know you can talk to me about anything, right?"

He exhaled slowly. "Same applies to you."

She tossed her hair back. "Luckily, I don't have relationship issues — probably because I don't have a relationship."

He snorted. "I'm beginning to think it's easier that way."

"Easier, but lonelier. I sometimes think it would be nice to have someone to come home to, someone to cuddle at night, but it seems I can't have that without all the bullshit."

Rob couldn't meet her eye. He knew they were both thinking the same thing.

The pay-as-you-go phone on the table rang.

CHAPTER 34

Rob stared at the phone, then at Jo. She waved her hands in a frantic *aren't you going to get that?* gesture. Only one person other than Will had this number.

Icequeen.

He reached for the device and picked it up.

"Hello?"

A throaty voice said, "Hey, baby, my name's Angelique. I heard from my friend Roxy that you were looking for some fun."

Angelique.

"Maybe." His heart hammered in his chest. Was this her? Was he talking to the woman who'd killed all four of his victims?

"She said you like it rough."

He forced a chuckle. Stay calm. Act the part. "*She* didn't, though. Stupid bitch."

"But I do. The rougher the better."

He paused. This was how she did it. She contacted the violent men and promised them just what they wanted, what turned them on.

"Are you going to teach me a lesson?" She was almost purring now. "Because I've been a very naughty girl."

That's for sure, he thought. *And I am going to teach you a lesson, but not the kind you're thinking of.*

"I'm busy tonight." He didn't want to be a pushover. It would be too obvious. He had to play it cool, lead her on, make her think he was a dangerous lowlife with no respect for women. "You'll have to find your fun somewhere else."

"I can wait, darling," she purred.

Rob met Jo's gaze and nodded.

She continued, "How about tomorrow night? Just you and me. Your place. I promise you a night you'll never forget."

"How much?" he growled.

"Honey, for you, I'll give you a discount. Half price. You'll be doing *me* a favour."

"How much?" he asked again.

"Seventy-five," she replied without hesitation. "Everything included. Whatever you want. I'm at your mercy." She even managed to inject some excitement into her voice. It was an excellent performance. None of the men she contacted would have any idea what she really had in mind.

"I'll think about it." He was taking a chance, but at the same time, he couldn't be too much of a pushover. He had to keep it realistic. "Give me your number and I'll call you tomorrow."

"Don't worry, honey," she murmured. "I'll call *you*."

The line went dead.

Rob placed the phone back on the table and stared at Jo. "I may have blown it."

"What did she say? Was that her?"

"I think so. She said she liked it rough, that she wanted me to teach her a lesson. She asked to come over to my place tomorrow night."

"And you said you'd think about it?"

He nodded. "Do you think I've ruined it? Scared her off?"

"No." Jo shook her head. "I think you played it just right. If you'd been any keener, she may have smelled a rat." She patted his arm. "Good job."

Rob still wasn't sure. "What if she doesn't call?"

"Did you get her number?"

"It's on my phone. It'll be a prepaid SIM, no doubt, but we can try and trace it, or at least analyse the call records. You never know, she may have used it before." It was unlikely, but worth a shot.

"Did you recognize her voice?" asked Jo.

He thought for a moment. "No, I can't say that I did. It wasn't anyone from the agency." They could be certain that the killer was using the forum as a hunting ground.

Jo finished her drink and this time, she got up. "I'm going to leave you to organize your sting operation. It's getting late and I've got an early start."

He stood up too. "This has been great, Jo. Thanks."

She grinned. "Let me know how it turns out."

"I will."

She leaned forward and gave him a peck on the cheek. "Be careful, Rob."

He inhaled her soft, vanilla scent. "Always."

CHAPTER 35

"I'm glad you called," Rob said. "I've been thinking about you."

It was mid-afternoon on Sunday and Rob was in the incident room surrounded by most of his team. Even the Superintendent had overthrown years of tradition and come in on the weekend to oversee the operation.

Rob had called Lawrence last night after he'd left the pub and told him about the phone call. The DSI had acted immediately. He'd instructed Rob to go ahead with the sting, that he'd approve any resources necessary. "Let's catch this woman and get her off the streets before she can do any more damage."

After that, Rob had assembled the team and they'd been planning the takedown all morning. They were to use Will's apartment in West Kensington. The block wasn't as downmarket as Rob would have liked but it was in the right area and Will, who was on the ground floor, had a back entrance leading to a small porch area, so the killer (or the cops) wouldn't be seen by the other residents in the block.

The phone was on the table in front of him, on speaker so the whole room could hear. No one dared to breathe while the caller was on the line.

"I've been thinking about *you*, Peter," she purred. "Are we on for tonight?"

Lawrence gave an imperceptible nod.

"Sure, why not?" He tried to sound casual. Was it working? He wasn't sure. His mouth was dry and the pulse beating erratically in his neck didn't help matters. *Keep cool.* The eyes of his team were on him. "What time?"

"How does six o'clock sound?" she said. "I'll come to you."

"Okay. I live in West Kensington. Clarendon Place. Flat four. Come around the back."

"I know it," the caller said. "See you later, darling."

He hung up. There was a moment's silence, then everyone started talking at once.

"Get on to SCO19," snapped Lawrence, talking about the Specialist Firearms Command. "We need them here ASAP for a briefing."

"You'll need a vest," said Jenny.

"Did we get a trace on the phone?" asked Mallory. They'd tried to get the call logs from the phone company but there weren't any. It seemed the caller had only used the phone to contact "Peter".

"No." Jeff was tapping away on his laptop. "She turned it off again."

Damn. Rob had been hoping for a fix on her location so they could monitor her movements. It would give them a heads-up as to when she was approaching Will's flat later that evening. He glanced at his watch. Nearly two thirty. They had to be in position by five at the latest, which didn't give them much time.

* * *

"You can't go back to the flat," Rob informed Will. "When I'm there, I'll remove the photos and any personal items that might give the game away."

Will's eyes gleamed with anticipation. "Sure thing, guv." He'd come from Vice, so this was right up his alley, and he was practically buzzing with adrenalin that the sting was going down at his apartment.

"Everything relies on us apprehending this woman tonight," the Superintendent pointed out. "If we fuck up, Will's been irrevocably compromised." The team sobered for a moment as reality set in. They were using a colleague's apartment, the place where he lived. If the killer cottoned on to the setup, Will's life would be in danger. Perhaps not tonight, but tomorrow, or the next day, or sometime in the future. They were taking a huge risk leading the killer there.

Rob would have much preferred to use a more neutral location, but they didn't have the time to find anywhere else. As he'd said to Jo, a motel was riskier and an Airbnb was out of the question. It would take weeks to find a place to rent and kit out.

"It was my call," Will pointed out. "I set it up. Besides, don't worry. We'll get her."

Rob wished he felt as positive, but his body was fraught with apprehension. She'd outsmarted them up until this point. He prayed she wouldn't figure out what they were up to and put on the brakes. They only had one shot at this.

"I'll call the firearms unit." Mike left the room.

"You can't go looking like that." Jenny inspected him from head to toe. "You need to mess yourself up a bit. Pull out your shirt, dirty your jeans."

Will nodded. "Yeah, you're not really the type to hire escorts, let alone rough them up."

"I can't do anything about the way I look," said Rob. Fortunately, he hadn't shaved this morning, just in case she rang back. He hadn't wanted to get his hopes up, but now it was all going ahead.

"You're too good-looking to be a punter," muttered Jenny, ruffling his hair.

"It takes all types," Rob remarked.

Will nodded. "True, we just have to make you look less like a copper and more like a biker. That's what I envisioned, anyway."

"Why a biker?" asked Rob.

Will shrugged. "My neighbour's a biker."

The SCO19 team leader came in twenty minutes later. He was a big, tough-looking guy with a buzz cut and biceps the size of Christmas turkeys. Despite his size, however, he moved with ease and deftly sidestepped the other members of the team as he made his way to the briefing room. He exuded professionalism and competence.

"Bruno Travis," he said in a deep, gritty voice. He extended his hand.

Rob shook it. "Good to have you on board."

They discussed the fundamentals of the operation. Rob was to be in the flat by four o'clock, getting into character. The armed police would conceal themselves in a nearby unmarked vehicle ready to act when the time came. A lookout would be stationed in the bushes facing the back porch, observing the killer as she approached. Will would open the back door when she arrived, and they'd take it from there. They wouldn't act until she attacked. The knife had to be in her hand before the team responded. If the worst came to the worst, they had clearance to take her out.

* * *

It was three thirty. Rob left the office, drove to Will's flat and got changed, attempting to get into character. He'd decided against the biker facade and instead wore dirty denim jeans with a grey hoodie over a Kevlar vest. The added layer bulked him up and made him appear more like the brutal bastard he was supposed to be. It was freezing outside, so he'd hiked up the heating. He hoped Will wouldn't mind. He'd also taken Jenny's advice and messed up his hair, using gel to make it stick up in all directions. By now, his stubble was a decent length, giving him a dirty, uncouth look. Hopefully it would be enough to fool the killer.

The wait was excruciating. The closest he'd ever got to being undercover was when he'd posed as a shopper to apprehend a credit card thief. This was an active sting operation to ensnare a homicidal serial killer. Talk about jumping in at the deep end.

He took all Will's personal photographs down. It wouldn't do for the killer to see a different man on display. It could raise some awkward questions. He messed up the apartment, cringing as he did so. He knew Will hated mess. He bounced on the bed, pulled some food wrappers out of the bin and scattered them on the kitchen countertop, left an empty coffee cup on the living-room table without a coaster and messed up the scatter cushions. He turned the television on to a game show, the false laughter filling the room and setting his nerves on edge.

Five o'clock.

Rob paced up and down the apartment. What the hell was he supposed to do for an hour? He pulled out his phone and called Travis to check his armed response team was in position.

"Do you have a visual on the back porch?" Rob asked.

"Not a hundred per cent," came the terse reply. "The road doesn't extend far enough around the block for a direct view. The best we can achieve is side-on, but the approach path around the back is in full sight, so we'll see her coming."

That would have to do. Rob had watched them get ready and had been impressed by their attention to detail. The team were dressed head-to-toe in black, and with their kit on they looked very intimidating. Beneath their long-sleeved tops they wore Kevlar vests with ceramic plates that were knife and bullet resistant — identical to the one he was wearing. They had walkie-talkies on their shoulders attached to a microphone for communication to and from their team leader. They were armed with specialist mid-rifles with optical sights and magnification for both close-range and distance shots. Every man wore an additional sidearm in a thigh holster for close combat. Completing the terrifying picture were the fire-resistant face masks and lightweight Kevlar helmets that not only protected their faces and heads, but also hid their identity from their target.

Rob felt this covert display of force might be overkill for one woman, but then she had murdered four men, overpowering several that were bigger and stronger than she looked in her hazy CCTV photo. It was better not to take any chances.

They tested the listening devices one more time. They'd been set up so that Travis and his team could hear everything that was being said in the apartment. "Reading you loud and clear," Travis confirmed.

Rob knew there was also a sniper hiding in the treeline surrounding the property. He would hole up and wait for further instructions. If they couldn't apprehend the attacker for any reason, the sniper would take the kill shot — and he wouldn't miss.

A chill went down Rob's spine. The next hour would be agonizing.

* * *

Rob glanced at the wall clock in the kitchen. 5.47 p.m. Thirteen minutes to go, assuming she was on time. Hopefully, the icy weather wouldn't put her off. So far, he'd avoided thinking about what could go wrong with this operation and it took all his willpower not to go there now. He was protected. There was an entire squadron of armed police out there. The revenge killer wouldn't get away.

Rob was tempted to switch off the telly. The beeps and pings from the game show were driving him mad. There was a beer bottle on the table. He'd poured himself a drink but hadn't had any. He'd even swirled some around in his mouth and spat it out so that when he breathed on her, she'd smell the booze. That was a tip Will had given him.

Finally, when the knock came, Rob's pulse skyrocketed. She was here! He peered through the glass door that led out on to the back porch and saw a slim, shadowy figure standing under the porch light. Pasting a lecherous smile on his face he opened the door.

CHAPTER 36

"You Peter?"

She wasn't what Rob had expected. The woman standing outside on the porch was of average height with a curvy body and enormous breasts, obviously enhanced. He didn't recall that from the CCTV photograph, but then the trench coat and grainy quality of the video could have hidden it.

The goth make-up surprised him. Her lips were a dark plum, almost black, and she was wearing a tight leather skirt and a low-cut top under a faux fur coat that left little to the imagination.

Is there a knife under there?

"Yeah. Angelique?"

She gave a sultry grin, her eyes raking over him. "In the flesh, baby."

Rob eyed her warily. At what point was she going to launch her attack? A scary thought shot through his mind. What if she wanted to have sex with him first? What if that's what got her going? Sleeping with her victims before she slaughtered them? But no, that wasn't her MO. He mustn't panic.

"You gonna invite me in, handsome?" Frigid air was seeping into the room.

He stood back to let her through knowing full well she was now out of sight of the sniper. "Yeah, you want a drink?"

She stepped inside and gazed around the open-plan lounge and kitchen area. In the light she looked older than he'd first thought. Maybe late thirties. "Sure."

He got a beer out of the fridge and handed it to her, careful not to turn his back. His senses were on high alert, braced for impact, but she accepted the bottle with a small nod of thanks and took a big gulp.

"Nice place you got here." She walked around admiring the quality of the sofa and the flat-screen television mounted on the wall.

"Thanks." What was she doing? Lulling him into a false sense of security? They hadn't prepped for this scenario. He'd been certain she'd attack almost immediately. Conversation had not been part of the plan.

Angelique, who was obviously used to such situations, sauntered over to him. She put her hands on his chest and smiled. "Do you want to get started? I've been waiting all day for this."

Rob hesitated, unsure how to proceed. Had she felt the vest beneath his hoodie? It appeared not. He glanced at the open porch door. The team outside wouldn't react until he was threatened.

He had no choice but to play along. But for how long? At what point did he call it quits? What if she didn't attack and he had to go to bed with her? Would he go that far to catch a killer? Maybe she was testing him?

Her eyes narrowed. "Is something wrong?"

"No." He cleared his throat and grabbed her by the arm. Maybe she needed a display of violence before she lost it and started stabbing him. "Come here."

She obeyed, dropping her coat on the floor as she did so. Nope, there was no knife under there. His eyes roamed over her body. Nowhere to conceal it on her person either.

Rob pulled her towards him and kissed her, hard. Hell, he hoped she was buying this. He let his hands roam over her waist and buttocks, ending with a hard squeeze. He heard her grunt in satisfaction. What he was actually doing was body-searching her. There was nothing hidden under her skirt, either. No concealed holster, no protruding weapon of any kind. She was clean.

The woman leaned back but he could feel her breath on his face. It was heavy, like she'd enjoyed his show of dominance. "Take me to the bedroom," she whispered.

Rob was about to lead her down the passage when there was a knock at the front door. Thank God.

"Leave it," she said huskily, reaching for him.

He pretended to hesitate. "I won't be a sec," and nodded towards the bedroom. "Get in there, I'll be right back."

Another knock, louder this time. Rob opened the door and saw Travis standing there.

"What's going on?" the SCO19 officer asked. He'd left his helmet and visor in the van but was still carrying his automatic rifle.

"It's not her," Rob hissed. "It's a false alarm. She must be a genuine caller."

"Bloody hell. Now what?"

"I'll get rid of her," Rob said.

"How?" asked Travis.

"It won't be hard. I'm Peter the prick, remember."

"Shit. This was all for nothing."

Rob felt his frustration. "It looks like it."

"Okay, we'll wait until she's gone before we stand down."

Rob nodded. "Thanks."

"You coming, babe?" called a voice from the bedroom.

Rob took a deep breath. "Hey, I've changed my mind. I'm going out with my mates. Get out."

The look on her face was anger mixed with disappointment. He felt like a real jerk.

"What? Are you for real?"

"Yeah, fuck off."

He stood in the doorway and watched as she got off the bed and put her clothes back on. She stormed past him, her chin up, shoulders back. "You're a cunt, you know that?"

"So I've been told."

She picked up her coat and faced him. "I want my seventy-five quid."

Rob took a menacing step towards her. He had a good two foot on her height-wise and was nearly twice as wide. "I said fuck off."

She turned and ran.

Rob sighed and locked the door after her, then went out the front.

* * *

"I can't fucking believe it," Rob fumed back at HQ. The armed response unit had been stood down. "It wasn't her."

"I can't believe there are actually women out there who will hunt down a known abuser and seek him out? That's messed up." This from Mallory.

They were all stunned and disappointed in equal measure. Rob had briefed the Superintendent on the way back to the station. There was no reason for him to come in. "Fucking waste of time and resources," were his exact words.

Rob scratched his head and paced up and down the small room. He felt like a caged tiger. How had they got it so wrong?

"What are the chances?" said Jenny. She handed out cappuccinos she'd picked up from Starbucks on the way back.

"At one point I thought you were going to go to bed with her," said Will.

"I contemplated it," Rob admitted. "I thought she might be testing me, seeing how far I'd go."

"Would you have done it?" Jenny's eyes were wide. They all knew he was married, and most of them knew the circumstances surrounding his marriage.

"Of course not." But deep down, Rob wasn't so sure. If it meant catching a killer — he just might have. At least he'd never have to find out now.

There were a few chuckles, releasing the tension. Rob slumped into the chair at the head of the table. "What now?"

"We go back to the drawing board," Mallory said. "She may still call you on that number."

"He's right," said Will. "We could bump up the warnings, create another profile lamenting the dangerous and violent Peter."

"Maybe Angelique will do that for us," Mallory murmured.

Rob shook his head. "I wasn't that hard on her. If I'd slapped her around a bit, maybe, but that would have been against the rules."

"Don't forget, she likes that sort of thing," Jenny pointed out. "She's unlikely to report him when she's actively seeking these guys out."

Mike shook his head. "Crazy chick, man."

"She's in the right business for it," Jeff remarked.

"What if we get Peter to call Daring Divas?" Mallory looked at Will. "He can ask for some light bondage, a little tie and tease, maybe some slapping. It may help to heighten his profile."

There was a murmur of surprised laughter. Rob stared at him. "Look who's down with the lingo."

"I've been reading up on it." Mallory grinned.

Just then Rob's phone buzzed. He glanced at the screen. *Jo.*

Now wasn't a good time. He ignored it, slipping it back into his jacket pocket. He'd call her later.

A short while later it vibrated again, two short ones. She'd obviously left a voice message or followed up with a text. Strange that she'd be calling tonight when she knew he'd have his hands full with the sting operation. A sixth sense made him glance at his phone a second time. She'd left a voice message.

"Excuse me, guys," he said, leaving the room.

He listened to her message and his blood went cold.

CHAPTER 37

"Rob, it's me. There's someone in my house. I'm in the hall closet. I'll keep the line open for as long as I can."

They could hear her controlled breathing as she waited for the intruder to find her. There wasn't a single person around the boardroom table who didn't admire her guts.

"Footsteps coming closer. Okay, this is it, I'll tell you what I know. Come get me, Rob. If this goes bad, come and get me."

There was a rustling as she slipped the phone into her pocket, followed by a creak as the cupboard door was wrenched open.

"Get out!" a female voice ordered.

"It's you," Jo hissed. "Rob, it's . . ."

There was a loud crack and a minute later the line went dead.

Rob felt his heart drop. They all stared at one another.

"She's got Jo," was all he said. A million thoughts flew through his head. Why had the killer gone after Jo? Was it to get to him or did she have something against the NCA agent? How had she even known Jo?

"But Jo's not connected to this case." Mallory rubbed his head in confusion. "I don't understand what's going on here."

"She was," said Rob. "She went undercover at the escort agency. She was the one who hacked into their database for us."

"Do you think the killer targeted her because of that?" asked Jenny.

"The killer is sending us a message." Rob pushed himself to his feet as a surge of adrenalin hit him. It cleared his mind, helped him focus. "She's saying, 'This is what happens when you mess with me.' Francine had Jo's details on file. Somehow the killer must have realized she was an undercover cop."

All the murderer had had to do was keep him under surveillance, and soon enough she'd seen him with Jo. It wouldn't have taken much to connect the dots. Once again, they'd underestimated her.

"Are we back to the agency theory?" asked Mallory.

"Yeah, the killer's shown her hand. Let's redo those background checks on everyone at that agency, and I mean everyone. Dig deep. One of them is hiding something that we missed before. Where are we with the friends and family?" They'd put that line of enquiry on hold when Angelique had contacted them.

"And what happened with the CCTV footage of the vehicles outside Yousef's place? Have we narrowed it down yet? Come on, guys, give me something. We've got to find her."

He paced up and down the incident room, trying not to give into the guilt assailing him. First Yvette, now Jo. The nausea rose in his throat. But Jo wasn't like Yvette. She was tough and well trained, she knew how to handle herself. She would be all right. She had to be all right.

Come get me, Rob.

Think, he ordered himself. He played Jo's message over and over again listening to every nuance, every background sound, the tone of Jo's voice.

"Hey, Mallory, come over here for a moment."

Mallory came over to his desk and perched on the edge.

He played his colleague the message. "Does it sound like she knows the killer?"

"It's hard to say," Mallory replied. "She could be saying 'It's you' as in the killer or she could be saying 'It's you' as in she recognizes her from somewhere."

"The agency. It has to be. Where are Mary and Francine right now?" Rob sprung out of his chair. "Send Uniform to their houses. I don't care where they live or what time it is. Do it now."

Mallory got on the phone. A few minutes later he'd dispatched police officers to the respective addresses.

Rob grabbed his jacket. "Mallory, with me."

They were just heading out when Mike came rushing up behind them. "Guv, I've just checked into Mary's background. She had a sister who died two years ago. It wasn't on her statement. She implied she was an only child."

"How did she die?" Rob fixed his gaze on him.

"She was raped and beaten to death," said Mike. "They found her body in a hostel in Brixton."

"For Christ's sake," snapped Rob. "How did we fucking miss this?"

* * *

Rob flew across town to Mary's flat, blue light flashing. The weather alternated between rain and sleet. He had to concentrate really hard not to have a head-on. Mary lived in Stockwell, a fair distance from Richmond, but also south of the river. Rob made it in a record-breaking fifteen minutes. Mallory didn't say a word the whole way there, but Rob noticed he looked rather green when they skidded to a halt behind a squad car. A uniformed police officer marched over to meet them.

"It's empty." He nodded towards the apartment block.

"Are you sure?" Rob scanned the run-down exterior of the block. A few dark heads could be seen in backlit windows, peering down on the street below.

"Yeah, we searched the apartment. It looks like she's cleared her stuff out, too. There's not much left."

Mary was doing a runner, but first she was going to give him something to remember her by. His throat swelled as he fought back his emotions. He needed to get to Jo before Mary killed her.

He took out his phone and called Francine.

"Where would she have taken her?" he barked into the phone.

"I have no idea." Francine's voice was high with tension. "I had no idea she was a killer. You have to believe me."

"Francine. Think carefully. Did Mary ever say anything about another property, anywhere she might take Jo?"

A pause. "I think her mother lived in Bracknell," she said finally. "I remember her saying she was going to visit her once when she was poorly."

"Okay, thanks." He remembered her mentioning her mother in the interview. Goddammit. They'd had her right in front of them and they'd let her go. He could have kicked himself.

Mallory was already on the phone asking for an address for Mary's mother.

"I've got it."

"Get the local coppers out there," ordered Rob. "Tell them to search the premises. If her mother doesn't let them in, they are authorized to break the door down." Mallory relayed the information to Will.

"Are we going to Bracknell?" Mallory didn't look too keen on the idea.

Rob shook his head. "I don't think she'd be so stupid as to take Jo to her mother's house. She'd know it's the first place we'd look. Besides, it's a forty-minute drive to Bracknell, more chance of Jo escaping. No, I think she's taken her somewhere local." Rob's phone buzzed. "Yeah?"

It was Mike. "Guv, we've whittled the vehicles from Yousef's house down to three possibilities. The first one, a blue Honda Prelude, is off the road, no tax disc. The second, a red Toyota Yaris, is registered to a Mr Thomas Ludgrove, who lives in Hounslow. We haven't been able to get hold of him to verify his alibi for the afternoon of the murder. The final vehicle, a grey Ford Focus is registered to a Zoe Bennet with a company address in Peckham — VL Holdings, twenty-seven Harris Road. That's near to where Jo lives, isn't it?"

"Yes!" Rob thumped his fist down on the hood of the car. *That's it. That must be where she's holding Jo — if she's still alive.*

"Another thing, guv," added Mike. "Guess what Mary's dead sister's name was?" He paused. "Zoe."

CHAPTER 38

Rob drove like a maniac. Luckily, traffic was light and he was able to shoot through Little Portugal into Camberwell, past the green and into Peckham Rye without much trouble. Mallory sat rigidly in the passenger seat beside him.

Harris Road was situated in the most dangerous part of Peckham, between Queen's Road and Nunhead. Rob knew from the police bulletins that it had a notorious crime rate, but right now, it was deceptively quiet. Late on a freezing Sunday evening, the streets were mostly deserted. The only people they saw were a vagrant huddled in a doorway and a drunk stumbling towards a bus stop. The windscreen wipers were working overtime.

He slowed to a crawl as they entered Harris Road and switched off the lights and sirens.

"Over there!" Mallory pointed to a sad-looking building.

Rob peered through the windscreen. *Smith & Sons* was just visible on the side of the wall and underneath, *Bake* but the rest of the wording was lost to crumbling, pockmarked concrete. The front windows — or what was left of them — were boarded up, but above the dirty green awning they could make out the number twenty-seven.

"It's deserted." With a sinking heart, Rob pulled over on the other side of the road and cut the engine. *Please don't let this be another dead end*, he prayed. "Let's check it out."

They climbed out of the car and approached the building. Icy rain pricked their skin and dripped down their necks, but that was the least of Rob's worries. He surveyed the block. Next door to the derelict bakery was a greengrocer, its metal security door locked and bolted. On the other side was some sort of community centre. The sign on the wall said, *St Matthew's Recreational Centre. Open 7 a.m. to 5 p.m. All Welcome.* It didn't look very welcoming with its corrugated roller door firmly locked in place and covered with graffiti.

"Nice neighbourhood," murmured Mallory.

"You go that way," whispered Rob, nodding to the left. He took off around the right-hand side of the building. A narrow litter-strewn alleyway separated number twenty-seven from the greengrocer. Rob proceeded with caution, avoiding puddles and looking for a window that he could see through. The alley reeked of urine and God knows what else. At the back he stopped and crouched down. Was that a glimmer of light coming from the basement window? It was so dirty that he could barely see through it. He rubbed it with his sleeve and peered through the grime. Yes! There was definitely a faint flicker down there. Mallory chose that moment to appear around the corner, making him jump.

"Sorry," he whispered. "There's a steel door on my side, but we'll never be able to break it down."

"Call for backup." Rob gestured to the horizontal window at knee level. "I think they're in there."

Mallory dialled the control room and issued the command into his phone, then crouched down beside Rob to have a look. "I can't see anything. It's too filthy."

"There's a definite glow coming from inside and I thought I saw movement." Or maybe that was wishful thinking on his part.

Please let her still be alive. He didn't want to think about the alternative. Christ, how would he live with himself? It had been bad enough when Yvette had been abducted, but Jo — his wonderful, shining friend, the woman he felt most comfortable with in the whole world — what would he do if she were gone? No, he couldn't go there. She was alive, he could feel it.

"How long?" he barked at Mallory. He was itching to get inside. Every moment counted.

"Ten minutes."

"Shit."

There was nothing they could do but wait. Mallory showed him the steel-enforced door. He turned the handle, slippery from the rain, but the door wouldn't budge. They'd need a battering ram to knock it down.

Next to the door was a window but it was boarded up from the inside. Rob tapped it. The glass felt thin. "We might be able to get in this way."

"They'll be here soon." Mallory peered behind them down the alleyway, looking for the telltale flashing lights, but it remained dark.

"Soon might be too late." Rob ran back to the car and reappeared with a baton. He took off his jacket, wrapped it around the baton and struck the windowpane. It shattered on the second knock, the glass falling forward into the alleyway, thanks to the cardboard that had been shoved against it. Rob ran the baton around the edges to get rid of as much glass as possible, then reached in and gave the cardboard a hard shove. It fell away easily, having been taped up against the window.

"Give me a leg up," he said.

Mallory looked uncertain but nodded. The window was fairly narrow, but Rob thought he'd be able to squeeze through. He laid his jacket on the ledge to protect himself from the shards, then climbed up, using Mallory's clasped hands as leverage. He glanced down. "Wait for backup, then get in here."

His DS nodded worriedly.

Rob shifted his weight over the ledge and dropped on to the floor on the other side. He shone his torch around the room. It appeared to be a back office of some kind judging by the old filing cabinets and a worn wooden desk. In a corner, he spotted a rickety armchair with the footrest out and a blanket thrown over it. On the floor beside it was a bottle of water. Was this where Mary was hiding out?

Heart hammering, he opened the door and stepped into a dark passageway. Somewhere, water was dripping and there was a dank, mouldy smell in the air. He shone the torch down the corridor. At the far end, he could make out the front door. It was boarded up and nailed in place. No one was coming in that way. He looked around and shone his light on to the lock of the steel side door. It was a double cylinder deadlock. No way was that opening without a key. It seemed his backup would have to barge their way in.

The hairs on his neck stood on end as a low groan sounded from the bowels of the building.

Jo!

He sneaked along the passage to a staircase that led down to the basement. The carpet had long since rotted away and the floorboards creaked as he descended into darkness. With every step he paused, listening hard, but the only sounds were dripping water and the creaking of the old building. He was halfway down the stairs when the door at the bottom flew open and light flooded the stairwell, temporarily blinding him. Without thinking, he threw himself the rest of the way down, landing on top of the person at the bottom. She howled and lashed out. He felt a sharp, piercing pain in his side and realized he'd been stabbed. Somewhere in the background, he heard a muffled shout that he recognized as Jo's.

He went for the hand gripping the knife and forced it back against the floor. The body beneath him kicked and squirmed, but he was stronger than she was. Now his eyes had adjusted, he could see it was Mary — a dishevelled, wild Mary. She was glaring at him, straining forward against his bulk, trying to bite him, kick him, scratch him, hurt him in any way she could. He grabbed her other arm and held it over her head while he got his breath back.

Looking up, he saw Jo strapped to a wooden chair. There was duct tape covering her mouth and she had a bloody temple and a black eye. But she was alive.

"Jo!" he yelled. He'd never been so happy to see anyone in all his life.

Mary was still twisting and screaming like a banshee beneath him. Through the basement window he saw blue flashing lights. Thank God.

There was a loud crash. Heavy boots thundered down the stairs. Voices shouted and guns pointed in his direction. "Get your hands up!" He recognized Travis's coarse growl.

He climbed off Mary, his hands in the air. She seemed too paralysed to move. An armed officer turned her over on to her stomach and cuffed her hands behind her back. He pulled her to her feet.

Her eyes blazed. "You bastard! They deserved it. They all deserved it."

"All right, Rob?" Travis lowered his weapon and removed his helmet. "You know you're bleeding?"

Shit. The side of his shirt was wet with blood. "I think it's just a flesh wound," he replied, hoping it was. With the adrenalin still pumping through him, he could hardly feel it.

Jo groaned as an officer peeled the tape off her mouth. Rob dashed over to her. "Jo! Are you okay?"

"Oh, Rob. Thank God you found me." The minute her bonds were cut, she collapsed into his arms. "Can you believe it? It was Mary all along."

"I know," he muttered into her hair. "I'm sorry we took so long. We eventually figured it out."

"That's okay." She smiled up at him. How come even with a smudged face, black eye and blood-soaked hair, she still looked good?

He feasted his eyes. "You sure you're okay?"

She touched the wound on her head and winced. "I think so."

"That doesn't look too good." He fingered the purple skin beneath her bloodshot eye. "Neither does this."

"It'll mend." She grimaced. "I'm just glad you got here in time. She knew you were after her. A few more minutes and that would have been it. I swear, I thought it was game over."

Relief rushed through him and he hugged her again. "So did I."

"There's an ambulance outside," said one of the armed officers. "Let's get you both checked out."

It was then Jo saw the blood. "Shit, Rob. You're injured."

"It's just a scratch," he said, faintly alarmed by how red his shirt was.

Jo gave him a sceptical look but didn't argue. Travis and the officer who'd unbound her supported her up the stairs. Her legs were wobbly and Rob suspected she had a mild concussion. He hobbled to the ambulance a few steps behind.

Mary was being bundled into a police vehicle, still protesting. "You were next," she hissed at Rob. With her hair plastered to her face and her mouth open in an ugly snarl, she really did look quite demented. He could picture her repeatedly stabbing her victims like a woman possessed. "After I killed your spying girlfriend, I was coming for you."

"She's barking mad." Jo watched as Mary was driven away. "Kept ranting on about how men were scum and deserved to die. 'Sick fucks', she called them."

"Her sister was raped and murdered two years ago," he told her. "They found her body in a hostel in Brixton."

Jo was helped into the ambulance, where a medic began tending to her head wound. "That explains a lot," she said. "Ouch."

"Sorry ma'am," he apologized, but continued to wipe antiseptic over the wound. "We'll have to take you in. That's a nasty bump you've got there."

"This way, sir." A second medic took Rob by the arm as if he were an invalid. "Let's take a look at you."

It was just a flesh wound. The knife had nicked his side, leaving a nasty gash, but he didn't need an ambulance.

"I'll meet you at the hospital as soon as I can," he told Jo.

She gazed at him, her eyes wet with tears. He'd never seen her so emotional before. She was usually the epitome of cool. A lump formed in his throat.

"Thank you, Rob. You saved my life."

He waved away the compliment. "It was my fault she went for you in the first place."

"No, it wasn't," Jo whispered. "It was *her* fault. We were just doing our jobs."

CHAPTER 39

"Mary confessed to all four murders," Rob said with a grim smile. He was sitting on the end of Jo's bed in the bright hospital ward, along with Superintendent Lawrence and Mallory. She'd been kept in overnight with no visitors, which was a good thing since it had been quarter to two in the morning by the time they'd questioned and charged Mary with four counts of murder and one of attempted murder.

It had finally started snowing, and by the time Rob had got to the hospital, the ground was covered by a fine layer of powder. The duty nurse kept giving them pointed glances, while the other two patients in the room made no attempt to mind their own business and were shamelessly eavesdropping on the conversation.

"It was so strange," Rob continued. "She was eerily calm during her interview. If I didn't know better, I'd never believe she was the woman we arrested last night."

"Was it all because of her sister?" asked Jo. She had a concussion, four stiches in her head and her left eye was swollen shut, but the doctor had said she was going to be okay. As far as Rob was concerned, that was all that mattered.

"So it seems. The police never did find out who murdered her. It destroyed their family. Mary's father died shortly afterwards from a heart attack, and without his salary, they couldn't keep up the mortgage repayments and lost their house. Her mother began binge-drinking to block out the pain."

"It's so tragic." Even after everything she'd been through, Jo could still empathize.

"It is," he agreed. So much about this case disturbed him. He thought about Ingrid, Christy, Bernadette and all the other girls prostituting themselves for money, unnecessarily putting their lives at risk, and was filled with a deep sense of sadness.

"Mary hounded the police," he explained. "I spoke to DCI Burton at Brixton nick and he remembers her well. When it became clear the perpetrator wasn't going to be found, Mary decided to take matters into her own hands."

"That's why she got the job at the escort agency," said Mallory, speaking for the first time. He'd helped Rob question Mary after her arrest. It hadn't taken them long to charge her. In addition to confessing, her DNA matched that found under Patterson's fingernail. The knife she had on her when she'd kidnapped Jo was the same one that had been used in all four murders. There would be no bail.

"Did she ever track down the man who killed her sister?" asked Lawrence, who was sitting beside Jo's bed on the only chair in the room.

"No, but that didn't stop her looking. She trawled the forum website and kept a close eye on the punters who called the agency. Whenever she found one that she felt deserved to be punished, she'd pay him a visit."

"So she didn't actually sleep with her victims?" Jo asked.

He shook his head. "With Aadam Yousef and Ken Billows, she waited for the escort to leave, then went round to dispense justice. Those were her exact words, by the way."

Lawrence made a scoffing noise.

"Dennis Patterson was a mistake," continued Rob. "She misheard the room number."

"Unbelievable," whispered Jo.

Rob thought about Patterson's family — his shell-shocked wife who suddenly had to raise two kids on her own, and the twins who would probably never be able to make sense of his death. There wasn't any sense to be made, that was the tragic part.

"And the third victim?" asked Lawrence. "The one that called the agency but didn't book an appointment?"

"Oh, Doug Bartlett fell right into her lap. Mary pretended to make a booking, but she didn't enter it on to the system. Instead, she went herself, pretending to be an escort. He was waiting for her, let her into the apartment, even began to undress — which was why he had his pants off — before she attacked him while he was going to the toilet. He didn't see it coming."

"Poor bastard," muttered Lawrence.

"She saw herself as a kind of 'avenging angel', getting vengeance for all the women out there who couldn't defend themselves."

"It's a noble cause, really," said Jo. "If only she'd gone about it another way."

"Well, she's in a psychiatric facility now, awaiting trial." Mallory told them. "She'll probably plead diminished capacity."

"I hope she gets the help she needs." Jo leaned back, her face almost as pale as the pillows propping her up.

"She needs to rest," the beady-eyed nurse said, coming over. The two other patients groaned and went back to their respective magazines.

Lawrence got to his feet. "Well, that's my cue to leave. Get better soon, DCI Maguire, and as always, it's been a pleasure working with you."

She grimaced. "I wish I could say the same."

He smiled and gently patted her hand before leaving the ward. The DSI was fond of Jo, Rob could tell. And he was a hard man to please. Mallory followed suit, saying he'd see Rob back at the station.

"How are you doing?" Rob took Lawrence's place on the chair beside the bed.

"My head feels like a herd of elephants has charged through it, but other than that, I'm okay."

He took her hand. "Let me know if you want me to leave."

She gave a weak smile. "Okay."

The nurse checked her pulse and blood pressure, then gave Rob a stern look. "You can stay but only if you don't get her excited. She needs to rest."

Rob grinned. "I'll do my best."

They sat quietly together, holding hands. He told her how they'd eventually figured out Mary was the culprit and how he'd broken into the abandoned building to find her.

"My knight in shining armour," she murmured.

"I'm not sure about that." He chuckled. "I literally threw myself down the stairs at Mary and got stabbed in the process. It wasn't a very gallant rescue. That honour goes to Travis and his armed response team."

She laughed, then groaned and touched her head.

"I'd better let you rest," he said. Now that she was safe, he ought to go back to the station, he ought to ring Yvette, but he found he didn't want to leave her side.

"Don't go just yet," she whispered and closed her eyes.

So he sat there, holding her hand as she drifted off to sleep, thinking he'd never felt so content in his life.

THE END

Thank you for reading this book.

If you enjoyed it please leave feedback on Amazon or Goodreads, and if there is anything we missed or you have a question about, then please get in touch. We appreciate you choosing our book.

Founded in 2014 in Shoreditch, London, we at Joffe Books pride ourselves on our history of innovative publishing. We were thrilled to be shortlisted for Independent Publisher of the Year at the British Book Awards.

www.joffebooks.com

We're very grateful to eagle-eyed readers who take the time to contact us. Please send any errors you find to corrections@joffebooks.com. We'll get them fixed ASAP.